THE
CRIMSON
VIXEN

DEE CAREY

The Crimson Vixen
Copyright © 2023 by Dee Carey

ISBN:

Paperback: 978-1-63945-589-8
eBook: 978-1-63945-590-4

Writers' Branding
1-800-608-6550
www.writersbranding.com
orders@writersbranding.com

Contents

To my family

who believed in me when I didn't.

The Legend

In the age before recorded time, all events were preordained. So, it was with the mystic isle. Ever green, Ireland's emerald promise was divined by Ancient Druids.

Like many other lands, Ireland was ruled in a cavalier manner. Whoever felt strong enough to wrest power from the current regent became ruler. Arthur, King of England, Scotland, Wales, and Ireland felt he needed a strong hand in Ireland, desiring to put into power an Irishman who understood the people and would be loyal to him as regent.

Entrusted by their forefathers with the protection of their sacred land, the Druids selected two children, royal and common, to rule with dignity and a true sense of the peasants under their care. Times were harsh. The Druid religion was under constant persecution by self-appointed Roman priests who drove the faithful closer and closer to the cliffs of the Isle of Clare.

The priests embroiled the populace to frenzy. The children had been chosen and the distinguishing mark placed upon the boy. With increasing anger, the people rose against the dwindling number of Druids, forcing them to place their plan in animated suspension. The encroaching Christians could no longer accept the faith of their fathers. In order to protect the girl, she was given the animal disguise of a fox. At the point when each realized their potential, the mark of the fox and the essence of the vixen would unite to hold the crown of Ireland.

Only the intervention of Merlin, greatest of all sorcerers, would release the children from suspension.

With her last ounce of breath, the mother fox willed her essence to transfer from her own broken body to the small one beneath her. As the spirit had been passed to her at the moment of her mother's death, so did she pass it to her last surviving female kit. With no knowledge of the purpose of the essence, she only knew her duty; to channel the power when she was no longer able to keep it in her own living body.

The true spirit of the vixen lay within the female fox until a perilous time of warring factions tore the country asunder as the soul of Ireland required a woman to be a leader and protect the chosen country. The male bearing a fox- shaped mole at the base of his neck was a royal orphan who would be raised to have honor and a strong sense of justice.

The essence could lie dormant for many generations, by being passed down countless numbers of times before the true purpose would be served. The orphan would unite with the vixen when the essence was passed.

This passing would serve the higher purpose and protect the war-torn isle.

Chapter One

Leigh almost passed over the frozen mound in the driving snow, but his mule paused to paw at the unyielding earth. Dismounting, Leigh knelt to scrutinize the mule's discovery. A pine bough marked the edge of the frozen grave, a part of the snare that had broken the neck of the fox that lay inside. A glance at the surrounding snow showed Leigh that the fox's babies had fallen prey to local predators.

As he started to remount, he heard soft crying sounds coming from beneath the dead body. Carefully shifting aside, the fox's body, he discovered a single remaining kit. He lifted the young kit from beneath its mother's body and held it in his hands. The winter wind intensified, whipping up the fallen snow so that it stung his eyes. He bent his shoulders to shield the tiny animal he'd rescued.

The kit's eyes flooded with fear. Ever so gently, Leigh tucked her deep into the folds of his tunic next to his chest. Her tiny heart beat a staccato against his own. As his body began to warm the small fur bundle, he could feel the animal relax and give itself up to the sleep it sorely needed.

Leigh felt warmth spread through his body. Alone for most of his ten years, now he would have a playmate. He smiled, visualizing the hours they would spend together.

"We'll have lots of fun, won't we, little one?" He held her as close as he dared while he remounted.

The kit was warm and safe next to his breast. He didn't know such comfort himself. Soon after he left the gravesite, it began to snow, a real winter storm that nearly blinded him. Suddenly, snow lightning flashed, clearly outlining the foreboding castle on the horizon. The castle stood high on a stone bluff, its towers slashing the eerie sky.

Illuminated by the bolts of lightning, the gaping main gate did not offer any sense of welcome. Relentlessly, he dug his heels into the side of the unwilling pack animal. The mule shook and tested his rider's mettle. Unable to unseat Leigh from the saddle, the mule lowered his head and pushed onward. Each hoof crunched in the tightly packed snow, making progress slow.

Leigh shielded his eyes against the driving wind and drew the kit ever closer to his body. The castle had been in sight for some time, due to its perch on the bluff, but at the moment it seemed unreachable. Still, he drove the mule onward through the storm.

Its hooves clattered against the wooden drawbridge, the sound echoing off the stone columns of the gate's archway. The mechanics of the bridge had long ceased to function. Once over the drawbridge, he returned the mule to the stable and entered the castle to look for his protector, Olyn. But he couldn't find the sorcerer. The old gentleman most likely had fallen asleep, as he often did when his wine consumption was high on a cold winter night.

Reaching into his shirt, Leigh gently petted the fox. Still warm and safe, she did not resist his touch. He took her to the highest tower, knowing they would be safe there from discovery.

"Shss," he said, holding his hand over her muzzle.

"We don't want Olyn to hear us. You are going to be my friend, not kept in any cage."

Tenderly stroking the kit, he carried her up a winding staircase. The cold, sodden air of the stairwell felt like it oppressed his soul, and the gray stone walls didn't offer any sense of welcome. The stairs were made of well- seasoned wood, each tread worn in the center from the countless feet that trod them in the past.

Now I have someone to care for, Leigh thought. How would he tend this creature that had already become part of him? Part of him, in ways he couldn't explain, even to himself. He had never seen a fox with eyes of green —no, not merely green, but a green as sparkling as the Irish Sea itself. Her fur was as brilliant a red as ever graced the most vivid sunset. Reaching into his tunic, he stroked her fur. Mayhap, she wasn't really a fox. How could this emerald-eyed creature, with fur of vermilion, be one of the common animals of the field? Where had this elegant wee being come from? And why was he the one to discover her?

Returning to his quarters in the high tower of the old castle, he placed her into his bed. Making sure she was safe and warm, he left her to sneak down to the kitchen area to obtain some milk. He was sure she was too young to be weaned, and milk would be just the thing to break what he was certain had been a long fast.

Carefully, he crept down the winding staircase, hoping not to disturb the cook. Deliberately, he placed his feet where he knew no sound would emanate. He knew Helga would question his request of milk. It was well known he, unlike other lads, didn't like milk. But Leigh knew the old woman loved him. She frequently would try to coax him to drink the milk she got from the goats wandering the grounds. She often provided scraps for the hapless animals he had in his keep, but Leigh knew she would reveal the presence of the fox to Olyn. He wanted her to remain his own.

Quietly, he held fast to the curving wall. Most of the time, he was totally unaware of the cold, damp, walls, but tonight the lack of warmth confronted him with a chilling foreboding. Why did this feeling haunt him so? Was the little fox in his bed responsible for this dread? What would happen when she was grown? When she was able to hunt on her own she wouldn't rely on him for food. He could only hope by then she would want him for other things. There was more to this little fox than met the eye.

Leigh located some trenchers and milk in a small jar. Helga was nowhere to be seen. Carefully tucking them in his tunic, he quietly found his way back up the winding staircase. In his absence, the little fox had begun to explore her new home. He found her peering under the bed. Only her full red and white tail protruded. He set out the milk for her and stepped back to watch. Milk would do for now, but eventually he knew she would need meat. As she grew, how would he continue to hide her from Olyn?

He heard her stomach growl. Apparently, her hunger overshadowed her curiosity as she drew near the milk trencher. She watched him as she sniffed the liquid, her green eyes peering over the edge of the vessel. She was too young to drink. He would have to feed her. The thought gave him a shiver of pleasure. He softly drew his hand over her fur and marveled at the beauty of it. To be responsible for the needs of another was a heady brew.

Taking a bit of clean worn cloth, he wound the corner tightly and dipped the twisted end into the milk. He offered the cloth to her. She looked at him, her head cocked to the side, then drew on the corner as if she were suckling her mother.

Leigh felt her lips and tongue as surely as if she drew upon his own body. Somehow, he knew this tiny animal was part of his true destiny, and she would remain a part of him forever.

The kit seemed intent on discovery of her new world. Sniffing, she explored every niche of the tower. Now more sure of herself, she leapt from stool to table to bed. Tired from her endeavors, she turned around and around, making a nest in the bedding. Quickly asleep, her breathing settled into a soft murmur.

A mew sounded from deep within the folds of his blanket. She poked her nose up from beneath the blanket and stared at him with one green eye. The other remained hidden under the coverlet. Her ear twitched as she watched Leigh approach her. She sniffed and backed under the woolen throw on his bed.

"Come on, little Kit, I won't hurt you," he said.

As if she completely trusted him, she ventured forth and licked his hand, but retreated when he attempted to pet her.

"Oh, little one, I've never hurt an animal in my life."

Quizzically, she looked at him, her green eyes holding questions of their own. Again, she ventured forth. As he extended his hand, she slowly approached and pushed her head into his palm. Circling his body, she rubbed against his back and returned her nose to his palm.

"Well, Kit, do I meet with your approval? Are we going to be friends?"

He swore she nodded. Somehow, she seemed to completely understand him, an understanding that went beyond any he'd known with other animals. This was a bond deeper than any other he'd experienced.

They slept together until the dawn broke.

Olyn's voice pierced the stillness. "Leigh, boy, are you coming? These biscuits won't stay warm till you roust your bones."

"Coming, Olyn, I'll be right down," he yelled. He carefully wrapped the kit in the coverlet and placed her in a box in the corner of the tower, where the sun would warm her through the day, until he was able to sneak from under Olyn's watchful eye and bring her food.

Leigh hurried downstairs and slid into the bench into the simple kitchen. Olyn and Helga provided his meager daily repast and he did his best to care for the two elderly souls.

Leigh had often caught Helga watching the old magician as he worked. Olyn moved with a great deal of grace for such a big man. He would whirl about and speak in an incomprehensible language, completely oblivious to those observing him. Helga would sigh and cluck about his tempting the fates. High in the abandoned stone fortress, the three forged a unit to the benefit of each.

Leigh knew, though he appeared unconcerned, Olyn cared deeply for the woman. His eyes lit up when she entered a room and whenever in her presence, he hummed. Neither Helga nor Olyn mentioned any family. Leigh had only known the cruel man who had beaten him unmercifully until Olyn had rescued him. His foster parents had used him for the most demeaning manual labor. He'd worked in the fields from the age of three. Unable to recall if they'd loved him as an infant, he dimly remembered a more caring woman who tended him.

Leigh picked at his food, then peeked at Helga.

"Helga, could I please have some milk?"

Shocked, the old woman raised her eyebrows.

"Milk is it, now, lad? Since when do you fancy milk?"

He looked up at her with as much innocence as he could muster. "I thought it might be good for me, if I'm to grow strong enough to protect you and Olyn when you are old and need protection."

Helga was not one easily swayed by the sly, and sly was how he was behaving. "Mightn't it be more like your pets need milk?"

Seeing his flattery was getting him nowhere, he nodded. The large softhearted woman reached over and ruffled his hair. "I'll give you a pitcher and, mind you, it wouldn't hurt if you were to have some as well. You're right about milk helping to grow strong, stout men."

"Helga." Leigh eyed her expectantly.

"Where are your sons? They never visit you. Are they well?"

Her withered hand pushed the strands of gray hair from her forehead. "Ah, my lads, they be well, but in a far off land. I fear I'll never see them again."

"Why not? Don't they want to see you?"

"I'm sure they would, Leigh, but they don't know where I am, and so many years have passed, I'm sure they think I've passed on." She swept a tear from her soft pink cheek. Quickly turning her head and wiping her hands on her apron, she gathered the few utensils from the table.

Leigh finished his biscuit and grabbed the pitcher Helga had set aside for him. Olyn reached for the boy's arm as he rose. "Lad, is there something you're not telling me?"

How can he know? Leigh searched his mind for a satisfying answer. Olyn stroked his stubbled beard and fixed his eyes directly on Leigh's. Haltingly, Leigh said, "Sir, keeping something from you? What do you mean? What could I keep from you?"

Thankfully for him, Olyn's powers were not as vast as they had once been. Morganna LeFay had seen to that.

Chapter Two

Leigh carefully carried the full pitcher of milk up the long winding staircase. The kit was not in plain sight. He looked about the room to discover her hiding place.

"Kit, you wily little witch, where are you?" he called softly.

She darted out into the center of the room, her paws catching on the rushes on the floor. Sneezing on the dust that rose, she fell back onto her haunches.

"Time to eat, little one. I've got some milk for you."

She approached the pan he set on the floor. Placing her snout close to the milk, she sniffed deeply and drew the liquid into her nose. Again she sneezed, and then softly growled.

It became clear she was not happy with this turn of events. She would not venture near the pan again. *I have to get her to eat somehow.* Taking a strip of cloth, he wound the coarse fabric around his finger and dipped the end in the pan of milk. Carefully he held it out to her. Clearly puzzled, she cocked her head to one side and tentatively approached him. She licked the cloth, then drew on it as if she were suckling her mother. He was surprised by the sensation. *How did she feel?*

Does she know she needs me, or am I just a substitute mother?

You fool, of course you are. She's an animal. Doesn't Olyn always say I read too much into the actions of animals?

The years passed quickly for the two. They played in the meadows and hid in the high tower each night. Olyn had grown less vigilant and more stout. Not only did he dislike heights, now he was unable to scale them. Kit and Leigh were safe from discovery in the lofty hideaway.

In the spring of his seventeenth year, Leigh went out into the field with a hawk he'd nursed to health.

"Can you fly today, most regal bird?"

Holding his arm high, he urged the bird to test its wings. The bird sprang from his forearm, spread its wings, and quickly caught a gentle wind that carried it on to greater heights. Swiftly, wings cut the air and the golden bird soared beyond Leigh's sight. Elated with his triumph, Leigh failed to watch where he was walking. Suddenly, a noxious odor assailed his nostrils, causing his eyes to sting and water. Now the stench seemed to be coming from his clothing. A skunk? *How in all my years of caring from the animals of the field did I manage to avoid this before; and why today am I a victim? Today all the creatures of the wild should rejoice in me. I set the great hawk free.*

How am I going to face Olyn? There is definitely no way I can avoid him. He'll smell me a mile off.

Slowly, Leigh headed back to the castle. As he climbed over a small knoll, he sighted Olyn stooped over tending the simple garden Helga had planted. The old man stood erect.

"Good heavens, boy, what is that stench? Have you been mixing with a skunk?"

"I'm afraid so. I don't think there is any way I could deny it."

"Deny it? Lad, I don't think you could deny it from here to the next town." Olyn threw back his head and laughed. His entire body shook with glee. The commotion caused Helga to stick her head out the window of the scullery.

"What is going on here? Oh, my word, what is that stink?"

"That, dear Helga, is our sweet lad. Doesn't he smell fine now?"

"He smells, but fine isn't the word that comes to mind." The old woman drew her head inside and began to hunt for a tub. She emerged from the castle, rump first, dragging a large tub full of water she'd been washing clothes in.

"Come on, boy, shed those clothes. I'll burn them, and Helga will scrub you down and see if we can make you pleasant enough to live with again," Olyn said with a laugh.

"Wait a minute, damn, I'm a man. I'll not have a woman scrub me like I was a wee child." He blushed as the old woman stared at him.

"All right, lad, but I warn you," Olyn said, "I might be a little heavy handed with the scrub brush." He held the boy fast and prevented him from leaving the tub. Turning to Helga, he nodded and indicated she was to withdraw. Her broad face began to color and she swiftly exited.

Olyn stifled a laugh. The humor in the situation, for the moment, escaped Leigh. He saw nothing funny in his humiliation. He'd always prided himself in being a friend to all animals, and now one had turned on him. *I'd better lose this aroma or Kit will avoid me.* How *would* she react to his predicament?

Olyn began to scrub him with vigor.

"Ease up, Olyn, you'll wash the hide off me."

"You don't think I can remove this stench with just a quick rinsing, do you?" The old man rolled up the sleeves of his robe and pushed Leigh deep into the tub.

Sputtering, he came to the surface. "What are you trying to do? Drown me?"

"Quit your whining, boy. You needed a good scrubbing anyway. The skunk just made it possible for you to have it done today."

"Olyn, you make it sound like I never bathe. I swim everyday," Leigh said, thinking how he loved to dive deep into the river and see Kit perched on the shore. She would often venture into the water, but when he dove deep, she would remain on the surface.

Wouldn't she just laugh to smell me? He knew normal animals didn't laugh. But Kit did, whenever he'd gotten himself into some fool circumstance.

As if bidden by unspoken thought, Kit peered around the corner of the scullery. She'd learned to hide herself from Olyn, and carefully crept toward the bushes near the tub. Leigh, used to finding his playmate's hiding places, spied her and scowled her into a retreat to the heavy shrubbery.

Mercilessly, Olyn plunged his head once again beneath the surface. As Leigh came up for air, Olyn lathered his neck and began to carefully remove all traces of the encounter. As he rinsed, he fingered a something at the base of his hairline. "Leigh, why have you never told me about this mole on your neck?"

"What mole?" Leigh asked, as he reached to touch it.

"Why, it's in the shape of a fox head."

Leigh wrenched himself free and, sputtering, emerged from the tub and ran into the castle and the solitude of his tower room.

Unmindful of his sodden robe, Olyn bent to the task of disposing of the stinking water. This tub would not be used by a second person as many others often were. It was no easy task to fill a tub and water was rationed carefully.

Olyn caught the glint of liquid green peering through the leaves of the shrubbery. A fox? Thinking her to be a wild creature, he knew if he paid her little mind, she would leave without incident. Still, he felt it would be prudent to leave the area.

Slowly, Kit approached the tub. Wrinkling her nose at the noxious odor, she ventured to put a single paw into the water. But she could not reach the surface. Jumping up, she balanced herself on the rim of the tub. Deciding the odor too unpleasant to explore further, she tried to leap from her perch and fell forward. She plunged deep into the water. Flailing, she pawed her way to the surface.

Olyn turned back to the tub, hoping the animal had left. He saw a slender hand gripping the rim of the tub. The hand of a young girl, nearly a woman, on the same brink of life as Leigh.

The child rose and stood in the tub. She peered anxiously about her and began to step from the water. Suddenly she slid and fell completely beneath the surface. Then a thoroughly drenched fox leapt from the tub.

Olyn was surprised beyond belief. *What can this mean? Did what I see actually occur? Was this a vision? A portend of things to come? Oh, how I wish I still had all my powers.*

But, he didn't, and no amount of wishing would make it so. He would have to do some thinking on the matter. How strange that today he had a vision and found a mole so like the royal mark on young Leigh.

Gathering his robes up around his ample thighs, Olyn hurried as best he could to the room deep in the dungeon, hidden from all, save himself. Neither Leigh nor Helga would dare venture anywhere near what was referred to as Olyn's place. Far beneath the ground of the castle's only remaining structure, the donjon, his area was well protected and thus suffered little from the ravages of time. This room held images of Olyn that reflected his old, greater powers. He well remembered when it held a full complement of sorcerer tools. When he had served the king he had been a respected wizard.

Olyn descended the broad, slippery steps with difficulty. It had been some time since he'd last ventured to his place. He had little need of spells of late. Far too long out of practice, he needed to force himself to concentrate.

He looked about the cold, unlighted room and set the torch he'd brought with him in the sconce on the wall. What little light the torch provided served only to accentuate the macabre air of the dungeon. He'd chosen this place partly because he knew neither Leigh nor Helga would venture down beneath the castle. Helga hated bugs and things that crawled, and Leigh did not like small, confined spaces. Nonetheless, it served Olyn's purposes. Grabbing a rag from the large table in the center of the room, he began to swat the dust from the numerous volumes lining the walls on makeshift shelves. His eyes, now acclimated to the darkness, sought out the tome that would give up the answer to his quest. Scanning his personal journals, he found nothing. At last his eyes beheld the Master Tome. The answers to the greatest questions of time were held in this ponderous volume.

He'd not consulted the tome since he'd left the King's court. In truth, he should not even retain possession of the book, but since Morganna had stripped him of everything else, he felt justified in keeping it. Carefully, he cleared a space on the large table. With reverence, he carried the Master Tome to the awaiting table. He opened the first page and scanned the table of contents.

A rat scuttled across the floor diverting his attention. When he turned back to the book, somehow it fell open to the directions for the "Mantle of Sorcery."

From the page rose a plume of smoke. It stung Olyn's eyes and blurred his vision. Suddenly, the smoke cleared and there, suspended above the page, was a vermilion cloak, trimmed with snow-white fur and edged with the finest black embroidery. As many years as Olyn had been a wizard, he'd never seen this marvelous cloak before.

Slowly, the cloak unfurled as Olyn reached up to it. Swiftly, the garment closed back upon itself.

"Do not seek to touch the mantle." A deep voice seemed to emerge from the very walls of the dungeon.

Olyn had heard of the mantle, but he'd never imagined he would ever see it. It was usually revealed only to wizards of the third level.

Those of his powers that remained reached the first level. He knew he should be frightened, but for some inexplicable reason he was not. He withdrew his hand. The pages of the book turned by some unseen hand. Words rose from the page, and the print took on sound.

"You are chosen." The voice boomed with the force of a hurricane. Olyn's eyes grew wide. "Chosen? By whom? And for what purpose?"

"You are an instrument of the Druids. The Druids have chosen you."

"What am I to do? What is my task?" Olyn asked, completely awed.

The cloak again unfurled and rent itself in two. The two torn edges licked the air with fiery tongues. From the smoke arose the image of Merlin. Merlin, the greatest of all the wizards, the wizard of the Third Realm to the High King Arthur.

Stroking his snow-white beard, Merlin began to speak. "Olyn, you recall when Morganna took your third-level powers?"

"I do, sir," Olyn said, wondering just what Merlin had in store for him.

"Tell me of today's events."

"Well, I got up, had some biscuits, and then went out to tend the garden." Merlin held up his hand and acrid smoke again assailed Olyn's nostrils.

"Not everything, only that which never happened on any other day." Olyn nodded.

"I understand."

Merlin glowered down at him. "Proceed."

"I-I saw young Leigh come over the knoll near the garden. He stank to high heaven. He'd been mixing with a skunk."

"Had he never encountered a skunk before this day?"

"No, Sir, I'm sure he saw many. The lad loves animals, but never crossed with a skunk before."

"And why this day did he?"

"He'd just released a hawk he'd been tending for a broken wing. It's my thinking he was watching the hawk and didn't see the skunk."

"I see. You bathed him to rid him of the stench?"

"Yes, and that's when I found the mark."

"You found the royal mark?" Olyn nodded foolishly.

"Yes, yes, in the boy's hairline at the base of his neck."

"How can you be so sure?"

"Why else would you be here?"

"Of course. You cannot call me with your first-level powers." Again, the old magician stroked his long white beard, looking thoughtful. "And what further events transpired?"

"Further events?"

"Yes, the mark alone would not summon me to a single-level wizard. What further event?"

Merlin was evidently not pleased Olyn didn't quickly reveal all that had happened.

"But, Merlin, I'm not sure it really happened. I thought it was my mind playing tricks on me. Did it truly happen?"

"It did. Now tell me exactly."

Merlin's demeanor left Olyn no room for doubt.

"When I went to empty the tub, I'd used to scrub the boy, I thought I saw a wild animal in a nearby bush. I caught the glint of its eyes. I left the tub thinking the creature would leave if undisturbed. Apparently, when I turned, it headed for the tub, instead of away. It must have fallen in. When I looked back, a young girl emerged from the water. She then slipped on the bottom and fell back in. Moments later, a thoroughly soaked fox leapt from the tub and scampered off."

"Did you follow this fox?"

"No, Sir, should I have?"

Merlin appeared deep in thought, withdrawn from the moment. Eyes closed, he seemed to be contemplating events of major import. Without another word, he vanished.

Alone, Olyn again questioned his sanity. *Did he really see Merlin? Did the Mantel of Sorcery arise from the book he'd secreted from Morganna? Would his treachery be discovered? Or if Merlin was really here, have I regained some of my powers?* No, that couldn't be. He would feel it. *Oh, what can all this mean?*

"Kit, where are you?" Leigh looked all around their quarters, but she was nowhere to be found. Then he heard it, an uncomfortable mewing. Kit's annoyed noise. She rubbed against his leg, soaking the area he'd just dried with a piece of linen.

"How come you're all wet? Did you mix with a skunk, too?" He sniffed her and noted she did smell faintly of the odorous creature.

Warily, she circled him. He waved at her with the piece of linen. She grabbed at the end and began to pull him about the room, growling as she did so.

"Shhh," he admonished, "Do you want Olyn to hear us?"

Emerald eyes flashed as she shook her head, now issuing a softer growl. Leigh let go of the cloth and finished dressing. Kit continued to shake the hapless rag. He grabbed for her and she escaped his reach. Tricking her, he came up from behind and gathered her in his arms.

"Now, you be quiet. I'm going to get you something to eat," he said, thumping her snout for emphasis.

She pulled back then reached out and playfully nipped him.

"Hey, that hurts. Is that the way to treat someone who cares for you?"

But maybe she didn't want to play anymore? His heart sank. How much longer would his playmate be with him?

Olyn carefully replaced the Master Tome to its position on the shelf in his secret room. Afraid to trust his own senses, he checked about the entire dungeon to see if anything was amiss. Somehow, he felt duty-bound to protect Leigh, beyond the protection he'd provided these past seventeen years. Protection from hunger, cold, and the everyday things that plague an average youth. But Leigh clearly was no average lad. If what Merlin had implied was true, Leigh would have many more enemies, and they would be far more dangerous.

Olyn scoured the room for answers. None were forthcoming. Again, Merlin came in the mist, more faint than before.

"Fear not these changes, Olyn. I wish you to remain here, but Leigh will be sent to King Arthur."

"But, Merlin, I've cared for the boy since he was a wee lad."

"I understand your feelings, however, for the moment you must do as you are bid. On the Isle of Clare is a young lass. For now, she will be your charge. You know the isle well."

"A lass? Merlin, I know nothing of girls."

"This is not a usual lass. You recall your fox?"

"I do."

"And the mark on young Leigh?"

"Are they somehow connected?"

"For the moment that is all I can reveal. You will be in no danger, but you will find yourself aboard Seamus O'Malley's ship."

"What am I to do?"

Merlin narrowed his eyes and stared intently at Olyn. "It will be unveiled in good time."

Seamus O'Malley was head of the clan and he ruled with an iron fist. Most of his holdings he'd obtained through pirating ships that had sailed too close to the offshore island. Captured between the mainland and the island, many were forced to give up their booty.

Seamus had been pirating for many years and had no son to take over the trade. Widowed, he'd been forced to bring his young daughter with him. She was a curious child. Her green eyes could bore through a man and most men on the ship steered clear of her. 'Twas not only her father's wrath they feared, but the child, who had a mysterious air about her, as if she were magic. Seamen were a superstitious lot and gave the red-haired waif a wide berth.

As Olyn waddled up the long dark staircase, carefully lifting his robe lest he disturb the vermin hiding there, he contemplated the recent events.

Will Merlin come again? How will I know my task? Will I be able to summon him, or will he come unbidden?

Suddenly, as he reached nearly to the door of the dungeon, Merlin again appeared, except this time he had less substance and his presence were more like that of a ghost. A figure in the mist.

Olyn leapt back, nearly falling on the wide stone steps. "What will you have me do, Merlin?"

"For now, you must wait. Summon me through the mantle on the full moon, and only when you have no other options. You now have that power. I have bestowed it."

Olyn reached for the sorcerer, hoping for clearer instructions. They were not forthcoming, and the vision disappeared. He blinked and reached for the heavy wooden door. The door was not opened frequently and did not yield easily. Throwing his bulk against the solid surface, he pushed, and nearly fell when it gave way.

"Good heaven's, man. What were you doing down there?" Helga asked, pulling on the door from the outside. Concern showing on her face, she lent him a sturdy arm. "Come, come," she said, gathering him up with her strong arms. She nearly dragged him to a nearby bench to rest.

"What have you been doing?" she asked.

"I don't know about the two of you. First Leigh with a skunk, and now you hiding in a hole in the ground." She chattered on, oblivious to Olyn's real distress.

"Helga, I'm fine. Just let me be."

"Let you be? I'll do nothing of the sort. Now come on, let's get you to the kitchen. Leigh is there eating some fresh biscuits and broth, and you will join him, Olyn."

Seeing she would not leave him to his thoughts, he acquiesced and reluctantly followed the rolling rump of the woman onward to the kitchen.

Chapter Three

Seamus O'Malley, the most feared pirate of the Irish coast, surveyed the calm sea before him. If only it could be so on his deck.

His precious ship was being boarded by the English, who'd pulled their ship alongside the pirate vessel. Men swiftly secured the boats together. Skilled sailors traversed the ropes and spilled onto the deck. They grappled hand-to-hand, neither side the clear victor.

Chest tight, he turned toward the deck, where bodies lay strewn everywhere, the captain's child among them. Sorrow lodged in his throat as a wave of emotion washed over him. A child, who up to this point in her short existence, was not really alive, merely a vessel for a spirit yet to come. She had no mother and had spent her lifetime at the side of her father, save for a brief illness. She lay on the blood-covered deck, her life force oozing from her. Startled, Seamus watched as the lass, dressed in man's breeches, rose and leapt onto the back of a man whose arm was around the neck of another.

"Let me pap go, English, or I'll slit your throat." In an instant, the child had a blade pricking the tender flesh of the man's neck as she hung on his back.

"That's a good lass, Kit. Now we'll rout these damned English." Seamus shoved his blade into the hapless sailor his daughter held at knife point.

She stood back from the man her father had just killed then stooped down to grab a sword from a fallen Englishman and swatted the unfortunate swabby overboard.

Seamus threw back his head and laughed. Once again, he'd bested the foreigners. For many generations, further back than he could remember, the English fought and taunted their Emerald Isle. Seamus pirated to arm a navy he hoped to build against the enemy. He prayed he'd live to see Erie free. His entire clan was behind him. He'd kept them safe and well fed for many years. For himself, his personal coffers exceeded his wildest dreams. Widowed with a daughter, he'd chosen an unusual occupation.

However, his daughter felt that his choice was ideal. She was nearly as ruthless as any man, and more so than many. She gave no quarter to those who would try to make things easier for her, preferring to do things herself in her own way. Her father had been appointed the "O'Malley" and ruled the entire island. He was fast securing lands on the mainland.

Kit was quickly learning her father's trade. Already she knew how to keep the tally sheets and the value of the pirated goods. She, and she alone, knew where the stores were kept. Her father trusted her completely, as he would a favorite son. She had all the savvy of the craftiest of men. And she had a plan. Someday, she would be mistress of the finest castle on the Isle of Clare. The one she had her eye on was the oldest and the best built in all of Ireland. She had learned young and often to take what she desired. She would restore the castle to its greatest grandeur.

Her father's first mate, a grizzled old salt, had deemed it his mission to watch over the girl. He tried at every turn to act as a mother to the lass who had none. Scilti had chosen himself her protector. Kit couldn't remember a time when he hadn't been there.

"Scilti, you scurrilous old goat, why are you hanging about?" Kit sidled up to the old man.

He crossed the well-worn plank deck and embraced her. The link between them could not easily be explained. Scilti had been with her at every momentous event in her life. At least, what part of her life she could remember. It was almost as if she had not lived until the moment the English threatened her father.

From that point on, she grew strong in her own right. Somehow, she sensed he was a conduit to greater power. He provided a safe haven, and with him, she shared her dreams and hopes. Nothing would deter her from the completion of her goals. Goals she had set the moment she realized she was not like other people, as she had no memory of a childhood. She would be head of the O'Malley's, and the first woman to command her own navy.

Leigh's life had changed in an instant. One moment, he was trying to rid himself of the unmistakable odor of skunk and in the next, presented to his cousin, Guinevere, the wife of King Arthur. The elderly wizard Merlin had taken him under his wing, in much the same way as had his dear protector, Olyn.

However, Olyn could have never taught him all that Merlin could. Since Olyn had found that odd-shaped mole on his neck, his life was no longer his own. Now here he stood in Arthur's court. The main receiving room lined with colorful tapestries, illuminated by the sunlight shining through the high curved windows, was more magnificent than anything Leigh had ever dreamed. He remembered Olyn's tales and realized they were true, not mere stories to entertain a lad. Guinevere sat on a raised dais beside her husband. Dressed in golden splendor, she smiled at her young cousin.

"Leigh, how you've grown. You were just a babe in your mother's arms when I saw you last." Shifting in her seat, she arranged the folds of her resplendent gown.

"Y-you k-knew my mother?" Leigh stammered, without the usual proper greeting to the queen.

Guinevere nodded and placed her hand on her husband's arm, as if to restrain him from correcting the lad.

"Yes, Leigh, your mother and I were very close as children. I was maid of honor at her wedding. When she was expecting you, she asked me to be your godmother. Later, I learned she and your father met an untimely death. I was deeply saddened."

Leigh bowed his head and backed away from the dais. Arthur beckoned him near again. "Leigh, you have been called to court due to the intervention of my most trusted advisor, Merlin."

"Yes, sir. I'll do whatever you say." Leigh held his sweaty palms against this stomach, hoping to muffle his roiling innards. Arthur smiled gently.

"No reason for apprehension, lad. You're here for a reason. And it is my charge to discover that reason."

Leigh knelt before the king. "Sire, I will do whatever you wish."

"Lad, I know most of the folk from your land do not favor English rule, and I trust you are no exception. However, the reason for your presence here at court may help to bridge the gap between our two peoples. My fair queen is from your land, and I would have no other. She is a true daughter of the Emerald Isle."

Leigh felt more confused than he'd ever been. It seemed all the events of his life had led up to his presentation at court. Why was everything happening so fast? *Why didn't Olyn come with me? What master am I to serve?*

As he looked at the opulent surroundings, trepidation grew in his heart. Everywhere he cast his glance, he found marvels beyond his imagination. King Arthur sat majestically in a hand-hewn throne. Carved upon the tall back piece was a bevy of foxes. An unusually dyed russet velvet covered the seat. Elaborate tapestries adorned most of the walls. Within these priceless wall hangings, he spotted flecks of golden thread.

A tall dark woman entered from behind the throne, an extremely attractive lady, who walked with the confidence of power. As much as Guinevere was light and goodness, this woman was dark and mysterious. She came around the dais.

"Good morning, my brother and my queen."

Her dark eyes flashed and seemed to glow deep amber, as if lit by an inner fire. Arthur acknowledged her with a nod. Guinevere, seemingly unfettered by the king's reticence, greeted her with a smile. Slowly, the dark woman turned and set her sight upon Leigh and smiled. Leigh could feel some hint of danger from this woman and his stomach tightened. Drawing near to him, she extended her hand. Instinctively, Leigh withdrew.

"Do not fear, lad, I shan't hurt you. I merely wish to welcome you to my brother's court." Her mouth said *welcome*, but her eyes clearly stated such a greeting was fraudulent.

"I have welcomed the boy, Morganna." Arthur spoke, not unkindly, but warily.

Leigh sensed the kinship between this brother and sister was not the usual familial relationship.

"Relax, dear brother, I know you have extended official welcome to the child. I simply wished to let him know he has a friend at court should he have need of one." Morganna drew herself up to her full height, which was nearly as great as Arthur's, and swept the dark cloak she wore around her. The cloak seemed so deep a black as to defy midnight itself. A rich fabric and trimmed with the fur of a black wolf.

"The lad is a relative of my queen and will have all manners of friends here." Arthur glowered at his half sister and stared her into silence. As unannounced as she'd arrived, Morganna swept from the chamber in the same way. Arthur turned to his wife. "We will have to watch her. She seems to have too much interest in young Leigh."

"Morganna." The stern voice seemed to come from nowhere.

"You take care. Do not interfere with young Leigh Longwurth."

Morganna's eyes narrowed to ominous slits. Merlin had foiled her plans more than once. If she were not careful, she would be unable to discern the true reason for Leigh's presence.

"Heed me, woman," he said, nearly shouting. His eyes fixed upon her with a steel blue determination. "You will not interfere with my tutelage of the boy. *I* will teach him what he needs to know, not you. Do you understand?"

"Of course, Merlin, I have never doubted your wisdom." Almost coyly, she tossed her dark tresses back over her shoulder as she turned to face the wizard. "I merely thought to expand the boy's knowledge of his family. We are related, you know," she said haughtily.

"I am well aware of your relationship to the royal family, but do not think for one moment you will be afforded the same courtesy as the king and queen." Merlin's eyebrows rose to accentuate his statement. He wouldn't allow Morganna to get her clutches on the boy. Leigh would be totally unprepared for her type of treachery. Merlin had given his word to Olyn the lad would be safe in his care. Whatever vigilance was required, he must undertake. He had given his word, a word as sacred as any vow taken by the clergy.

Morganna moved to the left of Merlin, out of his clear line of sight. "Merlin, I have no motive other than friendship."

Merlin nodded, knowing every utterance was a lie. "The person who has you as friend is indeed in dire straits. Do not try my patience, you witch!" Turning, he forced her to look directly into his eyes.

"You dare call me witch?" she retorted, her nostrils flaring like a spent horse.

"I dare call you what you are. You will never be more than a witch. And a demonic witch, at that." Merlin extended his arms over her as if he could repel her evil deeds with a sweep of his hands.

"No more than a simple witch, think you? Well, dear Merlin, you may be talented but even your talents are limited. I've been long from the kitchen. Herbs and potions are not my only tools." Spittle hung from the corner of her mouth. She wiped it with the back of her hand and glared directly into his eyes.

"You best watch closely, warlock," she threatened.

"Warlock? I am far more than a warlock, and you know it well. Mind your tongue, you harridan!"

"When I learn all there is to know about the young lad, I will have my way." She turned sharply and left the room.

"You will never learn the entire truth," he said aloud, to no one. "It is my sacred duty to protect this child, and by the heavens I will do so."

A strong resonant voice broke his introspection. "You appear to be alone, Merlin. To whom do you speak?"

"Ah, Arthur, my words were for your dear half-sister. That one is up to some sort of evil."

"I agree, and I feel it has something to do with young Leigh." Arthur's massive frame seemed to bend with the weight of his office.

Merlin noted that Arthur's hair was beginning to gray, small silver streaks among the deep brown. He was wearing a favorite tunic Guinevere had selected for him to wear while greeting her young cousin. The fabric was a clear blue nearly rivaling the color of his eyes. His ward's eyes now clouded with concern, for both his country and his young ward.

"Merlin, what are we to do with the lad?" Arthur asked.

"My king, at this point, I cannot tell you. It would not be wise for you to know. When the time is right, I will inform you. For now, see he's instructed as a page and prepare him for possible knighthood."

"Knighthood, Merlin? Does he realize what will be expected of him? Can he offer allegiance to the crown?"

"Arthur, do not question me now." Merlin drew back and settled down onto bench along the side of a whitewashed wall. The tapestry that hung opposite the bench depicted a scene very like the hunts at Camelot. Merlin marveled at the intricate needlework, much of it more complex than any of his spells. How he wished he knew the whole of Leigh's tale and how to block Morganna from her foul intent.

Alone and confused, Leigh paced in the small room set aside for pages. The narrow room was devoid of decoration so that a page might concentrate on the duty at hand. To Leigh, it was most magnificent, compared to the quarters he'd shared with Kit. *I miss her!* Without warning, Guinevere entered the cell-like room. Leigh struggled to quickly right himself.

"Your Queen-ness."

"I don't believe I've ever been called 'Your Queen-ness'," Guinevere said with a wide smile. Gracefully, she crossed the room and drew Leigh back down to the narrow bed.

"How do I call you?"

"Leigh, we are kinsmen, family. You may call me Guinevere, or, while we are in the company of others, 'Your Highness'. There is no need to be so formal. I am your friend as well as your cousin. I am here to help you."

"Cousin, I don't even know why I'm here or what kind of help I need. Do you know why I'm here?"

"No, Leigh, all I know is Merlin brought you here for a very important reason. What that is, I am not aware."

Leigh searched her face, hoping to find the answers in her features. She was very beautiful, but her expression revealed nothing. She placed her arm around his shoulders and brushed his hair back from his forehead. He grew nervous at her touch.

"Please, why am I here? I was doing fine with Olyn and Helga and Kit."

"Olyn, I know, and Helga, I think Merlin said, she did the cooking, but who is Kit?"

"You won't tell anyone?"

"Not if you don't wish me to."

"You have to promise."

"I promise." Guinevere nodded solemnly.

"She's my playmate. No, she's my friend."

"Oh, I see, a childhood friend, perhaps?"

"No, she's more than that, we always will be friends. She's my soul mate. She understands me. In ways no one else can."

Guinevere nodded and silently encouraged him with a quizzical look. "You don't want to hear about my life."

"Now, Leigh, that is not true. Allene and I were one another's soul mates, as close as cousins can be. I feel no less for her son. I understand the connection. Please, do tell me about Kit. How did you meet?"

"I found her under her mother's body."

"Under her mother's body? She was an orphan then, Leigh?"

"No, well, yes, her mother was dead, caught in a trap. I dug her out, put her in my tunic, took her back to the castle, and hid her in my tower room.

"How did you care for an infant?"

"Well, she wasn't an infant, not like a baby."

"I don't understand. Even if she were a young child, how could you care for her?"

"She isn't a person, she's a fox. And I fed her with milk from Helga's goats. When she got older she hunted for herself, but she always came back to the tower."

"Oh, I think I understand. She was a beloved pet."

"No, no, Your Highness, not just a pet. She's my friend. I never had a friend and she is. That's all, she just is."

Guinevere softly shook her head.

"Leigh, perhaps you would like to come with me to the faire in town this day? You are not to begin training until next week."

"I've never been to a faire. Is it as grand as Olyn says?"

"Olyn knows well the spectacle of a faire. When he was here with Merlin as a young wizard, I'm told he never missed a faire."

"Somehow it sounds odd that Olyn would have fun. At the castle, he worked long hours in the garden, just to feed us. I don't think he ever has any fun."

The look on the boy's face was full of longing for Olyn, as well as his playmate. The queen took his hand and began to lead him to the door. As she reached for the handle, the door seemed as if by magic, to open without her touch. In the casement stood Merlin.

"Good day, my queen. How is our lad getting along?" he asked majestically with a long sweep of his arms. He pushed his sleeves up as if to begin a complex task.

Guinevere acknowledged the sorcerer's presence with a deep smile and warm brown eyes. "Good day, Merlin. Yes, my cousin is doing well, but he misses his family."

"Family? I understood he had no family."

Leigh spoke up, somewhat timidly. "Not a usual family, but Olyn and Helga, they are all I know." He shot a glance at the queen, hoping she wouldn't reveal his secret. She returned his glance with a reassuring wink.

Leigh let out the breath he'd been holding. She would hold his confidence.

Merlin turned deep steel blue eyes on him. Leigh felt as if they were penetrating to his inner core. *He knows more about me than I know myself.*

The wizard crossed his now bare arms, closed his eyes, and seemed to withdraw from their presence. Guinevere touched Merlin's arm.

Quickly he turned to glare at her. "My queen, leave us!"

"But, Sir, can't she please stay? She's the only one I know in this strange land." Merlin turned his flint-like eyes on the boy.

"She is to leave." His demeanor left no room for doubt.

The queen bent her golden head and gracefully backed from the room. "Please, Sir," Leigh said, "I'm frightened. Let her stay."

From the doorway the elegant queen spoke softly.

"Do not fear, Leigh. Merlin will not harm you. I shall see you this afternoon in time for the faire." Leigh gave a timid nod.

"I'll do as you say, but I'm not sure of Merlin's purpose."

She placed her fingertips to her lips, blew the boy a soft kiss, and quickly withdrew. Leigh turned his attention to the wizard. In some sort of a trance, Merlin appeared totally oblivious to his surroundings. The dust from the floor rose about him in tiny tornadoes, until the magician became encased in a multitude of silver spirals.

Merlin snapped open his eyes and directed them at Leigh. The force in Merlin's glare frightened Leigh. *Is this part of the training of all pages?*

Merlin lowered his arms and the dust settled.

"Fear not, young Leigh. Nothing ill will befall you. I am here to help you realize your true destiny."

As fearsome as Merlin had been, in a moment he took on a more kindly countenance. Leigh hesitantly spoke.

"Merlin? Are you all right?"

"Your concern pleases me, lad."

"I've never seen anything like that. Can Olyn do that, too?"

"At one time he could, lad, before evil befell him."

"What do you mean? The bad woman he talks about?"

"Yes, lad, she is a truly evil person. Her only motive is discord among peaceful beings."

"You mean she hates all good people?"

"Yes, my boy, I'm afraid I do. At some point in her life she may have been good, but in the many years I've known her she has been a witch." Leigh felt his eyes grow wide. "You mean, she's truly a witch?"

"I do," Merlin said, with a finality that halted further questions.

Leigh sat back on the narrow cot in resignation. Whatever the wizard had in store for him, he would not question.

"Leigh, I know you do not understand all that has taken place. Do not concern yourself. There will come a time all will be revealed to you." With that pronouncement, he left as swiftly as he appeared. Before Leigh had time to gather his senses, he heard a gentle tap at the door.

"Leigh, it's Guinevere. May I enter?"

"Of course, Your Highness."

She pushed open the door and issued a clear melodious chuckle.

"You know, I rather like 'Your Queen-ness'." Her eyes twinkled with obvious merriment. Leigh stared, dumbfounded.

"But-but you said I should say 'Your Highness'."

"That is the proper term, but sometimes I like doing things that are not so proper. Don't you?"

Propriety was something Leigh was not familiar with. He always did what he felt what right. What needed doing, he did. Feeding Kit and helping Olyn and Helga were his responsibilities. He undertook them gladly.

"Leigh, are you ready to go?"

"G-go?" he stammered.

"Where, when?"

"To the faire. Now. Don't you want to go?"

"The faire? Oh, yes, 'Your Queen-ness'," he said with a pleased glint in his eye.

"Come on, cousin. Hurry, we don't want to miss anything." They hurried out of the castle and swiftly crossed the meadow, before the queen's attendants were able to join them.

"Leigh, we have so much to see," Guinevere said, grabbing a basket and filling it with wild flowers.

"Your Highness, why are you picking flowers now? They will be dead before we return," Leigh said.

"That is true, and what I intend. Dried flowers retain their smell much longer than fresh ones."

Leigh's interest quickly turned from the flowers to the joyful sounds he heard in the distance. "Oh, cousin, what is that sound?"

"Sound? Oh, 'tis music. Isn't it grand? Have you never heard music before?"

"Only the singing of the birds. This . . . music is so much more. What manner of animal makes such a sound?"

"No animal, Leigh. Men make the sounds using harps and pipes."

As they drew closer to the wondrous sounds, Leigh sniffed the air, catching such fascinating smells, the like of which he'd never smelled before. "Oh, Your Highness, what are those magnificent smells? This must be what heaven is like. The wonderful aromas make my heart sing and my stomach rumble."

"I know, Leigh, there are all manners of wondrous things to see, to hear, to smell, and to eat."

"What is the cause for such a happening?"

"This is the feast of St. John the Baptist. The crops are in the ground and there is much to celebrate after a long hard winter. Did you not celebrate feast days with Olyn?"

"Helga made cakes on Christmas, but that was all. However, they were very delicious cakes, and I enjoyed them very much." Leigh did not want to appear ungrateful to the pair that raised him and provided him with shelter for so many years.

"Well, now that you are here at court, we will have many celebrations and you shall have cake whenever you wish."

To Leigh's simple desires, this was like having a magic wand that could grant you anything. *I wonder if Olyn ever had all the cake he wanted? He certainly looked as if he had.*

As they approached the center of all the activity, Leigh noticed a man carrying an object shaped much like the wing of a butterfly. Strings seemed to be drawn across it. A man strummed his fingers over the strings and played such wonderful music. *Yes, that was what she'd called it . . . music.*

"Leigh, are you enjoying the troubadours?" she asked.

"Oh, yes, Your Queen-ness," he said with a twinkle in his eye.

"Does the man play only here and only on feast days?"

"He plays over the countryside. He is called a traveling minstrel."

"What of these others who jump about and the ones who throw so many things in the air and never seem to drop any of them?"

Guinevere captured the eye of one of the players and indicated he was to join her and Leigh.

"Good day to you, sir. Have you traveled far?" she asked, placing her hand on Leigh's arm.

"I come from Spain, my lady."

"My cousin has never been to a faire. Could you show him some of the wonders?" The juggler bowed low and swept his pins beneath his arm.

"But, of course, good sir, there is much to see and much to do. Where shall we start?"

The juggler took Leigh's hand, bowed to the queen, and quickly swept him up into the crowd. Again, Leigh found himself cut off from the familiar, only this time it wasn't so sudden. At least he could see where he might be going. He could see the queen making straight to a merchant, who had numerous bolts of material lain over a long table. He did not feel he was in any danger. Still, he would have liked to have known what to expect.

All of these strange changes troubled him, for it seemed he no longer had control of his own life. As a lad he hadn't minded Olyn and Helga making all of the decisions. It left him more time to spend with Kit.

Kit, I wish you were here. I'm sure these smells would tempt you even more than Helga's biscuits. Where are you?

Chapter Four

Kit gazed out at the sea, its waves as choppy as she had ever seen them in all her years at sea. She loved the ferocity of the storm. The sounds of the wind lashing the sails and the rigging slapping against the mast was music to her ears. All those under her command respected the courage of their leader. She never expected more of them than she did herself.

She scrambled over the rigging and shouted orders to her men. Her father had turned over command of his vessel, the *Storm Maiden,* when he lost his arm. He trusted her over any of his men and she was a far more capable pilot than he was. Many of her crew had more years at sea, but few had more expertise. Her father's right-hand man/woman for a full two years, at seventeen, she was the youngest sailor on the Irish Sea, probably the youngest ever to lead a crew. She maneuvered the narrows along the Irish coastline far better than her father and even his father before him.

She watched as Scilti struggled to keep his balance and hold the wheel as the deck tipped one way, then another. The pitch and roll tossed crewmen about the ship like jugglers' pins. This was the first journey her father had sailed in nearly a year. He was getting on in years and now preferred his time on land. He trusted her to handle all matters at sea.

She shouted to her father. "Da, get below. I can't spare men to haul you out of the sea."

"Don't you tell me how to ride out a storm. I rode out many worse than this." The old man shook his head and held fast to the main mast.

"I mean it, Da. I'm captain, and you'll follow orders just like any other man."

She wouldn't risk losing their precious cargo by stopping to haul in a man from the icy waters. A wave lapped beneath the ship, carried it high on the crest and then dashed the craft into the swell. Kit lashed herself to the wheel and shouted for the men to get below.

All complied, except her father. Screaming for his daughter to save him, he swept over the gunnels and out to the turbulent sea.

Kit stared at the dark angry sea and made the decision at the helm. The ship would continue to ride out the storm, without making an attempt to save her father.

As the seas calmed, Scilti unlashed himself from the mizzen to check on his ward.

"Kit, lass! Are ye safe now?" The old sailor squinted his eyes against the glare of the sun that followed the storm.

"Here, Scilti," she said, as she cut her bonds from the wheel.

"Did we lose any men?" The well-worn face looked like tanned leather.

Olyn, as Scilti, crossed the deck, not daring to show any real concern lest she dismiss him. She had to let him stay near her if he was to discharge Merlin's orders. It had been some time since he'd seen even the faintest mist of Merlin. But he knew his duty was nonetheless sacred. Wizards worked over vast spans of time.

He had watched carefully over his charge as directed. When necessary, he'd even protected her from her own folly. She often took unnecessary risks, not only with herself, but with ships and men. Scilti knew, however, each of these risks was carefully calculated. Kit had a goal in mind and every action geared toward that end.

"I did not see Pap below. Was he on deck, lashed to the mast?"

"He refused to lash himself and was washed overboard," she said.

"Overboard, lass? How long ago?"

He felt a stab of regret. Seamus and he had shared the care of Kit since she put to sea a few short years ago. The relationship between father and daughter was unlike most in that once Kit commanded a ship, she no longer did as her father bid.

"He went when the largest swell hit. He defied my order to get below." Yet no sign of remorse from the child. Why? Shock?

"God, we've no hope of finding him now." Olyn/Scilti felt it was his duty to comfort the girl over the loss of her father. She displayed no sense of loss of grief, like an animal only concerned with survival. But how could she not love her pap? He'd done everything a father could for his child. As Olyn, he'd been very concerned for Leigh's welfare and now Olyn transferred his feelings to Kit, the ward Merlin had assigned him.

With Kit's father the only man lost, Kit was in line to the 'O'Malley' since she had no other siblings.

"Scilti." Kit called for the man she knew would be her only ally. As she read his face, she found he feared the same as she. The men would be against a woman as the 'O'Malley.' The head of the clan had always been a man.

Kit stood on deck and called the men to order.

"Gentlemen, I have some bad news. Today my father was washed overboard. I am taking over as the 'O'Malley,' as is my right as his only heir."

The men turned to one another and the grumbling passed from man to man. They were definitely not pleased at this turn of events.

Scilti raised his arms and addressed the group. "Men, you all know Kit has done her best by you and will continue to serve as captain of this ship and as the clan chieftain the 'O'Malley,' as is her due."

"The hell she will," a man shouted angrily from the crew.

Another man said, "The head of the clan must be a man. There's no way around it."

Kit, her green eyes blazing, placed her hands on her hips. "Have I not kept your bellies full and amassed fortunes for each of you? You would turn against me now? This is mutiny."

The men, who at one time would have died for her, now were ready to kill her. They edged closer and closer. The first mate did his best to calm them. "Men, men, listen. Kit has done well by you. You owe her your allegiance. She is your captain."

"Captain, yes, chieftain, no. We'll not have a woman lead us."

Standing aside, Scilti saw the determination of the group and realized he must discharge his duties to Merlin and protect the girl. Quickly, he picked up a few belongings and grabbed her.

"Is this how you stand, Scilti? You want to be run about by a woman? Overboard with the both of them." A tall burley man lunged toward them, but they eluded his grasp.

"Kit, come with me. We have to jump. It's the only way." Scilti grabbed her and headed for the gunnels.

"Stay deep. They will try to get us."

The two dove deep. Scilti's girth rendered him buoyant. Kit's tiny form cut deeply into the ocean. The old gentleman searched beneath the surface. The girl was nowhere to be found. *I can't give up. I gave my word to Merlin. That can't be ignored. My God, Kit, where are you?*

The bubbles rose about his ample body. Forcing his eyes to open in the salty water, he searched for the young captain. He could not believe his eyes. A slender red fox swam a few feet away from him. *It can't be. Is this the same fox?*

Though separated from Leigh these many years, Scilti knew, somehow, that he was part of a master plan and that they would one day be together once more. The little fox was proof of that.

Swiftly, he grabbed the animal and struggled to the surface, the roaring seas fighting him every inch of the way. Once they broke the surface, for some reason, unknown to Scilti, he plunged the animal's head beneath the water.

At once the animal again became a woman. Kit.

Sputtering, she glared at Scilti.

"What are you trying to do, drown me?"

"Nay, lass, I was not taking your life, merely saving it."

"Saving is it? Seems a strange way to go about it."

"I cannot tell you my reasoning, only that I was ordered to do what I did."

"Ordered? By whom? I give the orders here, Scilti."

"Kit, you no longer have a crew or a ship. How can you give orders?"

Kit knew the old man was right, but she was born to lead. *I can feel the power within me.*

Swimming in the chilled waters, she strained to keep Scilti afloat as he was old and easily winded. As she pushed him upon the beach, he coughed and relieved his lungs of the sea he'd swallowed.

They soon found themselves on a desolate shore. The soft sea sand felt warm beneath her feet. Raising her face to the sky, she determined there would be little daylight remaining. They would have to settle in for the night and protect themselves from the damp sea air.

"Scilti, we have to find wood to make a fire for the night and in the morning we will make our plans. My people have not heard the last of Kit O'Malley."

"Kit, I wish I could tell you what will happen to you, but I am under oath."

"What are you babbling about? Were you in the rum stores?"

The old man closed his eyes, clasped his hands together, and spoke to the vacant sky.

"Help me, Merlin. What am I to do?"

"You call on Merlin? The English King's wizard? Have you not sworn fealty to Ireland? Where are your loyalties, Scilti?"

"Lass, never question my loyalty. My soul is the soul of Ireland. I owe no allegiance to the king, but as members of the same brotherhood, my sworn oath to Merlin is inviolate. Merlin is the highest wizard of all time."

The girl shook herself, much like an animal to dry its coat. She drew her bright red hair back from her face, discarding the scarf she always wore covering it, and looked to the distant hill. The hillside, covered with thick rich green foliage, welcomed them. Kit, ever the practical one, determined where they could secure wood and food. Running, she scrambled and caught a small rabbit. Wringing the animal's neck, she gathered the wood Scilti brought to the clearing. Once the fire was set, they would have enough food to get them through the night. In the morning, she would determine what would be their next action. Some deep hidden instinct told her this was the island of her dreams. Here she would find the castle she sought.

Tying the rabbit onto a spit over the fire, Scilti watched the girl carefully. He reached out, cut a slice of meat, and offered it to her on the point of his eating knife.

"Here, child, you will need to keep up your strength."

Absently, she took the offered meat and began to stare into the flames. Scilti did likewise and concentrated, hoping he could contact Merlin. Though the heavens did not display the proper circumstance, still he implored the stars. The smoke rose and he stared, mesmerized, into the flickering fire. It was to no avail; Merlin did not appear.

Gently touching her shoulder, Scilti nodded to the darkening sky. "Kit, we must seek shelter. There is not much daylight left."

She looked up at her first mate and then placed her gaze on the distant hill. The crimson sky seemed to bleed for her loss—ship and crew, all were gone, never to be replaced. Undaunted by circumstances, she determined to use them to her advantage. It was time for a new challenge in her life. It would take time to secure her position as chieftain. She'd been the first female captain and now she would be the first woman to own and restore a Viking castle. Finding one would be a simple matter as abandoned castles from ancient wars peppered the shores.

Her mind set, she followed Scilti into a thicket and settled down on the mat of pine needles he'd arranged for her.

Quickly, she dropped off to sleep, knowing Scilti would watch over her.

Chapter Five

As accustomed to solitude as Leigh had been, he now found the camaraderie of the other pages uncomfortable. He even shared his sleeping quarters since he'd been assigned a knight. The other pages envied his attachment to Sir Lancelot. Lancelot was on the list of favored knights and held the highest seat at the Round Table, on Arthur's right hand. Fair of face, his favors were sought by many of the ladies-in-waiting to Queen Guinevere.

Leigh served his knight well, taking care his armor was cleaned and protected from rust as well as, along with the other pages, exercising Lancelot's mount in the exercise yard. Lancelot found his page eager to please and quick to learn. Leigh quickly advanced from simple page to a valuable resource for the knight.

Lancelot crossed the courtyard with his mount's reins in his hand. "Leigh," he said, holding the leather bridle out to the boy.

"I think Cathaoimore's thrown a shoe. Please take him to the smith and tend to it."

Leigh led the horse across the courtyard to the blacksmith shop where he handed the bridle to the new smith. At once, Cathaoimore eyed the swarthy man with contempt. Nervously the hide on his back twitched. The stallion attempted to back away from the smith. The smith then pulled downward on his bridle in a move to control the large animal. Cathaoimore would not surrender to this handling. He reared and kicked his forelegs at the now frightened smith. The horse usually stood quietly while he was being shod. Today he would not.

Successful in freeing the bridle from the hands of the man he'd taken instant dislike to, Cathaoimore again reared, his hooves pawing the air frantically. Backward he danced then kicked the cooling pail and jarred the hot shoes from the forge. The molten iron ignited the dry straw. In seconds, the wall of the smith was afire. The massive horse's nostrils quivered fearfully as he smelled the smoke. Flames quickly leapt up the wall of the smithy. The smith ran from the lean to and Leigh reached for Cathaoimore's bridle. The horse's eyes were wide with terror. Leigh petted his muzzle and spoke to him in most gentle tones.

"Easy boy, relax. We'll get out of here. I won't let anything happen to you."

The flames licked up the side wall and caught on the cloth that served as a door for the smith. The courtyard, once a hub of individual activity, became as one to fight the blaze. Buckets of water passed from man to man and doused the fire.

Cathaoimore fought Leigh each step of the way, but Leigh firmly led him from the flames. Leigh petted the horse's muzzle and slipped him an apple.

"Here you go, boy. Remember, Leigh will never forget your favorite treat."

Most pages were uncomfortable around the powerful animal, but Leigh and Cathaoimore had formed a friendship that set them both apart from others.

Carefully, Leigh led the horse to safety outside the crude lean-to that served as the smithy. Only the forge remained untouched by the flames. Fortunately, the smith consisted of only one wall and the fire died quickly.

The smith ran over and grabbed the stallion's bridle. The horse resisted and shook him nearly senseless. The smith released his grasp and fell in a heap to the ground.

"What's wrong with that dammed horse?" he asked, rubbing the shoulder where he landed.

Leigh eyed him with as much disgust as he knew the horse felt. "There is nothing wrong with Cathaoimore. Have you never shod a stallion before?"

Continuing to brush his clothing, the swarthy man glared at young Leigh. "Who are you to tell me my trade? You're but a lowly page."

"I am, sir. And I serve my knight well, taking care of his armor and his horse. If you fail to care for Cathaoimore, I will be forced to inform Sir Lancelot."

"Oh, you're Lancelot's lackey. That fop. He wouldn't last a moment with me in a fair fight."

"Not so, sir," Leigh said, his eyes blazing, "No man can best Lancelot, fair or foul."

The man reached out and tried to grab Leigh by his free arm. Leigh dropped the reins and backed away from him.

"Come here, you sniveling little toad. I'll pound you and Lancelot both into the ground."

He moved quickly and grabbed Leigh by the scruff of his neck. Leigh kicked and squirmed with all his strength.

Lancelot came up to the burnt-out smith and saw the lad flailing his arms and legs trying to free himself from the grasp of a large sweaty man.

"You there, leave go of the lad. You've no cause to treat him so."

"I suppose you're the good Sir Lancelot," the blacksmith said mockingly. "I am, and I suggest you let the lad go, or I'll be forced to skewer you on my dinner knife."

"Your dinner knife?"

"I wouldn't waste a lance or fighting blade on a fool who feels he is brave by attacking a child."

The smith dropped Leigh, a look of utter surprise on his face. His surprise quickly turned to anger, and he advanced with both fists raised. "I told the boy you were a fop, and I was right. Come, meet me in a fair fight."

Leigh quickly scrambled out of the way as Lancelot crossed the distance between him and the smith. "What is your name? I hate to best a man without knowing his name."

"It's Ralf, and there is no way you'll be besting me," he said menacingly.

Shoulders bent and head down, he faced the knight. Lancelot sidestepped him, and the oaf stumbled forward and landed on his face in the dirt. Rolling over, he wiped the soil from his face with the back of his hand.

"Stand fast, coward."

"I am no coward. You are simply outmatched." The agile knight in full armor quickly averted a collision from the second onslaught of the massive man.

The smith grew winded, simply from the exertion of chasing the knight. Leigh began to laugh aloud at the clumsiness of the smith, which served to anger the smith further. He turned on the boy and reached out to grab him a second time.

"Sir, I warn you. If anything happens to that page, you will pay dearly. It's clear you are not an honorable man. Give me just a single reason to question your behavior, and I will see King Arthur learns of this."

Enraged, the smith turned and raced at Lancelot with the force of a driving wind.

Lancelot let him pass and hit his backside with the broad of his now drawn sword. "This is the last I will say on the incident. Now, see my horse is shod and the shoeing is correct, else you will be gone."

The burley man retreated and headed to the burnt blacksmith shop, hoping to find enough undamaged tools to complete the task the knight assigned. Wisely the fellow chose not to challenge the knight, as for a certainty the witch would learn and he would suffer more at her hand than Lancelot's.

"You fool," Morganna hissed at Ralf. "It does not pay to make enemies. I told you to behave as if you were the true smith and shoeing horses is part of that charade. Can't you handle the simplest of tasks?"

"I didn't know that horse of Sir Lancelot's would take such a dislike to me. He's a beast."

"Perhaps, but it's your duty to infiltrate the relationship between the knight and his page. I need to know the reason for young Leigh's presence. He is from the same land. He must know of the elixir."

"All right, I'll make amends with the lad, and try to befriend the good knight," Ralf said sarcastically.

"Mind your opinion of the favorite knight of the king does not further hamper your judgment."

Morganna had no problem manipulating the simple peasant, but that very simpleness could foil her plans. She needed the boy's confidence if she was to learn about his true purpose here at court. Majestically, she swept from the courtyard and into the castle.

So intent was she upon her plot, she ran headlong into Merlin. "Oh, Merlin, I'm sorry, I didn't see you there."

Merlin looked down his narrow patrician nose at the beautiful woman. "That much is apparent." Morganna seemed so driven by her own personal agenda, without thought for the welfare of others, he would continue to watch her closely.

"Where are you headed, Morganna?" he asked as lightly as possible, lest he put her on her guard. He needed her, if not to totally trust him, at least to respect him. She needed to know the force of his power, without feeling threatened by it. He would have to appear to trust her.

Warily, she answered the wizard. "I am headed to the solar. I've just thought of a pattern for a new tapestry and I wish to draw it before I forget the intricacies of the design."

"Ah, 'tis a matter of true import," he said.

She smiled widely, confident Merlin would not divine her true intent. "Yes, I am planning to portray the hunt with Arthur on a great white stallion. I believe it will be most beautiful."

"I'm sure it will be," Merlin replied.

Morganna gathered her skirt and headed up the stairs to the solar. As he watched her disappear up the staircase, Merlin puzzled over her haste to be out of his presence. *What is that witch planning now? How much has she already done in the matter of young Leigh?* Merlin knew there was no reason to trust that Morganna was inspired by a simple sewing task. She had more significant matters on her mind.

Morganna found the solar oddly deserted at the hour when most of the ladies-in-waiting would be about their sewing tasks. Morganna looked about, hoping to find a scrap to place the design upon should anyone question her about her presence.

Finding something suitable, she began to sketch a design, similar to what she told Merlin she would be using. Determined in her work, she failed to hear the footsteps on the stair.

"Morganna," a soft gentle voice called to her, "What are you doing here? Why aren't you with the others at the chapel?"

Slowly, Morganna lifted her eyes to the gaze of the queen. Careful to disguise her surprise, Morganna said, "I'm sorry, my queen, I was so drawn by the pattern for the new tapestry, I failed to note the solar was empty. Where did you say the ladies are?"

"It must be a very intricate design to absorb your concentration so completely," the queen said archly. "Do you care to join me, Morganna? I'm going to the chapel to see the others at vespers."

"Oh, thank you, Guinevere, I would love to join you, but if I don't sketch this design, the intricacies will escape me," she said coyly.

"As you wish," the queen replied in a tone the suggested she knew full well Morganna was capable of retaining any pattern indefinitely. Then with great dignity, Guinevere took her leave and descended the spiral staircase.

There has to be some clue about this boy. Morganna searched the solar, anywhere Guinevere might have left a letter or some scrap belonging to the boy. *He's old for a page and the queen seems all too friendly with him.* Morganna's gaze fell upon Guinevere's sewing basket. A small intricate piece of embroidered linen protruding from the corner of the basket caught her attention.

Looking about, she made sure she was not being observed. Opening the woven lid, she lifted the scrap of linen from the other sewing pieces and noted an ornate baptismal medal fastened to the cloth. The fine gold filigree was a depiction of the Virgin Mary and her tiny son, the infant Jesus. Morganna knew Guinevere was a Christian, even though her husband still followed the old ways and permitted the counsel of Merlin, the sorcerer. Searching her memory, Morganna recalled a similar medal given by Guinevere to a woman who had given birth and was having the child baptized. However, that medal had not been as costly as this. This was the work of a very talented goldsmith. Such a medal would only be given to a kinswoman, such as a beloved cousin. She was sure this was the medal the queen had ordered to be made for her cousin when she had learned she was to bear a child. Once Guinevere had learned of her cousin's death, it became clear she had kept the medal as a fond remembrance.

The strong smell of the balsam boughs beneath Kit's head woke her. She looked around and got her bearings. She was without her ship, without her men, and even without a father. As if that mattered. The morning fog was lifting, revealing a silver castle high on a distant bluff. The elegant structure shone like a crystal spire in the morning sun. The evening sky had hidden its magnificence.

She shook Scilti and found him difficult to rouse. His face contorted, as if he were battling a demon. She continued to shake him. "Scilti, wake up. I've found it."

"Found it? Found what?" He rubbed his eyes to clear away the slumber. "I've found my castle, there, up on the bluff. See it?"

The grizzled old sailor squinted against the sun and looked in the direction she pointed. "Sure looks purty in the sun, don't it?"

"Purty? Scilti, it's beautiful. It's mine. My castle, the one in my dreams. Come on, Scilti, we have to go there."

Slowly, they made their way up the rock-strewn hill to the outer walls of the manor then through the stones and over the mossy slopes into what had once been a magnificent courtyard.

Kit found herself filled with both awe and glee. Nothing would stop her from making this pile of misshapen stones into a castle fit for a queen.

In the center of the rubble sat a young boy rolling pebbles. Hearing them approach, the lad raised his head, grinned, then continued his play. Kit glowered at the interloper. This was her castle, not a playhouse for a simple child.

"Who are you, lad?" Scilti asked.

"Aaron," he said. Kit moved to the center of the courtyard and grasped the boy by the shoulder.

"Whose castle is this?" she asked.

"Kit, the lad is fey, leave him be," Scilti said. Wide-eyed, the boy looked up at her.

"Da's place," he said and returned to rolling his pebbles.

"Who's yer da?" Kit asked, a little less forcefully. Kit turned to Scilti for answers, as none were forthcoming from the dirty urchin. "What are we supposed to do with him? This is my castle, and I don't care who his da is."

Scilti shook his head in resignation. Kit was not a compassionate individual, but for some reason the fates had placed this child in her path and it was up to him to determine what was to be done with the lad.

Kit looked about the courtyard. Stones once placed in careful designs were strewn haphazardly and flowerbeds, which had once lined the perimeter, were now choked with weeds. Kit could visualize how grand the castle would be, once she realized her dreams. And the courtyard was the obvious place to start. Get all the rubble cleared and the ground raked smooth. Everywhere she looked, she could see work that needed doing. Undaunted by the vast undertaking, she began to plan. In her mind, she held a vision so clear, she could almost smell it.

She reached down to the boy and took his hand. Speaking in tones one would use to calm a frightened animal, she directed him to act as her guide through the castle. He nodded eagerly and began to tug at her arm for her to follow him into the main hall.

Once there, the true grandeur of the manor became more apparent. High, arched windows were cut in the deep stone walls where light entered and illuminated every corner.

The boy again tugged at her sleeve and bid her to go with him up into the tower. She followed closely, the dampness seeping into the very marrow of her bones. The gray stones seemed to have slipped from their original location. Only the main tower was fully intact. Within the donjon, the first floor lay crumbled upon the ground floor. From the second floor, a sturdy rope hung. Everywhere in the courtyard, pavers were chipped and broken. Grasping the rope, Kit ascended to the uppermost floor with Aaron close behind her. The worn balcony hung tenuously but the center room was perfect.

Elation filled her. This room would be the gemstone of her renovation. Though the whitewash on the smooth gray stones was almost completely washed away, giving the walls a clean coat would do wonders for the dark tower.

The lad tugged at her sleeve and drew her to a ledge with blankets on it. Pointing, he said, "Da's place."

She drew the boy back down the winding stairs and into the main hall once again. She looked about for Scilti and found him heading away from the raised dais in the center of the room. He glanced at Kit and withdrew from the hall.

Leaving Kit behind, Olyn found himself driven to continue deeper and deeper, until he arrived at the door restricted to all but him.

He raised his arms, his cobwebbed sleeves falling to his elbows, and suddenly the dark cavern bathed in light. The door sprung open. Power rushed through his body. It seemed as if he had never encountered the evil Morganna. His strength was nearly at its former level. His true purpose restored, for the moment.

Stepping through the casement, he noted there was not a trace of the passage of time. What little dust he found was the same as always. He had never been a fastidious housekeeper. In the center of his worktable sat the Master Tome, open to the page that had first revealed the "Mantle of Sorcery." Placing his hands on the edges of the opposing pages, he closed his eyes and raised his face to the ceiling. Not a sound heard, not a rustling of pages, not the scuttling of vermin; even breath itself was suspended. Opening his eyes, he saw, as before, a small puff of smoke and the cloak of brilliant red appeared. This time Merlin himself was wearing the Mantle. He began to speak in solemn tones.

"You call on me, Olyn?"

"Yes, I feel you must know what has transpired with the ward you assigned me."

"Think you, I do not know?" The ancient wizard's glare was piercing and unrelenting.

"Oh, no, Sir," Olyn said, sure he'd offended the great wizard.

"I just need to know what is next required of me."

"Yes, the time has come." Merlin closed his arms about himself and began to twirl like a dervish. His movements drew all the air within the chamber to wrap around him, taking all in its path, including him, with it. They traversed a long hollow tunnel, drawn by some powerful source. Olyn had never experienced the like of it. Even when he'd had his full powers, he had never known of travel without the usual types of conveyance.

Within moments, they were settled gently on the floor of a brightly lit, spacious workroom, much like the one they had just left, only larger, cleaner and consisting of a greater number of books. Olyn looked about in total awe. More books lined the walls than he had believed were in existence.

Timidly, he asked, "Merlin, have you read each of these books?"

Merlin hid a slight smile as he said, "I have written many of them myself."

Olyn stood dumbstruck in the face of such knowledge. "Why am I here, great Wizard? Do you not know all there is to know? What smattering might I have that you do not posses?"

Indulgently, the wiser wizard nodded and replied, "In this case, it is not a matter of *what*, but of *whom* that is important. You have close knowledge of both Kit O'Malley and Leigh Longwurth. It is their reactions to the knowledge I wish to impart that you have a feel for, more than I. You have lived with both of these young people. Further, you have been with them at critical parts of their lives."

"That is true, Sir, I've lived with them both and saw them through some very hard times. Each is very dear to me."

"Olyn, you understand your role in this matter is minor, but I feel you should be a part, since you, and you alone, have the confidence of each of them."

"I understand, Sir. I do not seek honor or glory." Merlin smiled.

"It is just for that reason you were chosen. You are a humble and gracious man. Leigh and Kit could not have chosen a better protector had they done the choosing themselves."

Olyn, who had been forcing himself not to appear a simpleton, nodded foolishly. Gathering his senses, he cleared his throat.

"Sir, what is required of me?"

Merlin raised his arms and appeared to be in another realm, speaking in some foreign tongue. Olyn raised his hands and tried to garner the sorcerer's attention.

Merlin's eyes turned on him and glared at him in obvious fury. Olyn withdrew his hand and bowed his head.

"I . . . I'm sorry, Sir." His humility went unacknowledged.

Merlin continued to recite some strange incantation. Between his fingertips a light flashed.

Morganna carefully descended the spiral staircase, moving as stealthily as an evening fog, down to within hearing of Merlin and Olyn. Holding her breath, she strained to hear what the two wizards were saying.

"Olyn, you are charged with bringing the two young people together. As Guinevere's cousin, the boy is the direct heir to the throne of Ireland. He is totally unaware of his destiny. Kit has realized a great deal of hers. What further the Druids have in store for her, is to share the throne with young Longwurth."

"And you wish me to tell each of them this?"

Merlin grinned, lines etching deep furrows in his face. "No, not at this point. I fear Kit will not want to share anything with anyone. She has worked hard for all she has acquired and will be more than unwilling to share. And young Leigh is still on the brink of greatness. All the signs must be in order and the Druid Priests will not allow us to interfere until all is ready."

"If we are not to interfere, what am I to do?"

"We must place them in situations where they might encounter each other. Has Kit learned how to use her unique ability?"

"I don't think so, but she is so clever, I'm not sure."

"Then some time must pass until you are sure. She must have full control."

Chapter Six

Further exploring the land surrounding the castle, Kit's curiosity drew her to the edge of the sea, atop a steep bluff. Lowering herself down the face of the cliff, she peered into the mouth of a wide, dark cave. Her bare feet padded in the wet sand as she entered. Looking about, she could see no one and, thankfully, nothing. Adjusting her eyes to the darkness, she proceeded deeper and deeper into the cave until she heard muffled speech coming from further back in the depths.

The voices sound strangely familiar. They were her men. The men she'd led for two years at sea. What were they doing there? Carefully, she worked her way along the side of the damp cavern, edging closer. Now she could see the open chests in front of the men. *Her* chests. The treasure they were dividing belonged to her! This was *her* cave. How different it looked coming in from the land. The sound of water lapping against the walls alerted her to the incoming tide.

The men must have heard it as well and turned toward the opening. She leapt into the incoming water to avoid being seen. Oh how she hated having her head wet. As she broke the surface, her hair clung to the sides of her face and drizzled down her back.

The men stared at her as if she were some sort of wild animal.

"Hey, Galen, look at this, some fool fox trying to catch mice nearly got itself drowned. So much for being clever as a fox. Ha."

"Well, that one seems a little short on clever."

"Come on, if we don't move this stuff, we'll miss the next outgoing tide." They turned their attention back to the goods they were looting.

They can't see me? Kit touched her nose, no longer pert and small, but now covered with fur. *Fur? What in the name of Seven Seas is happening to me?* Slowly, she made her way to the water's edge and stared at her reflection. *Damn, I am a fox! How can this be?*

Stepping back into the water, she padded, now on all fours, out the mouth of the cave. Careful to keep her head above the water, lest she change into something else, she clung close to the shoreline, swimming until she reached terrain that could be climbed. She raced up the grassy knoll toward the castle. Again, she heard the voices of her men. Looking back, she saw the men had carried one of the chests to the mouth of the cave. *How can I fit this into my plan? Will I ever be human again?*

Creeping through the tall grass, she strained to hear the men over the noise of the surf. Her ears twitched and caught the muted voices of the seamen. *I don't remember my hearing being this acute. This could serve me well.* One man, who had led the mutiny, motioned with his beefy forearm for the men to drag the chest out into the incoming tide.

"Come on, you fools, it's too heavy to float. We'll have to drag it through the surf. Leave the rest. The treasure's safe. We'll come back for it soon."

The men threw their backs into the work, each shouldering as much weight as he could bear. The chest itself was heavy, and, Kit remembered, the gold within was equally heavy. Not so heavy that she'd required help when she stashed it in the tide pool cave. She'd used a skid and hauled it along the wet sand alone. Her men relied on brawn, but she'd used her mind. Always self reliant, she reluctantly decided she now had to secure Scilti's help. This time she couldn't do it alone. Not as a fox, she couldn't. She watched the men put the chest on a raft and started back to the ship. Shaking to rid herself of the damp salt water, she continued on to the castle.

Scilti, working in the long-abandoned garden, spotted a tiny fox appear in the grass. He paid the animal little mind. There were many mice in the tall grass so the fox was no doubt searching for its dinner. Turning his attention back to his gardening, Scilti again saw the fox peering through the grasses. The animal did not seem to be looking for food. Strangely, it acted as if it were trying to get his attention.

I must be seeing things. I'm as bad as young Leigh, thinking an animal wants to communicate with me.

Next he heard a faint mewing, not the sound of an animal in danger, but one of confusion. He couldn't explain why he felt the fox needed help, but the feeling remained undeniable.

He stood slowly, lest he frighten the creature, and crept toward the sleek animal. It retreated deep into the underbrush. There was no reason to believe it was the same fox, yet stranger things had happened.

Scolding himself for his concern for a wild animal, Scilti returned to his task. He pulled several turnips from the ground and headed back to Helga's kitchen. The fox did not reappear.

Well, I suppose it found its dinner. I need to stop making too much of things. This business with Merlin has my mind playing tricks on me.

Carefully nosing out of the underbrush, Kit sat back on her haunches to think. She mulled over in her mind all the actions that had occurred since she and Scilti abandoned ship. The events seemed strangely connected. She'd landed on her island. Found her men and her treasure.

And, when they had first jumped from the ship, Scilti had called on Merlin. Perhaps the old fool wasn't just whistling in the wind. Perhaps there was magic afoot. There was no other explanation. *I wonder if I turned into an animal when we jumped overboard. That has got to be it. When Scilti said he wasn't trying to drown me, he was just turning me human again.*

Now the problem was to discover if Scilti knew for sure how to return her to her human form. Leigh wandered down the long hall leading to the queen's private chambers, hoping he might run into her and they could talk some more. Since their day at the faire, the queen had become his favorite person in the castle, almost like a friend. Nearing her door, he thought he heard sobbing coming from her sitting room. Tentatively he knocked, not wishing to intrude, only to offer solace.

"Come in," a tearful voice said. Leigh opened the door and peered into the room.

"Your Highness? Cousin? What is wrong? Are you hurt?"

Looking out the tall window, the queen had her back to him.

"Hello, Leigh, no, it's nothing. I'm fine, really." She didn't turn around.

"Ladies who are fine do not usually cry alone in their rooms. Can I help?"

Though she was older than he, the age span was not that great, as Guinevere was much younger than his mother. Leigh thought of his cousin as his only friend at court. Everything at the castle felt strange to him and Guinevere did everything to make him feel comfortable. He counted on her as a friend and wished to see nothing distress her.

Her shoulders shuddered as she stifled a sob. She turned and faced him, the tears streaking down her pale cheeks. Her eyes were rimmed with red, indicating she had been crying for some time.

Leigh quickly crossed the floor and gathered her into his arms. "Oh, Leigh, what am I going to do?" she implored.

"I don't know. What needs to be done?" he asked, ready to right whatever wrong was plaguing her.

"Leigh, do you remember I once kept a secret of yours?" Leigh nodded solemnly. Confidences were precious.

The tearful royal gestured toward a gracefully carved bench near the window where they both sat. Swallowing, she wiped the moisture from her face and turned her swollen eyes to him. Her delicate fingers traced the raised carved design on the back of the bench.

"Guinevere, what is wrong? I've never seen you troubled so."

"Oh, Leigh, I've fallen in love."

"Of course, the entire kingdom knows of your love for Arthur. He is a fine man. Women throughout Britain envy you."

"Yes, he is a fine man, and not deserving of one such as I," she said, weeping anew.

"Loving one's husband should not be cause for tears, My Lady."

"You are right, nor would it be, if Arthur were the man I love so desperately."

"You don't love the king?" Leigh asked incredulously.

"How could you not love the king? He is the finest of men, both noble and fair. While it is not something men dote on, he is fair of face as well. How can you not love him?"

"Leigh, I love the king, I just don't love him with passion. A passion he truly deserves."

"You are young. Surely the passion will grow."

"No, not while I love another."

"Tell me, Your Queen-ness, am I the object of your affections?" he asked, knowing full well he was not.

Her bright eyes, glistening with tears, gently closed. She shook her head. "No, Leigh. I love you as a cousin, not with this all-consuming passion. But, Lord, you do make me laugh."

"Are you saying this callow youth does not pique your interest?"

Guinevere laughed, her tears for the moment forgotten. Her hands wound about each other in her lap. Leigh took them in his own. "Tell me, my queen, how may I help you?

"Your distress wounds me deeply. Who is the man? Your lover?"

"You are a fine, caring lad. Your mother would be so proud of you. Someday soon, you will be a fine knight. Lancelot is well pleased with you."

"Guinevere," Leigh said with a gentle scold in his voice, "You are avoiding the question."

"I must not give him name. 'Twould only serve to wound me more."

"My Lady, I can't help unless I know all the danger. Is this man your lover or merely a man you love? You have not yet called him lover."

"I pray it would be ever so, as not, please, Leigh. There is danger in such knowledge."

"My Lady, I think the true danger lies in you remaining here at Camelot. You need to be away for a brief time to re-evaluate your feelings. To understand you are Arthur's Queen."

She brightened. "A trip? Leigh, that might just be the answer, but where would I go?"

"Lancelot and I are going to the land of the infidels. Perhaps you could join us. I'll ask King Arthur for his guard to accompany you." Feeling he had come up with the ideal solution, Leigh left before she could refuse him, eager to do what he could to aid her.

Kit crouched low in the grasses, looking for some way to communicate with Scilti without frightening him. Wishing she hadn't let him out of her sight before, she checked the courtyard, finding it empty. She would have to venture into the castle itself. Her heightened sense of smell led her to the kitchen. A fat woman stood over a cook fire and wondrous odors wafted from the pot over the hearth. A large man entered from the other entrance. He looked familiar, but she wasn't sure of his identity. She backed away and hid herself among the pots and pans. The man was dressed in robes, much like a cleric. Deep brown and very dirty. Who could this man be? The fat woman turned, a look of pure surprise on her face.

"Olyn, for heaven's sake, man. Where did you come from after all these years?"

"Surprised you, didn't I, old girl?"

The woman wiped her hands on her soiled apron, threw open her arms and enfolded the big man.

"How I've missed the two of you. It's a might lonely here. Is Leigh with you?"

"No. Helga, our lad is at Arthur's court. I've a lass with me now."

"Aren't you a little old for that sort of thing, Olyn?"

He smiled ruefully. "No, Helga, it's not that way. She's my ward, just like Leigh was."

"Well, I can't see you handling a young lass. How did she come to be your ward?"

"Helga, don't ask. For now, I have no answers."

Olyn? The woman had called him Olyn. *Odd, but he looks like Scilti.* Kit puzzled over this strange turn of events. She crept closer to the two. *They behave as if they are old friends. I didn't know Scilti had any friends.*

The fur on her back was reacting to a tender touch. First someone's fingers and now more firmly, a hand was petting her, as if she was a housecat. She turned, prepared to nip whoever would dare touch her. She hesitated when she saw the perpetrator. The simple boy, Aaron. He didn't seem to want to capture her, just to touch her.

A quizzical expression fixed on his face.

"Aaron." She and tried to speak. *Woof?*

A broad smile came across the lad's face.

"Woof," he replied, an exact duplicate of the sound she'd made.

Pointing to himself, he said, "Aaron," and then turning his finger to her, he said, "Woof." Getting down on his knees, he crawled toward her, then past her. As he did so, he turned, nodded his head, and indicated she was to follow him.

Slowly the duo made their way along the wall and out into a large storage area. It became apparent no one had used the area for some time. The dust they raised caused her to sneeze. Aaron stopped and then laughed at her.

Kit growled. Laugh at her, would he? But that only seemed to give rise to greater mirth. The boy's eyes twinkled and he covered his mouth with his dirty hand. The dirt on his hand mixed with the sweat on his face, rendering him almost black.

Kit fell back on her haunches and laughed at him. Looking at his hands, he realized what was cause for her laughter. Then Kit understood. He was not simple, merely unschooled. He could learn, but learn only that to which he was exposed. He had probably never heard anyone speak other than his father. Why?

Although, he'd only seen her as a fox, he'd mimicked perfectly. She could turn this to her direct advantage. All she had to do now was figure out how she became an animal and how to turn herself back. Olyn was the key. She had to get him to communicate.

Using her teeth, she grabbed the boy by his tunic. Tugging, she managed to get him to follow her. She was sure he thought it a game, but it was, in fact, a desperate effort. She had to get him to intercede for her with this Olyn person. Retracing the route they had taken, Kit led him back to the kitchen. The two adults were still at the table, where the woman had placed a trencher and some broth. The smell tantalized Kit. She'd not eaten, and her stomach growled with hunger. She walked right out into the center of the room while Aaron stayed hidden among the pans.

"My heavens," Helga said, "A fox. How did it get in here?"

"I think it's looking for me," Olyn replied.

"And why would an animal search for you? Is there something you're not telling me? Does this have something to do with the strange tongue you used in the past?"

"Ah, Helga, ever the wise. Nothing gets past you, does it?"

"Olyn, don't you try to evade the issue. What is going on here?"

"Helga, you must tell me what has happened here since I had to leave."

"Remember, you have been gone a long time. I was here alone for a while, then some years later a noble man came with a small child. He seemed despondent, unable to care for the child. I took the lad and tried to care for him, but the moment he could crawl he hurried away from me. I'm sure he's around here still. I set food out and it is consumed, but I never see more of him than a quick rustling of the grasses."

"What of the noble? Is he here still as well?"

"Sadly, he died. When he came he took to the tower and never again came down. The boy would venture up to see him, and take food to him."

Chapter Seven

Leigh could not rationalize his cousin's feelings. Guinevere was a queen. Did she know she had responsibilities? *You must fulfill the duty to which you are called.* She was fortunate she'd been called to such a lofty duty. To be Queen of England was no small prize.

Would that my destiny were that clear. After he closed the door to the queen's chambers, he leaned against its heavy oaken panels. With forced deliberation, he strode down the passageway to the king's council room. He tapped on the door, and Arthur bid him enter.

"Good day, lad, how are you enjoying your training?"

"It's going well, Sire, but I have much to learn.

"That you do, Leigh, but Lancelot tells me you learn very quickly."

Modestly, Leigh bowed his head. "Thank you, Sire. I-I have a request."

"Yes, what is it, boy?" Arthur raised an eyebrow. Pages did not usually make requests of the king.

"Lancelot and I are scheduled to be away from court for some time and I was wondering if it might be possible for my cousin to accompany us? Lancelot says we will be in no danger and I do feel Guinevere needs to be free from the duties of court for a short time. She's so young, and the duties of a queen are very burdensome."

Arthur frowned down at him. "What do you know of the burdens of royalty?"

"Nothing, Sire, only what my queen has told me. She seems very troubled, Sire."

"I will give the matter some thought. Now, you best be back to your training," the king said, dismissing him.

This was not the response Leigh sought, but for now, he would have to wait until Arthur made his decision. Then Leigh had another thought. Perhaps, if Lancelot intercedes for her, Arthur will listen.

As he headed down the corridor, he noted Lancelot coming from the queen's chambers. Guinevere must have also thought that Lancelot could ask the king.

Lancelot had not closed the door completely and Leigh heard him say, "Have no fear, 'twill all work out."

Leigh nodded. For a certainty, Lancelot had agreed to petition the king. Confident this was the case, Leigh approached the knight.

"Sire, are you to speak with the king?"

Lancelot forced his features into a detached smile. "I trust he will agree. It is in the queen's best interest."

"Yes, I believe she needs the time."

"Time? Oh, yes, you may be right about that." Lancelot's answers seemed, to Leigh, to be very oblique. Leigh wondered if Lancelot knew all about the matter in question.

"Then you will ask the king to allow my cousin to travel with us?"

Adjusting his tunic, Lancelot turned to go down the wide corridor.

"Lancelot, are you going to speak with the King? He is in the council room. The other way, Sire."

The knight turned his face, a picture of confusion. "Oh, thank you, Leigh. I guess I have much on my mind. I will confer with the king straight away." Abruptly, he headed for the council room.

A firm tap at the door alerted Arthur. Drawing his attention from the maps on the round table he said, "Leigh, I will need more time before I make a decision." Lancelot poked his head into the casement. "Decision, Your Highness?"

"Lancelot? I thought it was young Leigh, returning for my decision."

"Your decision on what matter, Sire?"

Arthur did not usually discuss his decisions with his champions, unless it involved matters of state. This was a personal issue. He would not discuss the queen with any man, member of his council or not.

Arthur drew himself up to his full height and glowered at the shorter knight. "It does not concern you, Lancelot."

"I understand, Sire, however young Leigh has asked me to petition you, that Guinevere might accompany us on our journey. The lad wishes to spend time with his cousin."

Arthur sat back down in the large chair reserved for him at the Round Table and said, "Where my queen goes is not your responsibility, Lancelot."

"Sire, I meant no intrusion, only that the queen's kinsman feels need of her company and asked I speak with you on his behalf."

Lancelot moved to the far side of the great table. The shadows were lengthening due to the lateness of the hour. Servants shuffled in with lighted torches, which they placed in the sconces around the entire perimeter of the room. Flickering flames cast golden planes on Arthur's face. He gave Lancelot such a piercing glare, blood should have been drawn. All were equal in the council room. The huge round table stood in the exact center of the room and was made of highly polished mahogany. So deep was the shine, each burl in the grain seemed to be an eye on the proceedings conducted at the great table. Around the table, comfortable and study chairs were placed, each the same, with nothing to display rank or privilege, other than the placement of Arthur's chair at due north, all conformed. Here in the council room, each voice had equal say.

Lancelot knew that in any other discussion his voice would be heard, but in a personal matter, the king kept his own council and would not tolerate intervention.

"Lancelot, your intent was clear, Sir. Watch carefully where you trod." Bowed, but not broken, Lancelot withdrew from the Great War Room.

Aaron gathered Kit into his arms and started to withdraw from the adult conversation. *I've got to make this boy understand,* Kit thought. *Somehow, he is the link to this Olyn, the man I know as Scilti. They look the same, but can two beings inhabit the same body? This will require the services of a wizard. That's the explanation! It has to be.*

Wriggling, she escaped Aaron's arms, scuttled across the floor, and nipped at the old man's ankle.

"Hey! That hurt," Olyn said, looking down at his feet.

"Be careful, Olyn, it may be rabid. Foxes don't usually bite unless they're rabid."

Aaron raced across the floor and swiftly swept her up.

"Aaron? Boy, wait, come here." Olyn reached for the lad, but Aaron escaped his grasp.

"Helga, close the door. We must not let him take her into hiding."

"Olyn, he is probably taking her as a pet, just like Leigh."

"Quite right, dear lady. Exactly like Leigh. It's the same fox."

"Olyn, that is outrageous. Foxes don't live that long. Leigh's pet is long gone."

"Not so, Helga, it is the same fox."

Olyn raced after the pair and grabbed the boy. He held the boy as tenderly as he dared while still keeping a tight rein on his capture. The fear apparent in the boy's eyes softened Olyn's grip. Aaron shook free, but the wizard held the fox fast. Grabbing her by the nape of her neck, Olyn looked deep into the eyes of the fox.

"Kit, is it you? Tell me you're in there."

The boy approached the wizard and tugged at his robe.

"Woof?" he said, pointing to the crimson vixen in the sorcerer's hand.

"Woof," Kit responded and tuned her gaze to Olyn.

"Boy, can you talk?"

"Aaron," he said. Again, he pointed to Kit.

"Woof," he repeated firmly.

"Helga, have you ever heard the boy speak?"

"Once, I heard him whisper 'Da's place,' but nothing other than that."

"Did anyone ever try to speak to him?"

"No, anytime I would try he would run away. I don't believe he's ever spoken to anyone, nor has anyone spoken to him."

"Well, he seems to have found some way of communicating with the fox. Now all we have to do is get him to talk to us." Wriggling, Kit freed herself from Olyn's hold.

"Woof," she said, and Aaron followed her as she ran from the room. Olyn quickly grabbed his robes and raced after them.

"Kit, Aaron, boy, please, stop."

Kit stopped, turned, and growled softly at the boy. He reached for her, a question in his eyes, *Da's place.* She nodded and followed him to the tower.

How can I make this boy understand?

Aaron set her on the shelf he used as a bed. Around and around, she turned in the bedding. The action seemed familiar. *I've been here before?* Lifting her head, she pricked her ears for recognizable sounds. Drawing in deep breaths, she hoped for comforting scents. And found them. *I have been* here before!

Though the scents were long gone, sounds produced an old, well known pattern. The wind gently blowing through the high windows, the gulls screeching around the high tower, those were the sounds of childhood. *I know this boy. The way he moves, how he smells. He's my friend.*

As sudden as her recognition of the boy, so was the pain of the depth of her feeling for him. No, not him, one very like him. Leigh? *Oh, where are you, my heart?*

Aaron stroked her fur. "Woof? Woof?"

Frustrated, she sat firmly back on her haunches. Aaron adopted a similar pose. She searched her mind for remembrances, not only of her knowledge of this place and this boy, but of how she became a fox. *Will this be the only form I take and will I be able to reason if I become another animal?* As a person, she had always thought the fox the most clever of animals. Perhaps that was why she became a fox?

Straining to concentrate on how the change had occurred, she wandered about the room, not really watching where she was going. Stepping into the water dish Aaron had left for her, she recalled getting wet had been the key on one other occasion. Thinking the fleeting thought to be an epiphany, she immersed her head in the dish. No change, nothing. Frustrated, she again sat back on her haunches.

Aaron held his position. He lifted his nose in the air.

Tantalizing smells wafted up to the tower. Kit could smell biscuits and honey, the scent wafting up from the bottom of the stairs. She eyed Aaron, who looked hungry and ready to be swayed by the temptation. Kit found herself drawn to the biscuits as well.

Slowly, the boy crept to the bottom of the stairs. Olyn hid himself in the shadows, waiting for the lad to come within reach. Kit followed close behind him. Her keen nose picked up the scent of Olyn from where he hid. As Olyn reached for the boy, Kit bit his breeches and pulled him back from the wizard's grasp. Olyn reached out further and enfolded the boy with Kit firmly attached to his butt. Kit quickly released her teeth.

Olyn's hand brushed her head as she tried to escape. "Kit, you're wet!" She halted her exit and turned to face the wizard.

"Kit, you've figured it out, haven't you?" He extended his hand to the animal. Tentatively she approached. "Kit, if you understand me, flick your tail."

She had never tried to consciously move her tail; she wasn't sure she could do it on command.

The thick-furred plume behind her responded.

"Oh, thank the fates, it's you. Are you all right?"

Again she flicked her tail. *Ah, a beginning. Now we need to get on with the business of transforming me.*

As if he read her thoughts, Olyn said, "Come, child, we have to make you human again."

Furiously she moved her tail and trotted up to the wizard.

"Oh, now you trust me, you clever fox." The old man embraced her.

"Oh, Scilti, how I've missed you."

"Helga, get me the old wooden basin. The very one we used to bathe Leigh after he mixed with the skunk. Do you still have it?"

The old woman looked wide-eyed at the old gentleman.

"Of course, who would steal such a thing?"

"Well, then, hurry and fill it. I need it right now."

"Whatever for? You haven't fallen in with a skunk, have you?"

"No, certainly not, do I smell?" Shaking her head, she rushed to comply. Carefully, she dragged the large tub from the scullery as she'd done many years before. It was hard labor to haul the water from the steep bank at the water's edge. The task had been difficult when she was younger. Now she struggled with each bucket she drew up the hill. After seemingly endless trips, the tub was filled. Olyn approached the tub and gingerly set Kit into the water. No change took place. Unceremoniously, he plunged her entire body beneath the surface. Sputtering, she struggled to the top.

"What are you trying to do, drown me?" she asked with a wide grin. She was back in human form!

"No, lass, I was merely trying to save you."

"I remember, Scilti. I forgive you."

"Oh, Kit, there is so much ahead of you. You are part of a grand design."

"Never mind grand design; we are going to get my treasure back."

Scilti shook his head. Kit was as incorrigible as ever. He had to apprise Merlin of this turn of events.

Chapter Eight

"Leigh, prepare for our journey. We are leaving today after we break our fast. Make sure Cathaoimore is groomed and shod."

Leigh knew what was expected of him. Irritated, he wondered why Lancelot had chosen to order him like a page in the first week of training.

I wonder what he thinks of me. Sometimes he treats me as if I am on the brink of knighthood and others as if I'm a simpleton.

His assessment of the king's favorite knight was changing. Lancelot had behaved in questionable manners on several occasions, and Leigh was concerned for the welfare of his cousin. Guinevere was a young regent and away from her family. He feared the worldly knight might easily sway her. Rather than question Lancelot as to his plans for his cousin, Leigh went directly to the queen.

He completed his duties and headed down the long, wide corridor. He noted the door to the queen's chamber was wide open and people were scurrying to and fro.

Knocking at the open door, Leigh peered into the large room. "Your Highness, may I enter?"

"Of course, Leigh, why are you not preparing for our journey?" she asked with a slight flush on her face. She seemed elated to be leaving court.

"Arthur has given his blessing on your journey?"

"Yes, Leigh. Thank you for asking him."

"I was happy to do it and I hope you realize that you are the most fortunate of woman to have a compassionate husband like the king."

A look of extreme guilt passed across her delicate features. She struggled to regain her composure. "Arthur is the most understanding of husbands. Thanks to you, he is permitting me to spend time with my only relative. It means so much to me, Leigh. Can you understand?"

Leigh nodded, not certain he did understand why a woman would be so eager to leave the comforts of court for the hardship of travel.

"Only a few hours ride and we will be at the ship." Lancelot pulled up on the large stallion. Cathaoimore danced backward into Guinevere's carriage. The carriage shook, then slowly stopped its rocking motion.

"Lancelot," the queen cried out.

"What's happening?"

The knight reined in his horse and said, "Nothing, my queen. We've nearly reached the sea, and Cathaoimore doesn't like the smell of the sea air." Leigh, too, could smell the sea. He'd lived at its edge, most of his life.

Riding his horse up to the knight, he questioned the direction the entourage was taking.

"Sire, why are we headed to the sea? I thought we were going to the land of the Infidel. I believe that is south and we're headed north."

Lancelot appeared to be uncomfortable with Leigh's question.

"Quite right, Leigh, we are headed north. I told the king I wished to visit my homeland before I continued my journey."

"Do we have provisions enough for the additional trip? You should have told me of your plan, Sir. I would have made sure our rations were sufficient."

Lancelot glowered down at him. "Leigh, you are but a page. You have no right to question my leadership."

While he had never before questioned the judgment of the knight, it seemed strange Lancelot had conveniently forgotten Arthur had given him the rank of squire prior to their journey.

Since Arthur had placed him in the stewardship of Lancelot, the knight had always treated him with respect. Of late, he'd been treating him as if Leigh were his personal serf. Even his cousin was behaving differently.

In Leigh's eyes, the shining knight was daily losing his sheen and honor. Once, Leigh would have defended his knight's reputation against all comers. Now, he had his own doubts.

Lancelot rode to the head of the group and ordered all to stand down and to prepare to board the ship that was pulling into shore. A fully crewed ship, whose mast pierced the red evening sky. The large broad-beamed vessel appeared to be of Irish ancestry. Leigh had seen many similar ships from his perch in the high tower he'd shared with Kit.

Guinevere looked apprehensively at the large ship and its crew. They seemed to be rough and savage men. Not the gentlemen she knew at court. "Leigh, do you know these men?" she asked in a shy little voice, alarm clear in her tone.

"Fear not, my queen, I'll not allow anyone to harm you. Lancelot surely has told them of your station."

Timidly, she searched the deck for the knight. He was astride his horse alongside the gangway, arguing with a large swarthy seaman.

"I'd take care what you think is your share. You follow orders, or your share will be mine." The knight rode his steed grandly up the gangway and swept the sailors' protests aside.

Leigh stared at Lancelot in total disbelief. These were not the types of men a true knight of the realm would associate with. Clearly, Arthur's favorite knight had a hidden agenda. Leigh assisted the queen from her carriage and walked her up the slippery plank to the deck. A massive man with a dirty, straggly beard bowed low and greeted Guinevere.

"Welcome aboard, yer Ladyship," he lisped through missing teeth.

Guinevere drew herself back into her cousin's arms.

"Leigh, I'm frightened, I've never been aboard such a crude ship. It's so bare and dirty."

"I fear, my queen, this is a pirate vessel." Guinevere's eyes widened in fear.

"Captain, I'm sure you have suitable quarters for the queen?" Leigh asked archly, certain the crude seaman had no concern for her welfare.

The captain blinked into the bright sun. "The queen? I'd no idear she's the queen. Are ye certain? The bloke said only she was his doxy. Don't sound like any queen ter me." Leigh, furious at the treatment being afforded his cousin, pushed her behind him. "Sir, order your cabin scoured and placed in proper order for Queen Guinevere and do so with utmost haste."

"And who is you ter be orderin' me about? Yer not the bloke what's payin' me. I take me orders from *him*." The taller man leaned menacingly toward Leigh pressing what he saw as an advantage.

Not intimidated, Leigh met his advance toe to toe. "I do not care who has employed you. You will do as I have stated or King Arthur will hear of your treatment of his queen."

"Oh, now if thet don't set me shaking in me boots. You talk ta yer master, boy, and don't bother me with yer high falootin' ways." Pushing both the Queen and her young cousin aside, the swarthy man strode to the upper deck and began calling out orders to prepare to set sail. Men scurried over the deck each to perform preset duties.

Guinevere shook in Leigh's arms. "Leigh, I've never been treated so meanly. How am I to manage?"

Leigh, who had endured situations far worse than this, shook his head and tried to comfort his cousin. "Don't fret, cousin. I'll make sure Lancelot sets the fellow straight."

"Oh, I pray so, Leigh, this is most upsetting."

Leigh smiled, certain his Kit, if she were a woman, would handle the situation with much greater ease than his cousin. Wouldn't that be grand? To have a woman as fair and brave as his fox?

Drawn from his introspection, Leigh looked up to see Lancelot approaching. The knight circled the pair and wedged himself between them.

"Come, my lady, I'll take you to your quarters."

"Well, Lancelot," she said, eyes blazing with indignation, her fear now spent. "And what provisions have been made for me? The captain did not even believe I'm the queen."

"Your Highness, I'm sure you are mistaken. The captain is well aware of the honor bestowed upon him, having you aboard his vessel."

The sea was on a constant roll. The canvas sails filled with wind moved the ship quickly through the angry sea. The queen felt very ill and went to her cabin. In truth, it was the captain's for none other would suit Guinevere, Leigh had insisted. The cabin was in the bow of the ship. Each time the ship cut into a swell the bow dove deep into the surf and rolled from side to side.

Nauseous, Guinevere held tightly to the edge of the bed and prayed she would either live through the journey or die quickly, so she would have to endure no more. In the three days they'd been at sea she'd seen the deck only on the day she boarded. Lancelot had not bothered to see her since they had left port.

She was ill, alone, and now fully aware of her folly. Lancelot was not the romantic courtesan, and he was anything but gallant. How she regretted her actions. He'd been so attentive, so courteous. Why had he changed so? Perhaps she misunderstood. Rising from the musty bunk, she asked a passing seaman to send Lancelot to her.

Many hours passed and still he did not appear. He truly had abandoned.

Living near the sea had given Leigh a keen sense of direction, and now he was certain they were no longer heading north. Wales, Lancelot's homeland, was due north and now they were heading west. Did Lancelot think to confuse him, that he may spirit his queen away? Leigh determined he would get to the heart of this matter. Even though he was still lacking his sea legs, Leigh rose from his pallet in the hold and ventured onto the deck, where he saw Lancelot standing at the wheel by the captain. Leigh headed over to speak with the knight, but paused when he overheard what the two men were discussing.

"Listen, mate, this journey better be as profitable as you say. I don't like changing course every few leagues."

"You'll change course as often as I say," Lancelot said vehemently.

The grizzled seaman clearly was not happy with this turn of events. He leaned forward and snarled at the knight. "Listen, Mister Knight of the Round Table, yer station in life don't matter a fig ter me. I'll run yer gizzard through jest as soon as look at yer."

Lancelot turned to leave the seaman and was yanked around by a large burly hand. He looked with disdain at the grasp the seaman had on his tunic. "Unhand me, you swine, or I'll see you flogged."

"You'll have me flogged? I don't think so, yer knightness. These men answer ter me."

The taller, more muscular man intimidated Lancelot. At Arthur's table, his word carried weight. On this pirate ship, it had the heft of a feather. The moon was full and all other circumstances were right. Oh, by the fates, this had to work. Olyn had even attempted to clean the workroom deep in the dungeon.

At once, the dust rose in the familiar spirals that heralded Merlin's arrival.

"I've been observing," the wizard said when he appeared.

"It seems our Kit has learned the key."

"Yes, she has discovered her alter identity."

"Does she know the extent of her powers?" Merlin asked.

"She has connected the times she's changed and observed that her senses are sharper as a fox. Kit is clever. She will use this information to her every advantage."

Merlin closed his eyes and looked toward the heavens. "Ancient ones, how am I to do your bidding?"

Olyn wondered which of the ancients Merlin was calling upon. This was the only occasion Olyn had seen Merlin appeal to a higher power. The prospect that Merlin did not have total control of the situation confused him. Who else was involved in this grand scheme? What exactly was at stake? Was it merely the simple isle or something beyond his comprehension? If the outcome were not as preordained, where would the fault lie? Would *he* have to accept the blame? Would it rest on the shoulders of the higher wizard or even pass to the ancients he'd called upon?

"And where do her allegiances lie? Will she be loyal to Arthur?" Merlin asked, returning his gaze to Olyn.

Olyn shook his head. "No, Merlin. Her only fealty is to Ireland, and I doubt she will want to share the throne with anyone."

"The Ancients have preordained events. She will have no say in the matter."

Olyn continued to shake his head, smiling wryly. "I don't think the ancients took into account our irascible Kit O'Malley. She has her own agenda." Her strength and single-minded purpose were the prime reason for her selection.

Merlin narrowed his eyes and carefully stroked his beard. "Olyn, do you have any influence over the lass?"

"Merlin, I've known her since she was infused to the body of Seamus O'Malley's daughter, and believe me, no one has influence over Kit. She's as clever as a fox when she is a woman, and as strong willed as a woman when she's a fox. In order to get her to fit into the plan of the Ancients, you will have to convince her the plan is one of her own making."

Clearly, Merlin would have to consult the Ancient Druids. The Ancient Order of the Druids would tolerate no breach of their ordination. One would do well to follow their tenets without question. Merlin would have to consult with them and apprise them of the situation. Such a circumstance was not one to Merlin's liking. For many centuries, he'd been the highest authority. All he'd been instructed to do by the Ancients had been carried out to the letter, without interference from any quarter. Now he must face them and beg for time to perform as he was instructed. Merlin was unaccustomed to begging from anyone, and to petition the Ancients was not a pleasant prospect.

"Olyn, open the book!" he ordered.

Olyn hurried to the center of the partially cleaned room. The Master Tome lay on the large worktable. Though there was no window, a breeze blew and gently turned the pages. The Mantle of Sorcery rose from the pages. The breeze became a fierce wind and gathered both of the wizards within its folds. Around and around they flew through the Travel Tunnel. The wind hurried with gale force, then slowly lessened and deposited the two wizards in Merlin's workroom at Camelot.

As clever as she fancied herself, Morganna often stooped to use truly mortal methods of deception. She crept carefully down the stairs to the room where none was admitted, save Merlin. Many years before, she'd found a secret niche in the wall where she could observe Merlin without being detected. She'd learned much from this observation point. Here she'd uncovered the secret of the *Sine Vitium*.

As she moved closer, the muffled voices became clear. *Is Merlin calling upon the ancients? And, who is with him? I've not heard this voice before.*

"Olyn," he said, his arm outstretched reaching for the other wizard. "Come with me. I need you to explain about Kit to the Ancients."

"I will accompany you, but I fear there is no explanation for Kit."

The cloak opened from one side and pulled Olyn within its folds. Together they entered the Travel Tunnel and began the long journey to the Realm of the Ancient Druids.

It was more magnificent than anything Olyn had ever seen in his entire lifetime, which spanned centuries. The room seemed to have no windows, yet it was completely bathed in light. The walls were not really walls, cloudlike with no real substance. Olyn reach out to touch the one that seemed to be nearest to him. At once it disappeared.

A deep voice came from the depths of nowhere. "Merlin, by what rare circumstance do you petition this sacred order?"

"Oh, Most Ancient Priest," Merlin replied with a tremor in his voice, "It is the matter of the crown of Ireland."

"It has been ordained. Have you not followed the tenets as you have been instructed?"

Olyn watched, fascinated. He'd never seen the most senior of all the wizards of the universe tremble before any power. In truth, he'd never known a greater power than Merlin's. Carefully, not daring to draw attention to himself, he drew back, searching for anonymity. It was to no avail. The Ancients knew his every move. Again, the voice boomed.

"Olyn, how is it a sorcerer of the first level dares to face this counsel?"

"Sirs, I am here at the behest of Merlin. The journey was not one of my choosing."

"Olyn is here to testify all has been done according to the tenets, but the result is not what you desired," Merlin said.

"Merlin, if all the tenets were followed exactly, nothing other than the ordained result can occur. Which of the tenets has been altered?"

Merlin hesitated again. "Oh, Great Priest, none of the tenets has been overlooked. With Olyn's assistance the children have been marked and groomed according to the directives. Nothing has been left to chance."

The voice boomed, vibrating off the nonexistent walls. "You, the most revered of the sorcerers in all the universe, require assistance from a first- level sorcerer? Surely you realize you have violated the most scared of the tenets? These were set up at the beginning of time and nothing can displace them."

"Ancient Priest, I only sought to utilize Olyn's intimate knowledge of the young people. He has shared lives with each of them. I felt he would be able to predict how each would react in given situations."

"Wizard, your excuses are useless. You were instructed to follow the tenets exactly, without any deviation. You have failed in your obligation to the Ancient Order of the Druids. The defense of your actions is without merit."

Merlin knew they wielded power far beyond his own, and under no circumstances would he try them further.

Chapter Nine

Though he'd been around the sea and seen ships all of his life, this particular ship was giving Leigh the tremors. Nothing was as he expected. The crew was a motley collection, the ship was in disrepair, and there seemed to be no discipline. Arthur would not have permitted such a ragtag bunch under his command.

Leigh crossed the filthy deck and strained to overhear Lancelot's conversation with a large bald man who seemed to control the rest of the crew. Eavesdropping was underhanded and Leigh did not normally condone such behavior, but he felt it fell within the providence of his duty to his cousin. Guinevere was a true innocent. She had been completely taken in by Lancelot's charm. Leigh knew he had to protect her from all harm, even from her own folly.

Leigh had watched Lancelot's control over the crew slip the farther away from Arthur they sailed. This latest argument had reached a fevered pitch. Lancelot stood waving his arms and shouting. He shook his fist in the face of the bald man. Baldy retaliated by pushing Lancelot full in the chest. Lancelot fell back several steps and drew his sword. A group of men had gathered behind Baldy and advanced on the knight. Leigh stepped back into the piles of supplies where he could not be observed.

"Look, you fool, if we don't find the treasure, no one will gain. Only if we work together will there be any booty for any of us." Lancelot shouted to be heard over the din of the advancing crew.

The bald man raised his arms and stopped his men.

"Listen, you swabs, he ain't running this ship. I am, and if yer knows what's good fer ya, you'll mind me. We're gonna get the treasure what's our'n and then we'll run the bloke through."

Murmuring passed from man to man through the crew. Grudgingly, they assented.

Guinevere must rid herself of this dangerous group of men. Leigh crept down to the cabin, careful not to draw any attention to himself. Gently, he tapped at the door. He heard nothing from within. Again he tapped. Still no response. Placing his ear to the door, he heard muffled sobbing. Pushing the door ajar, he peered in and saw the queen, her legs drawn up to her chest, sitting on the bunk and sobbing uncontrollably.

"Your Queen-ness?"

She raised her tear-stained face.

"Oh, Leigh, how could I have been such a fool? What am I to do?"

"We are going to leave the ship. We are very near the island where I was born. Can you swim?"

Choking back her sobs, she looked wild-eyed at his suggestion.

"Swim? Leigh, I can't swim. I've never tried."

"Well," Leigh said lightly, "If you've never tried you don't know if you can or not. It's not far, and I will help you."

"But, Leigh, what about my things?"

"Dear cousin, we will not concern ourselves with things. Your life is in danger."

"My life? Oh God, Leigh. He may not love me as I thought, but surely he wouldn't kill me."

"Lancelot's only thought is for himself. I heard him talking to the men. They are in search of a treasure and will stop at nothing until they secure it."

"Leigh, even if we get free of this ship and these horrible men, what will happen? We'll freeze in that water."

"Your Ladyship, we will not be in the water that long and I will make a fire on the beach. Once we are warm, we will search to find shelter. Now, quickly shed all those layers of clothing right down to your shift."

"Leigh, I can't do that. It isn't proper," she said.

"I thought you were the one who said, sometimes proper wasn't what you wanted," Leigh said lightly, hoping to jar her into action.

Numbly, she looked at him, her eyes glazed. Her fear was so great as to near have substance. Her hands shook as she tried to remove her gown. Leigh assisted her while she stood, complacent as a child with her governess.

Leigh stripped down to his chausses. He wrapped them both in the cover from the bed and pulled her with him out of the cabin. Slowly, they made their way across the moonlit deck. The deck was nearly deserted, save for the bald man. Most men slept below. Leigh noted the seaman's eyelids were struggling to remain open.

Guinevere drew in an audible gasp when she saw the man. Leigh covered her mouth with his hand.

"You must be quiet, my Lady. We don't wish to be discovered. These men aren't above having sport with you then killing you to amuse themselves."

They waited until the bald seaman's grizzled snore confirmed that he was fully asleep. Slowly, they inched past where he lay on center deck.

A slight creaking of the deck woke the seaman. "And where do yer think yer going, pretty ones?" Roughly, he grabbed the queen. "Ain't you the pretty piece? Let's us have a kiss."

Guinevere gathered the cover up around her shoulders. "I'll have you know I'm the Queen of England, and you will not treat me like a common trollop."

"Sure, and this bonny lad is the king, no doubt. If yer were the queen yer wouldn't be traveling with the likes of a traitor like Lancelot."

Guinevere eyes grew wide.

"A traitor? Lancelot? You must be in error, sir. He's the king's favorite knight."

"Guinevere," Leigh said, drawing her back within the coverlet, "Do not anger him further."

"If you'll excuse us," he said to Baldy.

"We'll return to the queen's cabin."

"Queen, me arse, and it's my cabin. You two will go down in the hold," he said, pushing them into the open hatch that led to the hold.

Leigh resisted and shoved the man aside. Other men began to spill on deck.

"Hey, Baldy, yer gon ta share the knight's doxy, ain't ya?"

Baldy narrowed his eyes and took a deep breath. "No, we're gonna leave her untouched. That Lancelot's a snake. She just might be da queen. We'll send a messenger and find if she's missin'. And, if I'm right, we'll hold her fer ransom. A treasure and a ransom could be a mighty profitable journey."

Leigh grunted as they landed roughly in the smelly hold. He looked around trying to adjust his eyes to the dark bowel of the ship. The smell was overpowering. This ship was not washed down after every voyage, as would Arthur's ships. Even then, a queen would not find her quarters in the hold of a vessel. Guinevere was crying, whimpering in fear and disgust.

Leigh smiled wryly to himself. Kit would deal much more easily with this situation. Oh, what a woman she would make. A match for a man, not a burden. Not someone who would need his protection, but one who would share any danger.

"Your Highness, Guinevere, stop your crying. It will not help. We must formulate a plan."

"Plan? Do we need a plan to die? Because that's what is going to happen. No one knows we're here, except Lancelot, and he doesn't care about me," the queen said piteously.

"Guinevere!" Leigh shook her.

"Take the blanket and sit over there on the sacks of supplies. And be quiet. I have to get us out of here. I need to think and I can't concentrate with your sniveling."

Contrite, Guinevere huddled deeper in the blanket and rubbed her cheek with the rough cloth.

The ship seemed to be changing course every few leagues. First hard to port, then suddenly to starboard, then back again to port. The queen was turning a definite shade of green. Leigh didn't know if it was the stench or the rapid turns of the ship that was making her ill, but unless he got her off this ship quickly, she would be even more useless.

Standing atop several bales of flour, Leigh peered through the single porthole and saw shore less than ten leagues from the ship. This had to be the narrows between Clare and the mainland!

"Cousin, we're going to jump ship during the next port turn."

"Leigh, I don't want to jump. I just want to sit here and die."

"You will die if you sit here. Get over here. Climb up with me. You will fit through the porthole if you drop that blanket. Now, come on, we haven't much time."

Guinevere clung to the blanket as if it were a coronation robe.

"Drop it, cousin. Now."

Numbly, she dropped the covering and scrambled up the sacks. "Oh, Leigh, I'm frightened."

"You'd be more the fool if you weren't. We have danger ahead of us. But the greater danger is remaining here."

The ship suddenly lurched hard to the right.

"Now, Queen-ness, jump." He pushed her through the porthole and pulled himself up and through the opening.

"Help me, Leigh. I can't swim!" Guinevere flailed her arms and legs in the cold dark water.

"Jus relax. Move your arms slowly and gently kick your feet. You will   stay afloat." She obeyed, as meek as a chided child.

He swam over to her. "Give me one hand. I'll pull you to shore."

"How can you find the shore? It's so dark."

"I spent a lot of nights swimming in these waters. I know the way."

"You know the way? How could you? It's dark and you've never been to Wales before, have you?"

"No, I've never been to Wales, but this isn't Wales. This is my homeland, not Lancelot's. He lied to the king."

"He lied to Arthur? Why?" she asked, now more comfortable since they were nearly to shore.

Leigh set her on her feet on the damp sand and looked around him for a way to make shelter. She would freeze if she remained in her wet shift. He knew the sheer cliff would not provide brush to start a fire. Their only hope would be some driftwood and shelter in a tide cave.

"Why, Leigh? Why would Lancelot lie to Arthur?"

"Several reasons. He wanted to get you away from court and he is trying to retrieve some stolen treasure. I don't know the whole of it, but certainly it is a foul deed."

Cold, tired, and defeated, Guinevere followed Leigh along the shore until they came to an opening in the sheer cliff, hidden from all except those who had ventured there before.

Carrying driftwood and helping balance the queen with his other arm made progress slow. When they reached the cave, Leigh set the wood aside and reached into his chausses to find his flint. After a few attempts, he struck a spark and ignited the sticks of driftwood.

Guinevere huddled near the edge of the fire, appearing more forlorn than anyone Leigh had ever seen. She looked like a child snatched from her mother's breast. "Your Ladyship, rub your arms to get the blood flowing and move your shift about so it will dry more quickly."

Numbly she complied. "Oh, Lord, will we ever be back to court and the safety of Arthur?"

"Guinevere, you should have thought of that when you chose to leave Arthur and Camelot. The rest of the world is not as fine nor as safe as Camelot."

Guinevere shook her head. "Oh, Leigh, I know that, now. How could I have ever been so foolish? I risked all for Lancelot, and he spurned me. Now, I have nothing. No clothes, no food, and no home."

"If Lancelot's spurning was the end of it, the situation would not be so grave. I fear he wants you still, but not for romance. The man is without honor. I feel he is after greater stakes."

The small fire cast eerie shadows on the damp walls of the cave, yet Leigh could still see clearly enough to pick out similarities between this and the cave he and Kit had often played in.

"Guinevere, I am going to search the cave. It looks like the one I played in when I was a child. If it is the same, I may find a blanket to warm you."

"Do be careful. I couldn't bear it if I had to be alone in such a horrible place."

Leigh shook his head. He would never understand women. How could she think of nothing but her own comfort? This did not bode well for Arthur. They could be at war if Lancelot was as devious as he believed. Guinevere merely closed her eyes and nodded. Leigh went deeper into the cave. Years ago, he'd hidden several blankets and some water in a cave much like this. In fact, he was certain it was this very cave. Quickly, he checked the old hiding spot and retrieved a blanket and the water skin he'd hidden. After walking back to the queen, he handed the covering to her.

"Here, cousin, this will help to make you more comfortable." Looking up with tear-stained cheeks, she gratefully accepted his offering. "I'm going to the head of the cave to see if we've been followed," he said.

From the mouth of the cave, Leigh looked out over the sea, calm in the dawn light. He was able to see a ship approaching on a course crossing back on itself. *Whoever captains this ship has navigated this narrows before.* As the vessel neared to the shore Leigh could see it was the boat he'd just left. What did Lancelot hope to gain?

The boat anchored just off the cliff and the men lowered a skiff. They appeared to be coming directly toward him. Hurrying back to the queen, he stamped out the fire and led her deeper into the cave.

"Be still, cousin. Lancelot's men are coming, and we don't want them to find us."

Leigh let instinct take over and found the narrow ledge he and Kit had used when they'd hid from Olyn. It was off the main corridor and several feet above the floor. Anyone could walk right past them and they would never be discovered. Lancelot's men, led by Baldy, did just that, dragging a sledge with thick, heavy ropes. They stopped midway into the cave.

Several shovels rested on the sledge. The men each grabbed one and set to work digging away a mound of dirt against the wall of the cave. Leigh frowned, not remembering this from his childhood, and when he saw what lay beneath the dirt, he gasped. The newly dug hole was filled with treasure chests.

Chapter Ten

"Kit, be reasonable, you can't take on your pirates with an old sorcerer, a boy, and a cook."

"You're right about Helga, but the three of us could do it," Kit said.

"By the heavens, how do you propose to accomplish such a thing? The boy doesn't speak. We're not certain he understands, and I am an old man, a fat old man at that. Neither of us have fighting skills," Olyn said with a sad shake of his head.

"We're not going to fight."

"All right, then how do you expect to retrieve your treasure?"

"They don't know I can change shape and would have nothing to fear from a fox. They've seen me once as a fox and thought I was just a stupid animal who would drown in the incoming tide. We can fool them again. They will be on guard against humans, but Aaron can hide in plain sight. I will trick them and separate them from the chests."

"But, how?" Olyn asked skeptically.

"I can only help with minor spells, remember. I'm only a first-level wizard."

Kit's eyes filled with glee. "All we'll need is an illusion spell. Nothing you can't handle. I remember how you fooled the men when they tried to pillage the ship's stores."

"You saw that?" Olyn asked incredulously.

"You never let on you knew."

"Of course I didn't. I'm clever as a fox, you know. Even when I didn't know I was a fox."

An expression of grave concern passed over the face of the old sorcerer. "And what will be Helga's part? I know she would be deeply hurt if we don't include her in our plans." Kit rolled her eyes.

"She'll make sure we have full bellies," she said dismissively.

Helga spoke up. "Listen, miss, I have cared for you and Olyn for many years and I want to be a part of this."

"You cared for me?" She had no memory of the woman.

"I knew Leigh had a pet fox and always made sure there was enough for you to eat," Helga said smugly.

Seeing contrition was the best course, Kit smiled.

"Thank you, Helga. I'm sure you were very important to my existence, I just didn't know. We have need of your skills. Food is important, no matter how small the army."

The old woman smiled and smoothed her apron, then quickly withdrew. Kit wondered if she'd gone too far. Could she have all she desired? If so, at whose expense? Concern for others was a new emotion to her.

"First, we have to scope out the cave after high tide, when they won't dare venture in. Once we complete our reconnaissance, we'll wait until the next low tide and surprise them. For now, get some sleep, because we might not get another chance for a while if this works as I think it will."

Guinevere sat huddled next to the small fire on the ledge over the tide cave hidden from the men who were intent on their treasure. Thankfully the shadows from the flame were above the vision of the men. Open, the chests revealed more gold than Leigh'd seen in Arthur's treasury. He was sure Arthur had greater wealth, but not all in one place. This treasure did not belong to these men who unearthed it! He just knew it.

He recognized Baldy and a few other men as those from the ship he and Guinevere had just left. At their hand did not lie the way back to Arthur. They must remain in hiding until another opportunity presented itself. In the meantime, he would have to feed and shelter the queen. She would be no help in her own salvation.

The men below were dividing up the spoils and bickering among themselves.

"Look here, I'm the capt'n, and I'll say what's whose. Yer gonna get yer share, but I'm takin' the best fer meself."

Leigh watched as the men growled and advanced on the captain, swords drawn. The captain stood his ground. He grabbed a torch that he'd placed in the sconce on the wall when he entered. He pushed it into the face of the nearest sailor. Quickly, he retreated, the men behind him stepping back.

"That's more like it. I'm the capt'n, and don't yer ferget it."

A figure advanced from the mouth of the cave carrying a lantern with his sword unsheathed. Leigh had to keep from gasping aloud. Lancelot!

"I believe I have more say in this matter than you, captain. Morganna and I outfitted your ship with the intent of retrieving this treasure, and I shall have it."

"Yeah, and how do yer think yer gonna get it?" Baldy asked, his eyes narrowing and nostrils flaring.

"You've forgotten my men have control of the ship. If you don't turn over the treasure, you will drown in the next tide. It's my men who guard the mouth of this cave, and they will let you pass only if I order it." Lancelot looked smugly at the motley crew.

From his perch on the narrow ledge high above the cave floor, Leigh saw the confrontation was over. The crew had yielded. Lancelot was directing them to place the chests on the sledge.

Leigh's heart began to beat faster. *I can't let them take the treasure. It belongs to Arthur.*

As Leigh began to make his way back along the ledge to Guinevere, he heard the rush of incoming water.

From below, Lancelot bellowed, "The tide is coming in! Secure those chests to the sledge and tie it off to a rock. We have to get out of here."

Kit knew her plan was without flaws. What was under her control would go smoothly. However, she could no longer control the men who'd once formed her crew.

"Aaron, I need you to cause a distraction. Do you know what that means?"

Aaron nodded and scooped up some pebbles and began throwing them, one at a time in various directions. Each time he threw another piece of rubble, all eyes followed the direction of the sound of the pebble.

"Aaron, that's a good idea. That will work. You wait until I say to throw the stones. Right?"

Aaron nodded and attempted to say right, only it came out "rut." Olyn glanced at Kit and nodded.

"I can see where Aaron can distract them. But how do you plan to get your treasure? We can't carry all that even if we do get it away."

"Scilti, search your memory. Do you remember only three trunks?"

A puzzled look crossed the face of the elderly man. "Only three? You never let on just how much there was, but I'm sure you made more than three trips."

"You're right. In all, there were nine trunks. I brought them in three at a time. It was all I could push on the skid. Unless they find the rollers, they will have a hard time moving the three they found."

"Are the others in the tide cave as well?"

"Yes, but they are hidden much better. I had to leave after I placed the last three. I thought I had been followed. Turns out I was right."

"Are you going to move these three with the others or are you going to take all nine and hide them elsewhere?"

Kit had a definite plan, part of which was not to let the whole of the plan to anyone. She looked out the window of the scullery. "There seems to be a storm building. If the storm rages, my scurrilous crew will have even less chance of stealing from me."

Olyn knew it was futile to have Kit reveal the whereabouts of the remaining treasure. Carefully, he lifted his broad frame from the bench, his joints protesting the movement.

"Kit, child, I don't think I can crawl in some damp, cold cave."

Kit frowned in concern, then raised her brows in surprise. She wasn't used to thinking about the comfort of others. "Perhaps you're right, Scilti. It is cold, and the ledge is very narrow. If Aaron can draw their attention, I can move the three to the safety of the others."

"Kit, why do you want to move them while the men are in the cave? Why not do it when they're gone?"

"That would be perfect, but the only time I can move the trunks is at low tide and those men know it's the only time they can move them as well. I just have to hope either they don't see me or if they do, that I have enough strength to move them as a fox."

Looking out to sea, Kit saw it was presently low tide. This was not the time for hesitation. She had to make her move now.

Motioning to Aaron, she led the way along the corridor to the entrance of the cave. Just off the kitchen, the passageway became narrower. Suddenly, the ceiling dropped off and the only way to continue was on their hand and knees. Onward she crept with Aaron close behind her. Below she could hear her men arguing. They were on the backside of the cave, farthest from the sea, about twelve feet above the floor. The tide was coming in quickly, filling the pool. Kit could see her men taking orders from some man who looked more like a soldier than sailor.

Turning to Aaron, she motioned for him to follow her out to the brink of the cliff. Aaron shook his head.

"Aaron? Come with me. I need you."

It was clear the boy understood, but he would not yield. He took her hand in his and led her back through the scullery, then on to a narrow passageway. Down and down, they went, deeper into the earth.

"Aaron, are we going to Scilti's workroom?"

Again, the boy shook his head and wiped away cobwebs that covered a large oaken panel. On the wall hung a stick wrapped with linen. Aaron reached into his tunic and extracted a piece of flint.

Kit nodded and scraped some shavings to make a fire. The torch ignited quickly.

"Aaron, well done. I'll carry the torch. I'm taller and can hold it higher."

Nodding, he said, "Woof, rut."

"You are rut, Aaron," she said, smiling. The lad was proving to be a valuable asset. When she recovered her treasure, she would reward him. She would? Sharing was an idea she had never entertained before. Aaron tapped the panel three times and it slid open. Kit looked approvingly at her young companion. He'd brought her to a ledge high overlooking the tide pool. Below her, men were scurrying to escape the incoming tide.

What would he do now? Leigh inched closer to get a better vantage point. Foolishly the queen had added more wood to the fire and the flickering shadows drew the pirates' attention. They'd scurried to capture her. Leigh watched the men lead Guinevere roughly from the cave. Cold gray walls, wet with lime, offered no sense of warmth.

The floor was treacherous and uneven. Great protrusions rose from the floor and hung from the ceiling, the lime dripping from the top forming teeth, which, unseen, could rip a man to shreds.

Leigh had traversed the dangerous floor many times, but in his absence the limestone teeth had grown both larger and sharper. As he raised his eyes from the view below, he saw the flicker of a flame on the far side of the cave. In the light of the torch, he saw a sight so beautiful, all thought flew from his mind. Never had he seen a more exquisite woman.

The men below were obeying Lancelot's orders, but without the sense of devotion they had displayed under Kit's command. They seemed to comply more out of fear, than loyalty. Lancelot was scanning the entire cave. Now he was looking toward her. She drew back along the wall tightly to avoid discovery. With his lantern raised high he examined the farther wall. A small whimper and scuttled movements riveted his attention. He walked closer, in ankle deep water.

"Baldy, get some men up there and bring whatever is up there down to me, and do it quickly. We haven't much time." Two men scurried up the rocky wall, cutting their hands on the sharp stone.

"Well, well, it's your doxy, Lancelot. How do yer suppose she got up here?"

"The queen? How fortuitous. She may even bring more than the treasure," Lancelot said maliciously.

The men brought Guinevere down to face Lancelot. She was cold, wearing only her shift. "You're certainly in a sorry state, aren't you, my queen?"

"How dare you treat your queen in such fashion?"

"Your Ladyship, you're in no position to make demands. Remember, you were never forced to make this journey. And you chose to jump ship. Where is that little traitor, Leigh?"

"Leigh is not the traitor. It's you who turned your back on Arthur. You who betrayed him."

"Too true," he said, sarcasm dripping from his tongue.

"Your Highness and I will not settle for his forgiveness. I will have the crown of Ireland and you will reign beside me as my queen."

"Your queen? Do you think I would even consider an alliance with you, after the way you've used me?"

"Even Morganna learned I use women as I choose until they are no longer of any use to me. You will be no different."

As cold and wet as she was, her eyes danced with defiance. He grabbed her arm and spun her around. She wrenched from his grasp and started to run. The cold stone and lime crystals cut her feet. Baldy was after her in an instant and threw her roughly to the ground.

Though he saw everything, Leigh did not dare to reveal his position. If they captured him, there would be no way he could save her. And save her, he must.

The tide pool nearly filled, Lancelot and his men filed quickly out of the mouth of the cave in chest-deep water.

Carefully, Leigh stepped along the slippery shale down to the water. The cold water and the salt burned the scrapes on his arms. The chill he felt was more trepidation for the queen than any discomfort of his own. He felt certain they wouldn't risk harming her, but at one time he'd been sure Lancelot was loyal to Arthur. He couldn't allow the traitor to compromise Arthur's wife.

Always a strong swimmer, Leigh easily sliced through the incoming tide and out to sea. Once cleared of the mouth of the cave he swam to the towering cliff's edge, his muscular arms cutting deeply into the surf. His hands cut and sore, he grasped each tiny crevice in the sheer rock face and pulled himself up.

Leigh scrambled over the edge of the cliff and looked around. He headed up a small knoll he was sure he'd traversed before and looked toward the imposing castle in the distance. As he reached the other edge of the knoll, the view before him was the same as the day he'd mixed with the skunk. Olyn was leaning over in Helga's garden and the old woman was leaning out the window as she always did. He raised his hand in greeting as the now older, more hunched, wizard lifted his head.

"Olyn" he shouted, "Is it truly you?"

"Leigh, lad," Olyn said as he ran toward the boy, his ample arms out stretched in greeting.

As the two embraced, Helga ran up with tears in her eyes. "Oh, Leigh, how I've missed you. I thought I would never see you again," she said as she embraced him.

"How you've grown. I thought you were at court with King Arthur."

"I was, Helga. I am still in the service of the king, but the knight I was assigned is a traitor and has kidnapped the queen."

"Kidnapped the queen? You can't mean he's taken Guinevere?"

"Yes, Olyn. He courted her and ensnared her. And when she'd discovered his treachery, she left the ship with me and we hid in the tide cave."

"Is she still there?" Olyn asked.

"Why would you leave her?" Leigh bristled.

"I did not leave her. She was taken from me."

"Won't Arthur send aid to find her?" Helga asked, her expression incredulous.

"If he doesn't hate her for leaving him, he may, Helga."

"Leaving him? You mean she was so besotted she left her husband? Why, she is yet a bride."

"'Tis true, but Lancelot tricked her into believing she would be able to clear her thoughts and spend some time with her cousin on the journey Arthur sent us on."

"Lancelot? But Leigh, he is Arthur's favorite champion."

Helga's eyes grew wide. "You don't mean you're the queen's kin?"

"It seems I am, dear lady," he said, embracing the woman who'd been like a mother to him.

Olyn scowled. "Does Arthur know what has transpired?"

Thunder rumbled overhead. They all looked to the darkened sky. Placing his broad arms about him and Helga, Olyn said, "Come back in to your old home, Leigh. We will figure what we can do. Arthur must be informed."

Impatiently Leigh stamped his foot. "Informing Arthur will take time. We have to rescue her ourselves."

"And how do you propose we accomplish that? We are but two old folks and an unarmed youth. How can we hope to overcome one of the finest knights of the realm?"

"He may have been one of the finest, but now greed has dulled his senses. He wants the throne of Ireland for himself, and expects Guinevere to reign with him."

"What has given him this foolish notion? He is not royalty," Olyn said, his brow furrowed.

Leigh signed. "I fear, my old friend, it is not what, but who."

"Who?"

"The king's half-sister. She is the most sinister person I have ever encountered."

"Morganna? Morganna is at the bottom of this . . . this plot?"

Olyn knew this matter was greater than he alone could handle. He had to contact Merlin. And, he must do so without delay. The queen was in danger. More danger than she could possibly realize. More danger than even Leigh could imagine.

"Aaron, the incoming tide is coming much faster than I'd hoped. The men are leaving, but they've left the sledge, which means they'll be back."

He nodded. "Rut." He scurried back into the farthest wall of the ledge. When he turned back to her, he held several ropes with tackle and pulleys. "You mean get them now?"

The boy was the strongest ally she'd ever had, not counting Scilti, of course. A wizard and a small genius, they were a formidable army. This battle they would win, regardless of their small number. Aaron laid out the ropes and tackle. The pulleys were old and worn, but well greased and functional. Kit could feel the heft of the ropes. They, too, were old, but well cared for and sturdy.

Slowly, the boy lowered the rope over the rim of the ledge, using a worn piece of wood to protect the rope from the sharp rock. The ropes and pulleys secured, Aaron began to lower himself.

"No, Aaron, if they see you they will kill you. If it's me I will change and they won't believe their eyes. What a tale they'd tell that dandy of a soldier."

Aaron protested, flexing his muscles to prove to her he could handle anything. Kit placed her arm about his shoulders.

"No, Aaron. You are too valuable a man to loose."

Surprised, he responded, "Aaron mon?"

"Yes, Aaron, you are a mon and a fine one at that."

Carefully, she let herself down the ropes. She had to keep her head above water if she was to use her hands. Paws wouldn't be of much use in tying off the chests.

The water was cold as she slipped into it, her feet reaching about for the chests. Feeling the brass fittings on the curve of the chest with her right foot, she quickly formulated a method of tying off the lines.

She threaded the rope through the staple of the hasp on the side of the chest. Knowing the moment she put her head under the surface she would change, she had to secure the line with her feet. No easy task, but she did it. Swiftly she tugged on the line and Aaron hauled the chest upward.

Slowly it rose, swinging back and forth on the rope. One chest was safely on the ledge, now she had to secure the other two. Aaron threw the securing line down again. Hanging onto the stationary rope, she lunged for the line. Nearly losing her grasp she slid further down into the water. The tide rose around her, the water up to her shoulders.

"Woof?"

Olyn was clearly agitated by this turn of events. He needed a higher power's help. Morganna was obviously in league with the finest of Arthur's champions, and Leigh believed that Lancelot was not the knight in shining armor Arthur thought. Olyn knew Leigh would not wrongly accuse a man on mere speculation. He had seen for himself the dastardly manner in which Lancelot had handled the queen.

"Leigh, we have to summon Merlin at once."

"Summon him, Olyn? How can we contact a wizard miles away in another country? It could take weeks. We have to rescue Guinevere now, not in weeks." Shoulders slumping, he gazed out the window. The sun had set and the moon was on the rise.

Olyn followed his gaze out to the rising moon.

"Yes, Leigh, I can summon him. He has bestowed me with special powers that enable me to contact him in moments of dire need. The kidnapping of the queen is dire. In fact, I can't imagine a more dire situation."

"All right, Olyn, how can I help?"

"As I recall, you were not fond of enclosed places. Has that changed since you became a man fully grown?" Leigh blushed.

"Actually it wasn't me that disliked tight places it was . . ."

"Your pet fox, right, Leigh?" Helga interjected.

Olyn held up a restraining hand. "Helga, in due time."

"You knew? And you, Olyn, did you know as well?"

Leigh looked nervously from one to the other, as if he'd been caught filching goodies from Helga as he had when he was a child.

"Why is it small boys think the adults around them have no idea what occupies them?" Helga giggled and smothered her face in her apron.

"Leigh, we know about Kit, but there is more to the story. For the moment, we have to concentrate on freeing the queen."

"Why do you need me to be in tight quarters? Down in your dungeon?"

"Yes, lad. I am too old to take the steps as quickly as I use to and haste is most important." Olyn hitched his robes up around his thighs.

"Take my arm and help me down those old slippery steps."

"All right, Olyn, take it easy. It won't do for you to break a leg," Leigh said, hurrying down the steps as swiftly as he dared.

Olyn let out the breath he'd been holding as he descended the stairs. Standing in front of the warped oaken doors, Leigh pushed his muscular shoulder against it, forcing it open.

Helga had followed, though not closely, with a lighted torch.

"Here you go, lads. This will help, but I'm not staying down here. I hate bugs."

Cobwebs festooned the walls like lace curtains. Each step they took lifted billows of dust into the air. Leigh sneezed.

"Too bad we couldn't get Helga to stay. This place needs a woman's touch," Olyn said.

"A woman's touch?" Leigh asked.

"This mess requires a battalion of scullery maids."

"We cannot bother with cleaning now. We must contact Merlin without further delay." Going to the large table, Olyn swatted dust from the Master Tome. Reverently, he turned the pages.

Smoke rose from the open pages, a pink mist that reddened as it rose. Concentrated, it formed the 'Mantle of Sorcery'. The cloak rested lightly on the shoulders of the Greatest Wizard of all, Merlin.

"Olyn, why do you risk my wrath? I instructed you never to summon me unless your situation was so grave as to require my assistance." Leigh looked on, awestruck.

"Sire, I understood your instructions, but I have grave news to impart. Our queen has been kidnapped."

"Kidnapped? Kit? But how? She was in your care, Olyn."

"No, not Ireland's future queen, England's present queen."

"Guinevere? Who would dare to incur the anger of King Arthur?"

"I fear you will find it difficult to believe me," Olyn said haltingly.

Still amazed, Leigh ventured to speak. "Master Wizard, I was with our Queen when Lancelot tricked her and spirited her away."

The senior wizard turned and glowered at the young squire. "Aren't you his squire? Where is your loyalty? You were to serve Arthur's champion, not accuse him."

"Merlin," Olyn nearly shouted.

"Leigh would never betray a trust if he felt it was well deserved. Lancelot broke trust with Arthur, by seducing the Queen, misusing her and, finally, by holding her captive."

"Sir, he speaks the truth. My loyalty and duty are first and foremost to Arthur and his queen."

Merlin, calmer now, stepped out of the Mantle, still suspended over the table. He began to pace, stroking his long white beard through his slender fingers. From one end of the narrow table to the other he strode, each step placed carefully among the many books and papers. He stopped pacing, raised his head, and stepped out into midair. Leigh looked on in amazement. As many times as he'd secretly watched Olyn, the wizard had never walked on thin air.

"We must return to Arthur," Merlin exclaimed.

"Great Wizard, how are we going to accomplish this? We have no ship, and the journey would take so much time, I fear Guinevere would not fair well over a long period. Can we not send a pigeon with a message? Arthur must have troops somewhere nearby."

Merlin glared at the youth. "Do you doubt my abilities? We will inform Arthur. All of you prepare to come with me."

Olyn gasped. "All of us, Merlin? Only you and I are wizards. How can that be accomplished?"

"Now, you doubt me? How dare you?"

"Excuse me, Great Wizard," Leigh ventured, "I have no question you can accomplish what you say. I simply fail to see how."

Merlin's countenance softened, and he winked at Olyn. "Olyn, isn't this the lad you told me about?"

"Yes, Sire, but that is not the plan the Druids had for him, so I feigned ignorance of his desires." Glancing back to Leigh, he silently begged his pardon.

The senior wizard arched his eyebrow and descended to the floor. He turned, a rustling sound catching his ear.

Chapter Eleven

"Not a bad day's work, Aaron. We have them all, and no one will ever find them."

"Rut, Woof," the boy replied, his eyes ablaze with pride.

Kit smiled, realizing this was the first time she'd considered anyone, other than herself, capable of grand plans. "Rut you are, Aaron. Great teamwork. Now, let's get back to Scilti," she said, grabbing his hand and heading back the way they came.

Aaron withdrew his hand and shook his head.

"You don't want to go back the same way?" she asked, firmly convinced the route was sound. Aaron took her hand in his and led the way back into the tide cave.

Once in the cave, she protested, "Why come back here? Did you forget something?"

Aaron held his finger to his lips. She threw him a glare, halfway between anger and puzzlement. He had no right to give her orders, yet he'd been right each time he changed her course. She would trust him once again. Quietly, she followed, placing each foot solidly in front of the next. They made their way back to the ledge where the treasure was hidden. The ledge became even narrower. A misstep could result in disaster. Carefully and firmly, Aaron placed her hand on a line drawn along the wall attached to several pitons. There was no room to walk along the narrow edge. Movement was made by shuffling one foot, with the other close behind and hanging firmly to the line.

The ledge began to widen and Kit noticed a break in the wall. Once through the break they were in a narrow corridor. The roof above was rounded, as was the floor below, as if a giant worm had made a tunnel. Aaron reached to a sconce on the wall and found a torch bound in linen. Reaching into his tunic, he withdrew his flint, struck a spark and lit the cloth bound stick. At once, the flame drew further down the narrow tunnel.

They stopped and Aaron held a restraining arm across Kit's chest. Turning his head, he pointed to his ear. Kit turned and heard muffled voices.

Softly, she said, "It's Scilti and the cook and two other people. Do you know the voices?"

Aaron shook his head and crouched down on the floor of the tunnel and pushed aside a heavy wall hanging allowing Kit to see into a room off the worm-like cavern.

"Aaron, where is this? A part of the castle?"

"Olyn place," he responded.

"Olyn? You mean Scilti?" The boy nodded.

Kit peered into the chamber, which was filled with people, two of whom she did not know. She drew the curtain back further and attempted to garner the attention of Scilti.

"Scilti," she hissed, hoping he would hear her and not the others, but instead one of the men she didn't know, the old one, older even than Scilti, turned his face toward her.

"You there, come in here at once."

Not like being ordered about, Kit bristled at his command. Who did he think he was? She darted back through the opening.

Aaron firmly pushed her back through the aperture.

"Woof?" he admonished.

She shook her head in disgust and continued into the small, windowless room. The cold gray walls were unadorned except for the wall hanging over the opening. Even though there were only four people in the room, if felt crowded.

Determining she would be in control, she addressed the group. "Well, gentlemen, what is the reason for this gathering?"

"Young lady, while you have reason to be at this meeting, you have no authority. Be still, while I determine what course we will undertake."

"And what gives you the right to make that decision?" she replied saucily.

Eyes flashing, the older man's voice boomed. "Kit O'Malley, one day you will be a woman of consequence, but for today you are nothing. I am Merlin, Wizard of the Third Realm to the High King Arthur. My powers have no equal. I will make all decisions in this matter."

Merlin, ah? "What matter? Getting my treasure? I worked hard for that and no one, not even some high wizard, is going to take it from me."

Scilti crossed the small room, put his arms about her shoulders, and quietly admonished her. "Kit, this matter is bigger than your treasure, greater than you can even imagine. For now, you must follow Merlin's orders."

"Scilti, I follow orders from no one." Firmly she stood her ground and did not move, even with the wizard's gentle urging.

"Kit, please?" Aaron moved to her side.

"Woof, Olyn's place."

"All right, I understand, Aaron. This is Olyn's place and he sets the rules. If he wants this old warlock to be in charge, so be it," Kit said acquiescently, turning from the group, as it became apparent her voice would not be heard. Aaron moved closer to Leigh and began to stare intently at the young squire.

Pointing to himself, he said, "Aaron." Pointing to Kit, he said, "Woof," and finally pointing to Leigh, he said, "Da's."

Olyn spoke up. "No, Aaron, he's not your father."

The boy was adamant. "Da's."

"Scilti, who is this person?" Kit demanded with slight arrogance.

Scilti glared at the young woman.

"Kit, mind your tongue. This squire is to be the future King of Ireland."

"By what right are you to lead my homeland?" Kit demanded of the handsome young man.

"I only know what Olyn has told me. That I am related to the queen and I'm destined to rule."

"You're destined? I make my own destiny and no one will alter what I choose."

Leigh's eyes danced with merriment. This woman intrigued him. No, not merely intrigued. He felt something much more. In a flash of insight, he knew this woman was the love his heart ached for, the one that would complete him. Merlin, clearly agitated, interjected.

"Woman, you have no authority here. Keep your place."

"Aaron says I should respect this place as Olyn's, but what reason do I have for respecting you?"

Merlin sputtered, "I am Merlin, Wizard of the Third Realm to the High King Arthur, and my word is law throughout Arthur's holdings.

And you, young woman, will do as I say, and will do so without question. Do you understand me, Kit O'Malley?"

Kit's eyes flashed. "How do you know my name?"

"Woman, I know all things. I am here to fulfill the tenets of the Ancient Druids. And nothing you can say or do will change that."

"I told you. I make my destiny, not some group of ancient priests."

Olyn's eyes grew wide. "Kit, child, please be still. This is more powerful than you or any mere mortal."

Kit refused to be intimidated, even though her ever-present Scilti appeared humbled by the mere presence of the king's High Wizard. Maybe there was something more to this so-called wizard, Merlin. Maybe he did have powers. She'd seen many strange things in her time at sea. There didn't have to be a logical explanation for everything. After all, she was a fox.

Kit turned, Scilti's arm still about her shoulders. The rest of the group stood speechless in the dim light of the torch, the flames flickering across the planes of their faces. No one spoke, as if they were trying to find the right words to suit the occasion. Merlin, brows drawn together, broke the silence.

"I understand you are a headstrong young woman. And you made a tidy treasure in piracy, so I'll not dispute you are without merit. However, the tenets of the Druids bend for no man or woman. You will follow them as I instruct you."

Scilti tightened his hold on her and begged silently for her compliance. Kit looked down at the dirt floor and then raised her eyes to meet those of Merlin. "Sir, much has happened to me in a short time. I understand I might be part of some master scheme of things ordained, but that does not explain why this squire is to rule my homeland. By what right is he to rule? How will he treat me?"

Leigh knew Merlin would not take to Kit interfering. He had to do something. "I am a direct descendent of the queen and will rule both fairly and justly, when the time is right. What is important now is the rescue of the queen. She is being held, most probably, for ransom." Though he knew his duty was to the crown, he found it difficult to draw his attention from the woman he'd immediately desired.

"I suppose that dandy of a solider is the one who took her," Kit said, her voice filled with disdain.

Merlin glanced first at Olyn, then at Leigh. His eyes narrowed and he stroked his long white beard. Throwing his head back, he raised his arms to the roof of the cold drafty workroom. A shaft of light appeared directly in front of Kit. Quickly, she jumped back. Turning to her first mate, her green eyes flashed and she sought an answer to explain this strange phenomenon.

Leigh met her glance with a questioning look. The two of them joined hands and encircled the wizard. Merlin lowered his arms and stretched out his hand to Olyn. At once, the familiar twist of the Travel Tunnel began to pull all four of them into its vortex.

"Woof," Aaron frantically shouted. "Da's."

Kit released one of Leigh's hands, then grabbed Aaron and brought him into the circle. Around and around they spun, faster and faster, all the time spiraling upward. Without warning, the spiraling ascent ceased and each person within the tunnel landed gently on the floor of a larger workroom.

Aaron shook with fear. Kit's chest tightened. Poor lad. She patted him on the back in long soothing strokes. The feelings of the young boy strained at some strange emotions in Kit. Did she actually care for the boy?

Olyn patted the boy's shoulder.

"Aaron, lad, things will be all right. Merlin and I will make it so." The boy nodded, his lip trembling. Merlin turned, his gaze settling on Aaron.

"Olyn, how has this lad come with us? The chosen ones naturally would be swept up with us, but what is this boy's lineage that he would be drawn in as well?"

Olyn looked to her for an answer. "Kit, who is Aaron? Do you know who his da is?"

Kit shook her head. "I found him alone playing in some nearby ruins."

Aaron scuttled across the floor and placed his hand in Leigh's, then leaned his head against the young man's side.

Kit began to study the two carefully, assessing their appearances. There was a strong resemblance. Eyes the same shade of crystal blue, the hair blond and slightly curled, the two could be brothers.

"Merlin," she said, "Could Aaron possibly be related to the squire?" Merlin's eyes shot with a flame of understanding.

"Kit, you can communicate with the boy. Ask him. Will he understand?"

"I believe that's what he meant when he said the squire was Da's," she said.

"They belong to the same father." Her anger now defused, she began to deeply study the squire. So like the boy. There was a warmth about him. Familiar, like the dear friend of her youth.

"Leigh?" she inquired, her eyes rising expectantly. The young squire stared at her, mesmerized by her beauty.

"How do you know my name?"

"We were friends in another life, when we were children."

"How can that be? I knew no other children. My only playmates were my pets."

"Is that all I was to you, a pet?" she asked tauntingly. Immediately Merlin strode to the center of the room, black cloak flowing behind him, and faced a large table. She and the others followed, then stared at the book Merlin was fingering through. The sun coming in the tall, arched windows illuminated a duplicate of the tome Olyn used to contact Merlin.

Kit immediately took a step back, her fingers clamping her nostrils together. Little Aaron did the same. From the pages rose a stench, not unlike that of a skunk. Leigh's nose caught the noxious odor, triggering a memory long forgotten.

"You mean you're a skunk?"

Kit eyebrows rose in exasperation. "No, Leigh, I was the fox. Your Kit."

"But how? How can this be? Here before me you are the most beautiful woman I've ever seen, and now you tell me you're a fox? What magic is this?"

Olyn looked up from the book and motioned Leigh and Kit to the table. Merlin's long slender finger traced over the edges of the page.

"Here is written the proclamation of the Druids. You are the chosen ones."

"Chosen for what?" Kit asked impatiently.

"Does this mean I get my treasure?"

"For the moment," Merlin said, "Your treasure will remain where it is." Kit's nostrils flared, her eyes sparkling with fire.

"Until I move it, it will remain where it is. Only Aaron and I know its location."

Leigh watched as Aaron moved protectively to her side and slid his hand into hers. The two had certainly bonded. Though she'd hesitated at first, Leigh noticed she gave Aaron's hand a reassuring squeeze.

"Treasure? How can you think of treasure when the queen is in danger?" Leigh asked angrily.

"Kit, Leigh, you must listen to Merlin," Olyn said.

"He only thinks to protect you and teach you the reason for the strange happenings that have occurred."

"Leigh, you know you are cousin to the queen, are expected one day to rule Ireland and were brought to England to help you learn your role in the lives of those you will serve," Merlin said.

"Kit, you have less information as to your station in life, but nonetheless your role is just as binding as Leigh's." Leigh shook his head in disbelief. "How can a person be a fox? I must have proof. There is no way this woman, though very beautiful, could be my Kit. Her fur was soft as down and as brilliant as red fire. Her eyes were liquid green."

Kit turned those limpid pools of emerald to stare him full in the face. Without taking her eyes off Leigh, she said, "Fetch a tub of water and you shall see I am truly your Kit."

"Lass, this is not some game nor trick. Your transformation is not to be taken lightly."

"I understand, Scilti, but it is the only way he'll believe." Merlin closed the book and directed them to a large tub and bid Leigh drag the empty container to Kit's feet. "This will not do. There must be water. I must be totally immersed or there will be no change."

Merlin scowled, his eyebrows drawn together in frustration. "Have you forgotten I am Merlin? I will place the water in the tub." He drew Aaron back into the room as he was leaving to find water.

A faint smell of skunk still hung in the air. Without warning, water cascaded from a vessel suspended above the tub. Leigh looked on in awe. Merlin was truly a great wizard.

Aaron, though usually speechless exclaimed, in a very soft tone, "Magic?"

Kit stepped into the tub and began to remove her tunic. Leigh's heart started to pump faster as heat flooded his body. Surely she wouldn't disrobe in front of him.

Olyn rushed up to the side and stilled her hand. "Nay, Lass, simply step into the tub and plunge beneath the surface," Olyn said. He shot a knowing glance toward Leigh. "You'd only confuse the lads."

She shrugged then stepped inside the tub. When she nodded at him, he approached and, shocked beyond words, saw that her feet were no longer and fox paws had taken their place.

Back and forth Morganna paced, each turn drawing her closer to the niche in the wall. Here she learned many of Merlin's secrets. It had been many weeks, and still no word from Lancelot. Perhaps the wizard would know something of the queen's whereabouts. Silently, Morganna crept ever closer to the unseen niche. Seeing she was unobserved, she quickly drew back the tapestry and slipped into the small space. She heard the voices of a number of people. Voices she did not recognize. Merlin's voice was clear, as was that of the other doddering fool of a wizard. She thought the other male voice to be that of the boy, Leigh. Still, there were others she could not name.

Merlin's voice rose above the rest.

"Olyn, she knows of the transformation. Can she control it herself? This is most important. If she is subject to anyone other than herself, she has not full control. And full control is what is required."

Kit glared at the senior wizard. "You question my control? How is it you let the queen be taken? I control myself and my destiny and will not submit to the direction of others."

Behind the tapestry, Morganna watched as the female stepped into then out of a shallow tub of water. Her heart caught in her throat. When the woman was in the water, her feet took on some animal's guise, a fox maybe. Yes, definitely a fox. When she was out of the water, her feet returned to human. *This woman is a fox! Could this be the fruition of the ancient ordination?* The one she'd learned of in this very place on another occasion when she'd chosen to eavesdrop on the King's High Wizard?

Chapter Twelve

Damn that Lancelot. He'd ruined the entire plot. Morganna, though cramped in her secret niche, had expansive plans. She would have the throne of Ireland, and neither Merlin's sorcery nor Lancelot's incompetence would keep her from her heart's desire.

Turning her attention back to the proceedings in the workroom, she noted Merlin appeared to be deep in thought. She peered through a slit cut carefully in the inner tapestry.

"This young lad here must indeed, have some ties to the royal lineage," Merlin said.

Aaron drew close to she-fox's side, seeking safety within her arms. "Woof?" His eyes glistened with fear.

"Don't worry, Aaron. Leigh and I will keep you safe," she said, inclining her head to what the fools believed to be the future king.

"Kit, how can we protect him? We are not even certain of where we are. Lancelot's men will no doubt be searching for us."

"Leigh," Merlin said, "You and I will handle the matter of the Queen. Olyn and Kit will return to Clare and commence Kit's training."

"Training? What could I possibly need training for? I can recover my treasure without any training. I captained a ship, you fools."

Despite herself, Morganna found herself admiring the spirited woman. She'd discovered there were far too many men with self-proclaimed power. Olyn put a restraining hand on his ward.

"Kit, calling Merlin a fool is not very wise. Be careful of what you say."

Kit's eyes flashed a brilliant green. Her nostrils flared as she drew in and held her breath. "I'm sorry, Scilti. It's just I've been handling my own affairs for some time and find it strange anyone would think I need more training."

"Kit, as a seaman you are without equal. You have more than proved that, but as a regent you lack polish."

"All right, I'll do as you bid, sorcerer," she said almost defiantly. Merlin raised his long, thin arms and twirled his index finger in a circle.

From behind the tapestry, Morganna observed as Scilti and Kit became engulfed in a Travel Tunnel. As she was royalty she, too, could travel in the tunnel. Carefully, while the room was in turmoil, she crept toward the swirling funnel and grasped the final spiral. She fought against being pulled into the tunnel like the others, and easily retained her grasp on the tail. Without a sound of any kind they flew over the countryside and out to sea.

As they approached the sheer cliffs of Clare, Morganna spied the boat she'd secured for Lancelot. Then the tunnel swept low over the countryside. Her heart leaped as she spotted Lancelot and his crew. She released her grasp. Her billowing skirts slowed her descent and landed her gently on the grassy knoll above the castle.

Quickly, she hid behind a gnarled tree, following her first and foremost mantra. *There is more to learn from observation than confrontation.*

"Come on, we'll get to the castle and inform them we have the queen. They will pay dearly for her return."

Lancelot ordered his men to secure Guinevere with leather bindings and place her in a makeshift lean-to on the edge of the castle grounds.

Baldy glared boldly at the knight. "Thet castle don't look like no one could pay any ransom. Have yer thought of that, Mr. Dandy Knight?"

"I'm sure they have some means of contacting the King. Even if they have to send an emissary, I will have my queen, my treasure, and the crown."

The sailors were grumbling among themselves. "Thet fool. Who's he think he is? The bloody king? He's in fer a fall, he is."

"Will have me queen, me treasure, and me crown. The fool is bloody daft."

"I don't care what he has, long's I gits mine. He's promised more than he can deliver, the way I sees it."

Morganna's keen ears quickly picked up on the men's rumblings. *Lancelot has made a fool of himself once again. What's worse, he's compromised me and the throne. Wants Guinevere to rule as his queen, does he?*

Whipping her skirts around, she stepped into the open clearing and called for Lancelot. Hearing his name, he whirled toward her, his eyes wide in disbelief.

"Morganna, my precious, how do you come to be here? I thought you were still at Camelot."

"Dare you call me precious? You idiot, did you think I would not learn of your desire to rule with Arthur's queen? Perhaps you would like to rethink your plan. It is not clever to try to deceive me." Her dark eyes blazed with a fire so vivid, one could almost hear the crackling of the flames.

"Now, Morganna, please, it is all part of the plan. Arthur might give up the throne of Ireland. It's a country of little use to him, but he would never give up the Queen. We need him to confront us. Else we will be powerless." Carefully he played out the words, pausing frequently and judging the effect on the king's half-sister.

Morganna was not one easily fooled. *Why must I suffer such shoddy incompetents?* Carefully masking her feelings of disgust, sweetly she replied, "Of course, Lancelot, I know you would never betray me." *Not if you want to keep your head, anyway.*

Using his well-practiced art of flattery, he sought to soothe her. "Morganna, you well know Guinevere is sorely lacking in the skills to run a regency. You will be my queen, and none other." Taking her hand, he bent and gently placed his lips to her palm.

Forcing herself not to withdraw quickly, lest she tip her hand, Morganna smiled coquettishly and glanced at him through her thick smoky lashes. "Lancelot, you are to trust no one and nothing you see. There is magic afoot. Beware of deception. The King's Grand Wizard has a hand in this matter."

"Certainly, my queen. You are most wise."

"Of course, I knew you wouldn't toy with my affections. After all, you have more to gain with me as your queen," she replied in a superior manner. Haughtily, she swept her skirts over the damp grass and indicated he was to lead her to the castle above the knoll.

"I don't think it's wise to have you appear at the castle with me and my men. We need to keep your presence as a surprise should we have need of you. Your talents are formidable and I wouldn't want to waste them on a simple ransom demand," Lancelot said.

Wary, but agreeing with Lancelot, she requested his men find her suitable lodging.

Lancelot appointed Baldy to see to Morganna's needs. "I warn you, Baldy. Have a care when dealing with this woman. She is not a mere queen. This one has powers we do not wish to challenge."

"Fer a landlubber, you sure has yer woman problems, don't ya, Mr. Fancy Knight?" The sailor moved to grasp her arm.

Morganna glared down on the captain and informed him he was not to touch her person.

"All right, missy, jest follow me and I'll fix ya a place ter stay while were in this godforsaken land," he said leading the way to the lean-to where Guinevere was tied.

"Fool, do you think I would seek shelter in a shabby lean-to? Leave me. I will construct my own lodging," she said, dismissing the sailor with a wave of her hand. After she constructed her shelter she went to visit the queen.

Guinevere strained at her bonds and bid her sister-in-law to free her. "Please, Morganna, this is no way for a queen to be treated. Release me," she said, her eyes pleading.

Morganna looked down on her brother's wife. "Well, I guess you have learned Lancelot's company is not what you expected, is it, my queen?"

"No, he's not to be trusted. You must help me Morganna. Untie me and perhaps we can find Leigh and get word to Arthur. He must rescue me."

"Now why would my dear brother choose to rescue such an ungrateful wife who would run off with his favorite champion?"

Sorrowfully, Guinevere hung her head. "You are quite right. I do not deserve to be saved. My treatment of Arthur is shameful, and I will probably pay with my life."

"I don't think there is that much at stake. If Arthur chooses to pay the ransom Lancelot demands, you will survive."

An expression of grave concern passed over the queen's features. "What do you know of Lancelot's plans? Are you in league with the rogue? What will Arthur say when he learns both his champion and his sister plot against him?"

"If he's wise, he will pay the ransom and turn the Irish crown over to me," Morganna said with the conviction that there could be no other possible outcome to the queen's situation.

"Olyn, how are Leigh and Merlin going to rescue her ladyship if they are at Camelot and she is here on Clare? Aaron and I can get her. Wizard reasoning makes no sense to me."

Olyn sighed as Kit continued pacing back and forth in front of him. "That's because you are not a wizard and seem to have little respect for them." How could he convince his ward to trust someone other than herself?

"Now, Olyn, you know I respect you. I even like some of your spells. You know, that illusion thing."

Gently he shook his head. "Yes, child, I know you respect me, but you seem to lack an understanding of the scope of Merlin's power. He can and has changed the destiny of nations. In this matter, even he must follow directives of a higher power. No one can alter the instructions of the Ancient Druids."

Resigned, she shrugged her shoulders. "What would you have me do? Can we at least look for Guinevere?"

"Woof?" the young lad said.

"Aaron, Woof look?" Olyn blew out a breath. Nothing less than an active role in the scheme of things would satisfy his Kit.

"Yes, you may search for her, but when you find her, do nothing. Come to me and tell me where she is and I will contact Merlin. Remember now, Kit, do nothing. Do you understand me?"

Eager for the fray, Kit grabbed Aaron's hand and led him out of the workroom. Quickly, they left the castle and headed to the cliffs above the cave.

"Aaron," Kit said.

"I think it best if we look to the mouth of the cave. They would have to move her to avoid the evening tide." Aaron nodded and pointed to the reddening sky.

"You're right, there isn't much daylight left. We'll camp here and watch for a fire. Surely, they will look to her comfort. It wouldn't do to have 'Her Highness' cold," she said somewhat disdainfully.

All she'd learned about the queen did not instill any reverence for the woman. The woman was weak and easily duped. Aaron pointed north, below the knoll at a thin wisp of smoke. "Woof, look."

"I see it," she said, crouching low to the ground and brining Aaron down with her. "They won't try to move her tonight, so we'll act at dawn." Aaron shook his head, his eyebrows raised. "Olyn, nothing, rut?"

"Yes, that's what he said, but we are going to trick them and draw Fancy Knight and my men into the castle. If Merlin is as great a wizard as Olyn says, he can turn them into butterflies or something." Aaron threw back his head and laughed.

Heart pounding, Kit placed her hand over his mouth.

"Shh, we don't want them to hear us. We need to surprise them. Now, lay down on the pine bough and sleep. We need to be very clever and well rested if we are to pull this off."

Arranging the pine boughs to accommodate Aaron, she bid him lay down and rest. As she studied the boy, she wondered what it would be like to have a child of her own. He acted as if he hadn't a care in the world. Smiling, Kit lay back on the boughs and faced the moonlit sky.

The warmth of the sun and the crowing of a faraway rooster awakened Kit with a start. She jumped to her feet. Aaron was slower to rise. He rubbed his eyes and stretched his arms over his head.

"Come on, sleepy, we have much work to do," she said, kindly ruffling his hair, noting how alike his curls were to Leigh's.

The lad rose and quickly brushed off the few bits that clung to his clothing. Kit sat down on the ground and found a twig. Clearing an area to draw, she drew the cliffs, the cave, and the secret entrance.

Aaron dropped to his haunches and pointed to the area of the wall entrance.

Nodding, she said, "You are rut again, Aaron. Behind the panel door is too direct. We'll use the break in the wall. They'll never figure it out and we'll have them trapped. Baldy's so wide, he'll never make the ledge, but that dandy will try. The man is a fool. I cannot understand how the queen was so entranced."

Aaron grinned. "Woof rut. Queen not."

Kit broke into a wide grin. "Each day you learn more and more. I wish you would pretend not to know all that you do. Ignorance is a valuable tool when dealing with the devious.

Solemnly, Aaron nodded.

Kit then scattered the boughs and wiped out the plan she'd drawn in the dirt. "Come, we'll go into the cave from the kitchen. Helga will not be up and we can slip in unnoticed."

Carefully, they made their way though the dew-kissed grasses up to the dilapidated castle. Only the front intact. It was apparent it had been a glorious structure not so very long ago. *It will be that way again. I will make it so.*

Through the gaping gate and into the rubble-strewn courtyard they made their way to the area where Olyn had made some repair. It served as a kitchen, though Kit was sure that was not its original function.

Aaron moved to the hearth and began to set a fire.

"No, Aaron, we do not want them to know we have been here. Helga will only worry and Scilti will rant on about the fates, Druids, or some other such thing." Taking the lad's hand, together they followed the path he'd shown her only a day ago. *So much has happened it seems as if I've always known of these strange occurrences, yet none of it makes sense.*

"We may have to wait for them to enter the cave, but I believe they will come back to the place they found her."

Carefully, they made their way along the narrow ledge above the tide pool. There was no sign of the men or the dandy knight.

"We'll just have to wait, Aaron."

"Rut." He nodded and settled back to wait.

A chill wind blew through the workroom at Camelot. There was no source for the wind, yet it chilled both the sorcerer and the squire.

"Merlin, what would you have me do? You can send me back to Clare and I will assist Kit, without her knowledge, of course."

Merlin let out a puff of breath in mock disgust. "She certainly won't accept your help, if you offer, but you're right. We have to act and quickly."

"Can you send me alone?" Leigh was eager, not only to rescue the Queen, but to see his Kit again.

Merlin furrowed his brow and glared down on the squire. "For a certainty, I can, but I will not."

Leigh, ignorant of the reason for Merlin's disapproval, pressed the matter further. "But why? If you have the power, use it."

"Oh, give me patience," the wizard said, raising his arms and imploring unseen spirits. "Lad, think. You are but one man against a crew of cutthroats and a member of the Round Table. These men have considerable skills in dispatching their enemies. They would have little trouble with an untried squire."

Sadly, Leigh hung his head and brushed his hands back and forth over his thighs. "But we have to do something. We can't let Lancelot take the queen or allow him to take over my country."

"True, these matters are of great import, but the Proclamation of the Druids is the greater need. Alone we can do nothing. Neither sorcery nor confrontation will settle the matter. We will inform Arthur of the situation and ask for his assistance."

Looking at the wizard skeptically, Leigh asked, "Will he help, knowing his queen left him of her own accord, and that I requested she be allowed to travel with the man who holds her for ransom?"

"Quite right, Leigh, he will not be eager to aid us, but I feel he will see the right of it and help us. Love is more powerful than anger," Merlin said with the wisdom of one who has witnessed the power.

Together the two headed to Arthur's War Room. As they opened the large oak door, they saw the king bending over the Round Table, his eyes focused on a map. Hearing them enter, he raised his head.

"Good day, Merlin, Leigh," he said with forced cheerfulness. "Merlin, I have need of your sorcery. I wish to know of Lancelot's whereabouts."

The sorcerer let out the breath he'd been holding since he entered the room. "Arthur, I already know where Lancelot is to be found."

"And where is my queen, then? I entrusted her to your care, Leigh." Arthur stretched to his full height, his eyebrows raised in expectation.

"Yes, we know of her approximate location," Merlin replied as stoically as possible.

"Approximate location? Merlin, what does that mean? Either you know where she is or you don't," Arthur said impatiently, quickly crossing the floor to confront the wizard toe to toe. "Merlin, as your king, I command you to tell me what you know of the queen and Lancelot."

"Sire, I have learned Lancelot has betrayed your trust."

"Betrayed me? How?" Leigh cleared his throat noisily.

"You, lad, what part do you play in this betrayal?" Merlin stopped the squire before he was able to speak. Laying his long thin arms across the boy's chest, he pushed him aside.

Clearly angered by his High Wizard, Arthur reached behind Merlin and grabbed the boy by the arm. "Leigh, I demand to know what your part is. I trusted you and Lancelot to keep the queen safe. And now Merlin knows only of her approximate location. Lad, you have failed me."

"Arthur, gather your senses. The boy has not failed you. The failure is with Lancelot. Your most trusted knight has broken that trust."

"Sire, I did all I could to save her, but those brigands took her from the ledge. If she had remained quiet, as I bid her, she would have been safe."

Merlin stepped back and allowed Leigh to talk to the king directly. "Forgive me, lad. Please, tell me what transpired."

"Sire, when we set out, it was my belief we were traveling to the land of the infidel, which, I believe, is south. I realized we were in fact heading north. When I questioned our direction Lancelot said you had allowed him to visit his homeland, Wales, before continuing our journey. Suddenly we were headed due east and we were at the coast. Lancelot assured the queen you knew of the plans and she should not concern herself. He said he would make sure she was safe and comfortable."

"East? Then you were headed out to sea in the direction of Ireland?"

"Correct, Sire. We were then led onto a ship. Clearly it was not one of your ships. It was very dirty and the crew showed Guinevere no respect or consideration. I demanded she be provided with the best accommodations available."

"You demanded? Had not Lancelot provided for her lodging?" Arthur asked incredulously. Leigh hesitated and glanced at Merlin who bid him continue.

"Your Majesty, Lancelot was not behaving like a true knight of the realm and certainly not in the manner of a member of the Round Table. He had not a care for her comfort or safety. The men on the ship were crude to say the least. They did not believe Guinevere to be the queen, said Lancelot told them she was his doxy."

Arthur fairly sputtered. "They did not believe her to be the queen? Why did Lancelot lead them to think she was a lowly trollop?"

Merlin interjected, "Please, Arthur, she is the lad's only kin. Be kind."

"Yes, yes, I'm sorry, boy. Then what happened?" he pressed.

Looking down to the floor Leigh continued his report of the happening. "I settled her in the captain's cabin and she became ill, as the sea was very rough. Lancelot never came to see how she faired and I overheard him talking to his men of a treasure they were to steal."

"Treasure? I have no treasure hidden in Ireland. However, since I am regent of the land, whatever treasure is found belongs to the crown."

Leigh did his best to suppress a grin.

"I know, Sire, I tried to tell her, but she says it's hers."

"Hers? Of whom do you speak?"

Nervously Leigh glanced at Merlin.

"Continue, lad, he'll need to know all of the tale."

"Kit, the pirate. It's treasure she captured from what she calls the dreaded English."

"A pirate with the unlikely name of Kit? Merlin, of whom is he speaking?"

Merlin inhaled deeply and slowly let out the breath. "Your Highness, the woman is the one I hinted would hold the crown of Ireland with young Leigh here."

"The ancient Druids said a pirate would hold the regency of such a valuable trade market? What strange method of reasoning is this? Do the ancients take into consideration the Resurrection Fluid?"

The import of the fluid would turn the balance of power to any regent who discovered it. Arthur had been searching for the wondrous liquid for many years. Presently, he had troops in Northern Ireland hoping to discover the elusive prize.

Merlin's eyes grew wide. How did Arthur dare to question the Druids? "Hold your tongue, Sire. The Proclamation of the Druids is not to be trifled with. What they have ordained must be fulfilled without question. Not even questions from the King of England."

"I take it you see the merit of this ordination?"

"I do, Sire," Merlin said with conviction.

"Very well," he said, resigned.

"But still, we must rescue the queen."

"Please, Sire," Leigh said,

"Forgive me. I should never have asked you to allow her to accompany us. I felt she needed to realize what a wonderful husband she had and not to follow the first dandy who flattered her. She was behaving foolishly. I only sought to permit her to find her true path."

Arthur's brows drew close together and his eyes narrowed.

"You mean to say Guinevere was smitten with Lancelot? She followed him out of lust?"

Merlin shook his head sadly. "I'm afraid, Arthur, that is the truth of the matter. Leigh only thought she would come to realize her love for you is greater and return a better wife for you."

"Is this true, boy?"

"Y-yes," he stammered.

"I meant no harm. I did not know Lancelot was the one she wanted, or that he would play her false."

"I understand, lad. One would have every reason to think a Knight of the Round Table would be honorable."

Merlin led Arthur back to the table and gently lowered him to his chair. The regent seemed to sink with the weight of the knowledge.

"Merlin, what am I to do? Should I even rescue her if she has no desire to reign as my queen?"

Leigh's fear he had failed the king grew with this pronouncement. Had he ruined the future of Arthur, Camelot, and England? He crossed the room to stand at Merlin's side. Gently, he took hold of the wizard's sleeve. Merlin looked down at the boy.

"Do not fear, Leigh. He's just overwhelmed. He had a great concern such a young woman would not be able to handle the crown and now he feels his concerns are justified. But in truth he loves Guinevere with a love greater than he has ever known. He will save her. For the moment, leave us. I will contact you when we have a plan."

Leigh nodded and slowly went out the large oaken doorway, looking back only briefly. Sorrowfully, he returned to his quarters in the page wing. What could he do to make things right?

Chapter Thirteen

Kit could hardly contain her excitement. The long wait had proved fruitful.

Aaron pointed to the floor below. Kit saw Lancelot and his men entering the cave. She smiled. *Now we have them where we can entice them into the wall.* Slowly, she crept down close to the tide pool. The soft glow turning her hair to a brilliant burnished copper. It had been years since her hair was free of the scarf she wore to impress the men with her dedication to the sea. The men saw her and were at once entranced. She was a truly beautiful woman. They had no way of recognizing her as their captain, but they knew a lovely piece when they saw one.

"Hey there, dandy knight. There's a woman really fit ter be da Queen. She looks like she might have more spunk dan the uder," the seaman observed as he circled Kit.

"She is truly beautiful, but what is she doing in this godforsaken place?"

"Let's follow her and find out," Baldy said eagerly.

Swiftly, they jumped into the tide pool and waded to the far side where Kit was scaling the wall. Aaron lowered a rope for her to grab and swing into the hidden niche in the wall. Looking back, she saw that their plan had worked so far. Lancelot's men appeared confused, and were searching uselessly around the cave for some sign of her.

From her perch many feet above the pool, deep within the wall niche, she and Aaron stifled laughter. Aaron pointed to the antics of the men below, with his hand over his mouth, lest he give away their position. Kit watched the men until they had come as far as she wanted, and then stepped out from the wall.

Baldy yelled, "There she is. Get her, men."

"Forget the woman, we're here for treasure. She may be just an illusion," Lancelot barked.

"What d'yer mean, illusion? There some magic afoot here?" the captain asked warily.

"Pay her no mind. We've work to do. Push those sledges in and start loading the treasure." Lancelot directed his men.

Baldy looked around the shallow pool and found nothing. "Hey thar, little Lancelot, looks like someone ran off with yer treasure."

"What do you mean, someone ran off with it? I directed you to secure it before we left the cave."

"We tied it off, but now even the sledge is gone. Do yer think she took it?" he asked, pointing to where she poised above the pool.

As the men lowered their eyes to find their footing to scale the sheer face, Kit and Aaron exchanged broad grins. As the men ascended the wall, they would now see a small boy in her place.

"What manner of magic is this? Morganna must have a hand in this," Lancelot said. Again, the tide was rising in the pool.

From her hiding place, Kit watched as Lancelot directed his men to pull the small skiff out into the open water.

"We'll regroup before the next tide. First, I want to confer with Morganna. I need to know what we're dealing with."

"And, I serpose, she's magic and will know how to handle this ghost."

"Don't be a fool, Baldy. You don't mix with that you can not understand," Lancelot said.

Kit signaled to Aaron to draw back into the wall. Slyly, she grabbed the rope and lowered herself to the surface of the pool. Releasing her hold, she dropped into the water.

At once, she rose again as a fox. The men became frightened and crowded into the skiff to escape this perceived danger. Someone pushed Lancelot overboard, and the men paddled furiously out of the cave, leaving him in the quickly rising tide.

"Wait, you fools, don't you see it's a trick? We have been duped. This is not real. Use your reason. No woman becomes a fox," Lancelot shouted to his departing men. He slapped the surface of the water, dove in, and began to swim out of the cave.

"Woof?" Kit again submersed herself and rose from the pool a woman. "I'm all right, Aaron. Pull up the rope. Did you see that dandy sputter?"

Laughing, Aaron quickly hoisted the rope. "Woof rut, he sput."

"Oh, he sput, that's for certain. Those sailors will never follow his orders now. They think he's bewitched. But we still have to get him into the castle and find where the precious queen is."

Aaron pointed out to sea where Lancelot was fighting the tide. "Aaron save dandy."

"That's a good idea. You're a boy. He would not fear you have any other motive than saving him. When you get him to shore, direct him to the castle. He'll be wet and scared. He'll follow you to safety and warmth."

"Rut," he said as he plunged into the sea. He dug his arms deep into the surf, quickly reaching the floundering knight.

Lancelot clung to the boy as if he were the only one standing between him and certain death. When they reached the shore, Aaron set him on the sand and allowed him to catch his breath.

"Thank you, lad, you saved my life. You shall be rewarded when I reach my treasure."

Aaron smiled and placed his arm beneath Lancelot's. Slowly, they headed up the knoll to the castle.

Kit grinned and took pride in Aaron's rescue as she and Scilti watched the unlikely duo come up the knoll toward the castle. The knight seemed less magnificent in his sodden tunic and cloak. Once he crossed the threshold, Scilti would bind his arms and force Lancelot to reveal the whereabouts of the queen.

Aaron led him into the makeshift kitchen and bid him sit. After he was lowered into the straight-back chair, Scilti quickly bound his wrists behind him.

"What are you doing?" the knight demanded angrily. "Did you save me just to bind me? What will my capture gain you?"

Kit stepped into the room, her eyes narrowed at the knight. "I believe you owe me the return of my treasure and the location of the queen you took."

"I owe you?" He spat.

"I don't owe you, or anyone, anything. What I have discovered is mine."

Kit smirked, her emerald eyes flashing, and lowered her head to speak with careful deliberation. "Knight, you owe me. The treasure you stole is mine, and the queen is of value to friends of mine. I do not quickly shift allegiances, as you seem eager to do."

Struggling against the leather thongs that held him fast, Lancelot attempted to free himself. His head fell to his chest in desperation. Scilti poured warm water over the bonds.

Kit nodded and indicated he should withdraw. Scilti slowly shuffled out as Aaron came around the chair to face the knight.

Lancelot raised his head, grimacing in pain as the drying leather binding grew tighter around his wrists.

"Do you now wish to tell me the location of the queen? I can have the bonds doused again. Each time they will dry tighter," she said with the conviction that this dandy of a knight would capitulate before the leather was completely dried. The pain would be great. It was one thing to suffer pain and wounds on the battlefield, and quite another to be reduced to a quivering mass by a woman and an old wizard.

Drawing in his breath and raising himself to as straight a posture as he could, Lancelot stared her directly in the eyes.

Kit met his gaze with an equally belligerent stare. "No man takes what is mine. Be he knight, king, or wizard. What I gather is mine, forever," she said. "My men will be searching for me. How long do you think you can hold me? A woman, a boy, and an old fat man," he said, his voice dripping with disdain.

Kit would not allow him to bait her. She pivoted on her heel and held her arms at the elbow. Back and forth she paced in carefully measured steps, each move calculated to give Lancelot more time to realize she not only held him, but the men he trusted would not rescue him. Aaron sat down near the knight and softly laughed to himself.

Kit spoke not another word and the knight began to squirm, clearly realizing he was indeed in dire straits. The sweat stood out on his forehead then ran down the back of his neck, each drop landing on the leather thongs. Tighter and tighter they grew.

Minutes passed as if they were hours. Finally, Kit spoke. "Do you wish to tell me something? Surely you know the men you hired were once mine and are not coming for you. They will follow the leader who will gain them the most treasure. They have no loyalty that cannot be transferred if fortunes change."

Dejected, the once proud knight hung his head.

Kit grabbed his forelock and pulled his face toward her own.

"Not so cocky now, Sir Knight?" she asked, her face only inches from his.

Lancelot swallowed, his throat constricting. "I'll tell you where she is, but you will have to let me go to her. She will be afraid of strangers."

"Since when does a captor care for the tender feelings of his prey?" Kit asked.

Aaron shook his head. "Woof, not. Trick."

"Don't worry, Aaron, I am aware the knight is as slippery as an eel." She glanced across the room and saw Scilti enter with a plate of food.

"Surely you two must be hungry. Come, Helga made biscuits. Remember how they melted in your mouth when she drizzled honey over them?"

Kit did remember. It was a memory nearly forgotten and one to be savored. The knight's stomach rumbled. He'd not eaten and the biscuits tantalized him. His wrists were beginning to chafe against the shrinking leather.

"Well, Dandy, wouldn't you like to eat? Helga's biscuits are delicious. Simply tell me where the queen is hidden, and I'll free you. You can eat, and I'm sure we can find some salve to soothe your wrists."

"I'm a Knight of Arthur's Round Table. You cannot treat me as thus," he said with as much dignity as he could muster.

Kit would not be bullied, nor impressed, by the knight's credentials. "I've heard of you and your treachery. Arthur would do well to divest himself of your services. A false knight is no better than a traitor. You have used the king's trust to play him fool. Worse, you duped his queen. The Round Table is better for your demise."

"Surely you cannot mean to kill me. You're a woman," he said incredulously.

"Being a woman has never determined my course and it will not start to do so now."

The thongs squeaked as they shrank. Aaron cocked his ear and nodded solemnly to Kit.

"Well, if that is your response, we'll leave you out in the courtyard where you can watch the stars. I'll give you till morning to decide."

With Aaron on one side of the chair and Kit on the other, the two carried the hapless knight into the open courtyard. There were no trees to offer shelter or buffet the wind of the cold fall evening.

Lancelot's breathing quickened. Dead leaves swirled around the chair and the wind cut at his face, as did the bindings at his wrists. His soul cried out at the anguish of his folly. Was there no hope?

Merlin entered the room and studied Arthur as he bowed over the Round Table. The tall man straightened his shoulders and greeted the wizard. "Good day, Merlin. Have you learned anything further about the queen?"

"No, Sire, no matter what incantation I employ, I am unable to learn more of her whereabouts."

"Morganna has been strangely absent from court. Could she be blocking your spell?" Arthur asked.

Worry clearly imprinted on the brow of the wizard caused Arthur to question him further.

"Merlin, is that a possibility?"

"That is a definite possibility and combined with her absence could very well explain the barrier."

"Could she know of the resurrection fluid or the Ordination of the Ancient Druids? Can she alter the course of events?"

"The possibility of her having knowledge of either is very dangerous. Arthur, we must contact your troops in North Ireland and have them meet Morganna and Lancelot on Clare."

"Meet them? Are you certain they are both on the Island? How can that be?"

"It involves more than I can explain, your Highness. Trust me, I must contact your troops."

Arthur's shoulders fell and he wrung his hands over and over.

"Very well, Merlin, do what you must."

Arthur slowly shuffled across the room shaking his head in sadness. As he reached the door, he heard a gentle knock. He pulled open the wide oak door and saw Leigh standing in the casement.

"Good day, Sire. Has Merlin learned anything more about my cousin?"

"Sadly no, Leigh," Arthur said.

Leigh rushed into the room. "Great Wizard, what are we to do? We must save her. She's gotten into some mess I don't even understand."

"Quite so, Leigh. Her folly may very well endanger not only England, but your homeland as well."

"What are you saying, Merlin? She's barely a woman. What possible reason could she have for placing the countries in jeopardy?" Leigh asked. "We must save her from this absurdity. It is not of her making."

Arthur turned slowly back from the door. "I hesitate to utilize the crown for a foolish woman. However, Leigh, you're right. We must save her and our countries. Merlin, do what you must. Send the troops. Whatever it takes." "Great Wizard, can you send me to join the troops? Like you took me in the tunnel?"

"The tunnel? Merlin, how is it this boy knows of the Travel Tunnel? I understood only sorcerers and royals could use the tunnel." Arthur reached down and grasped the Wizard's shoulder.

Merlin looked down on Arthur's hand and then glowered up at his face. "Unhand me, Arthur. You overstep your bounds. The boy's knowledge comes from experience. He is a true royal and bears the mark."

"What foolishness is this? Have you two taken leave of your senses? It is not wise to anger the Wizard of the Third Realm to the High King."

"Merlin, it is you who has taken leave of your senses. It matters not if either I or the lad touches you. The queen and our lands must be saved whatever the cost to your dignity."

The ancient sorcerer shook his head and nodded. "Yes, yes, forgive me. My vanity is misplaced. Arthur, have I your leave to dispatch the resurrection party to the Isle of Clare?"

"Most certainly, and do so with the greatest haste." Morganna listened from her elaborate tent as Baldy called his men together. The ragtag group gathered just out of sight of the lean-to where Guinevere was captive. Baldy seemed to be chastising them for their foolhardiness in believing the transformation of Kit was a sign from the devil. "Who else but the devil would make a woman a four-legged animal with a coat of red? It's a sign, I tell you," a crewman protested.

"Yer are truly a fool if yer believe that. The devil is after men's souls, not some foolish girl who changes into a fox. It's magic, and that witch what pitched her fancy tent is the one behind it. You mark my words, we'd best have a care and get that one on our side, fore we make any foolish moves."

Another crewman protested, "I ain't messing with no witches. Let's jest leave the damn queen and head out to sea. I'd rather take me chances with the weather than some witch."

"Witches is fine. Ya jes have ter know how to handle them."

One of the smaller men to the back of the group wedged himself closer to the head of the crowd. In a small squeaky voice, he said, "I suppose you know all about handling a witch?"

"Look how she set that tent out of thin air. She can move things and make things appear and I reckon if she takes a liking to ya she can do the same for ya. We jest need to get her to see our way is the way she wants. Then she'll be no threat as long as she gets what she wants."

Fools, thinking they can best me. I'll allow them to believe they have control. Slowly Morganna began to sashay toward the group in a coquettish fashion. Men are so easily fooled. She tossed her long dark hair over her shoulder and smiled at the captain.

Seductively, she swayed her hips as she approached the naïve crewman. They'd been at sea a long time and were easy prey for the sorceress. Facing the captain, she reached out and drew her hand along his cheek. She blew him a phantom kiss and placed her fingertip under his chin.

The rugged seaman blushed. He threw a look of conspiracy to his men, designed to show he was in control. In truth, Morganna was completely in charge. She was master of the situation. Using her powers and every feminine wile at her disposal, she would soon have the entire crew in the palm of her hand.

Baldy ordered his men to assemble. "Listen ter me, we have the queen and this beautiful sorceress. She must know where our treasure is and she will help us to get it back," he said, throwing Morganna a confirming look.

She returned his gaze with affirmation. She would allow him to think he was using her.

"You remember the fox we saw in the tide cave? And then we saw the woman. I think she is bewitched, and if we have her, there is no telling what riches we can have. We will be rich beyond measure."

Baldy grinned. Morganna smiled. It was so deceptively easy to fool the simpletons.

Lowering her lashes, she spoke to the captain. "Sire, I think you're right, we must find this fox woman and hold her for more ransom than the queen. There are many queens but there can be only one fox woman. It is the making of the wizard Olyn."

A murmur rushed through the crew. Fear spread like wildfire.

"I ain't messing with no Olyn. He got too much power. He can see everything. You can't hide from a wizard."

Another man said, "Let's jes' take the queen and head back to Camelot. Arthur will pay for her return. If we tamper with the wizard, we'll have nothing."

The men advanced on the captain. He raised his hands in an effort to halt their progress. "Stop, men, don't you realize we are in control? We have Arthur's queen and the witch. She can hold any action from the sorcerer. Woman have more hold over the realm of magic than men."

Morganna grinned. She could not have planned it any better. They were falling right into her hands.

Chapter Fourteen

Morganna heaved a great sigh and steeled herself for what was to come. She would have to pretend empathy for her sister-in-law. Slowly, she walked to the lean-to where the men held her captive.

"Guinevere, dear? How are you faring? Can I get you something to eat?"

Guinevere lifted her head and glared at the woman. "How do you dare inquire as to my well being? It's not as if you care. What do you have to gain?"

"Tut-tut, my lady. Not true. Of course I wish to see you returned to my dear brother. Further, I wish you to be unharmed, and I will take special care to see you are not injured or compromised in any way."

"I suppose I wouldn't be of as much value if I were dead."

"Of course you have more value alive, and I would think it is the way you prefer to remain. Simply cooperate, and you will be safe at home in Camelot's court as soon as Arthur sends the ransom."

"It will take weeks for Arthur to learn of my plight and more weeks for him to send the ransom. How long to you expect to keep me tied like this? If you don't feed me properly, I will die or succumb to disease. I don't think Arthur wants an emaciated or sickly queen."

"How wise, my queen. Then you see the importance of your cooperation?

If you understand there is no escape, I will allow you to share my tent."

"You have my word, Morganna. I will not try to elude you."

"That is most judicious, Guinevere. I will summon Merlin and he will contact Arthur, and we will have you home in no time. However, my queen, your hands will remain tied."

Morganna swept from the lean-to and instructed two crewmen to release the queen's ankle ties and take the queen to her new quarters in the tent.

Baldy came up to her. He lowered his voice, lest the others hear him. "Well now, Missy, how do yer perpose we gets that fox woman and more ransom from Arthur?"

Morganna laughed a deep, throaty laugh and smiled at the dirty captain.

"First, good captain, we must rescue Lancelot. He's being held in the courtyard of that rundown castle above the knoll."

"Oh, how does yer know that? You got one of them crystal balls er somethin'?"

Morganna smiled to herself. "Something like that. I simply know what happens to those I prize or despise." She shot the captain a warning look designed to give him pause. No one dared question her or suffer a dismal fate.

The sky had grown completely dark. Though the moon was full, clouds passed over its face, casting eerie shadows in the courtyard. Everywhere Lancelot turned, there seemed to be evil lurking. He strained against his bonds. Since the sun had dipped below the horizon, the drying went slower, but they shrank nonetheless. His wrists were bleeding, the blood running down the back of the chair. Some of it was now dried and gave off a stench.

In all his years of battle, he'd never been in a situation so hopeless. At least then he'd had troops who would rescue him. People had respected him. He would have that again. *This time as King. People would look up and revere him.* Only one thought kept him going. If he could just live through the night, surely Morganna will free him.

But it proved a night of a thousand hours. His eyes strained for the morning sun to appear. The biting cold in the open courtyard had chilled him clear to the bone. He'd never been this cold before and he vowed he'd never be this cold again, once Morganna came and they ruled their kingdom together. Even if all she wanted was that *Sine Vitium*, whatever it was. They would rule and the potion Morganna desired would protect their realm. He drifted off to sleep, dreaming of better times.

A slim line of sunlight appeared. Kit rose and looked out at the courtyard. Men were creeping toward the chair where Lancelot sat tied. They looked about carefully. Baldy took his long knife and slashed the leather bonds. Lancelot was too weak to stand, so the large swarthy pirate slung him over his shoulder and proceeded out of the courtyard.

Kit felt a tug at her sleeve. Aaron held her by her tunic and placed a finger across his lips. It was as if Aaron could read her mind. She nodded. She'd expected them to finally come and rescue him.

When they were out of earshot, she said, "I expected them sooner. They must be afraid of the dark. Come, we'll follow them. They will lead us to the queen."

Aaron nodded and said softly, "Rut."

They followed at a safe distance. She would need more than a simple transformation to free the Queen. Her men were easy to fool, but having been fooled once they would not be so easily duped again. She had to devise a plan.

Morganna's tent came into view. As Baldy took Lancelot in, Kit got a glimpse of the queen through the open flap. Guinevere did not seem to be bound as she had bound Lancelot. They must be treating her well. "Come, Aaron, we need Olyn's help."

Aaron nodded solemnly, and they rose from their observation point above the knoll and headed back to the castle.

There, they found Helga in the kitchen bustling about, and Olyn sitting at the table, his head in his hands. As he heard Kit and Aaron approach, he rose and greeted them.

"Good morning, did you two manage to sleep well?"

"Yes, Olyn, I slept quite well. Too well, in fact. The knight has been freed."

"Ah, you call me Olyn. Then you realize Scilti is simply another name for the same person?"

"I do," she said, hearing the pride in her voice. "Olyn, we must use some of your magic if we are to free the queen and retrieve my treasure."

"Free the queen we will but, child, you must realize the treasure belongs to Arthur. He is King. The isle is part of his kingdom."

"I understand, but he must have greater riches than three trunks of treasure."

"Kit, three? I thought you told me there were nine in all. What of the other six? They all belong to the king."

"Well, what he doesn't know won't tempt him. I think the six others should be mine for rescuing his queen."

"You may be right, Kit, but that is for him to decide, not you."

"Olyn," she said, with the patience of one who knows they no longer hold the winning card, "I earned that treasure and it is not going back into the hands of the English. Even if you feel this Arthur is a just king."

"Very well, Kit, we will deal with the treasure another time. Now we must free the queen. Did you see her? Is she all right?"

"I saw her. She's fine, sitting in a fancy tent with a tall dark woman. She didn't appear to be bound, but it did look like the woman had some hold on her."

"Describe this dark woman. Did she have long black hair the same shade as midnight?"

"That's her. Who is she?"

"She is the king's half-sister and perhaps the most evil person I've ever met. We must be very careful if she is on the scene. I fear this is beyond my capabilities. I must contact Merlin. He will determine what is to be done."

Arthur watched with trepidation in his heart as Merlin withdrew from the room. A breeze of indeterminate origin became a gale and swept the wizard away. "Leigh, come, we will await Merlin in the counsel room at the Round Table."

"You think he'll return quickly? Will he have news of our queens?"

"Our queens? How is this woman you desire to be a queen? Of what country?"

"Merlin has told me only that I am to rule beside Kit and our kingdom will be Ireland. How this is to come about, I do not fully understand."

"Nor I, lad, nor I. Merlin works in ways even a king cannot comprehend. Trust only that his is the way it shall be."

"I will, Sire," Leigh said, his words full of confidence he did not truly feel in his heart.

"Leigh, are you aware I have a searching party in your homeland?"

"Your Highness, my experience is very limited. I'd never been off my island, till Olyn sent me here, after he found the mark on my neck."

"The mark, boy? What mark? Show it to me."

Leigh approached the king and knelt before him. Arthur pushed aside the boy's hair and found the fox-shaped mole. He felt his eyes grow wide in astonishment.

"By all that's holy, you truly are the chosen one. Merlin told me there would come to me a ruler for the wild island. This man is to unite the two lands and bring peace to both countries. Leigh, lad, you are that man."

"I believe what Merlin and Olyn have told me. What is your party searching for?"

"Searching for? I'm sorry, Leigh, your revelation distracted me. They are seeking the *Sine Vitium.*"

"*Sine Vitium?* What is it? I've never heard Merlin or Olyn speak of such a thing."

"I do not believe any other than Merlin knows of its existence. It is the heavy weight in the balance of power. With this elixir, a wound, even a mortal wound, is healed. Such a thing must not fall into the wrong hands. It could save a country or destroy it."

"If no one knows of its existence, how is the search party to find it? Wouldn't they need to know what they are searching for?"

"Leigh, son, your reasoning is definitely that of a king. How will they find it, indeed? Merlin has enlightened them. They know only what it looks like and approximately where it can be found. However, it is well hidden. The Ancient Druids have for many centuries been keepers of the *Sine Vitium.*"

"Why not make sure all kings have this? Then all powers would be on equal footing."

"That is logical, Leigh, but men are not all logical. Some seek to destroy others and rule unjustly. The Ancients foresaw this and hid it from all, save Merlin."

"Does Merlin go to find the *Sine Vitium* or to rescue the queen? Which is his highest priority? To render your troops to be without flaw or to save the Queen of England?"

"I understand your frustration. Many times Merlin has kept me in the dark about his plans. I can only trust he will do what must be done. Even he answers to a higher power."

"The Druids?"

"Yes." Arthur placed his arm about the shoulders of the young man and together they entered the room wherein the Round Table stood. He circled slowly around the table, carefully noting each place and the name borne upon the chair placed there. When he reached Lancelot's chair, he began to weep. This man he'd trusted so deeply had betrayed him. Lancelot had not only stolen the queen, *he'd* been robbed f his most trusted champion. He reached down and took the ceremonial sword that lay at the knight's place and turned it. The tip of the blade now faced the chair, signifying disgrace. All the other swords were placed blade tip facing the center of the table.

Leigh stepped back to allow the king time to bear his grief alone. Heading for the door, Leigh placed his hand upon the handle and drew it open. There, in the opening, stood Merlin.

Carefully, Olyn traversed the slippery steps down into the dungeon where his workroom now stood dark and empty. Without Leigh to guide him, the trip was indeed dangerous. His girth rendered the journey even more difficult. *I must summon Merlin. This is too formidable a task for me to undertake alone.*

Leaning his stout shoulder against the door, he pushed. The door gave way, raising clouds of dust. He searched in there, settling for a hint of the spiraling that foretold Merlin's coming. No spirals appeared. Merlin would not come unbidden. Not this time.

Olyn shuffled to the center of the room to his worktable. The Master Tome lay in the center where he'd placed it only a short time ago. The room remained unchanged as well. He placed the torch he'd carried with him into the sconce on the wall. The torch threw off a soft, almost gentle glow onto the pages of the Master Tome. From the center of the page rose the smoke as before, but then nothing. No cloak, no scarlet plume, simply smoke. "As a wizard, I'm useless," he said to the walls. He'd lost his powers to that demon witch, Morganna. He'd been unable to help Leigh, the boy he'd so tenderly raised. Unable, even, to keep the girl safe.

"Olyn not rut," Aaron said, startling Olyn.

Olyn allowed him to lead him up the stairs into the kitchen, where Helga was preparing a meal.

Hearing their footsteps, she turned away from the cook fire and smiled at them.

"It's so nice to have someone to cook for. And to have you sit at table with us, Aaron. We're a family again, aren't we, Olyn?"

"I suppose you're right, Helga, but the head of this family is unable to protect its members." Olyn sighed heavily.

Aaron shook his head vehemently. "No, Olyn save."

"Aaron, how can I save us if I don't even have the ability to reach help?"

The boy slid along the bench where they sat and placed his hand in that of the old wizard.

Helga walked toward the two and embraced them both. "Now, we're all together," she said, patting them both on the shoulders.

Olyn looked up in horror. "No, we're not. Where is Kit? Was she not with you, Aaron?"

"Woof, behind, trick dandy."

"You left her? Oh, may the Ancients protect her from herself. Come, Aaron, we must contact Merlin. Help me down to the workroom. I must try again."

The wizard rose from the table and there in the sunlight streaming through the window stood a shadow. A shadow so foreboding it was cold. Dampness permeated the air.

The ominous silhouette spoke. "You wish assistance, oh great wizard?"

The voice was one he knew all too well. Morganna. She, who so many years before had stripped him of his Third Realm powers. In all the known worlds, this was the only truly foul personage, who cared only for her own gain. No one else mattered to her. Not kith, nor kin, nor child, not even a lover. She placed herself above all other mortals, her gain above all else.

"Take yourself from this place, Morganna. You have no reason to be here. There is nothing for you to gain, no jewels, no treasure, nor bounty of any kind. This is a broken-down castle and we are but poor inhabitants."

Majestically, the witch seated herself on the bench and drew the wizard down beside her.

"What is it you fear, Olyn? If you have nothing, then you have nothing to fear. I would not steal the very bread from your mouths," she said with sarcasm so thick it could be cut with a broadsword. "I am the king's sister. It is my responsibility to care for the subjects under his rule."

"Morganna, you never cared for Arthur's subjects. All you desire is Arthur's wealth."

"That is not quite true, old man. There is more I desire, and by holding Arthur's queen, I shall have it."

"You have the queen? Where is she? You have not harmed her, have you? If you have, that would be most unwise."

"I am no fool. I take no risk upon myself. Lancelot is the one who holds her, not I."

"You're in league with Arthur's rogue knight? Have you no shame, woman?"

While Olyn was busy with Morganna, Aaron slipped quietly off the bench and out of the kitchen, briefly touching Helga's skirt. She pulled her skirt wide to hide his escape as he scrambled from the room.

Retracing his steps, he searched for Kit. She was no longer on the knoll, nor was she in the cave. Aaron feared the worst. *Dandy has her.* Somehow, he'd managed to get those dark and dangerous men to help him. *If only the squire were here then they could save Kit and the queen they prize so much.*

He went back into the cave. Finding nothing, he dove into the sea. Just off shore stood a pirate vessel. Slowly and quietly, he swam up to the boat, where could hear voices.

"Thet witch will gain us all measures of bounty. All we has ter do is keep her on our side and hope she doesn't want us to share her tent."

A drunken sailor wiped his gin-soaked chin and laughed. "She's pure and certain a witch, but I don't think I'd mind sharing a tent with her. She's a beauty, even if a dangerous one."

The captain glared at the foolish sailor. "Now, you men, take heed, she's not one to be messed with. She'll turn us all into swine. As long as she stays in thet fancy tent with little Miss Highness we'll be safe. Jest don't cross her."

Aaron treaded water and then swam back to shore. He would trick them, just as Kit had done. He covered his face with mud and climbed up to the knoll where the tent was pitched. The darkness would hide his dirt-stained face. He approached with the stealth of a cat hunting its dinner.

A single lamp outlined the knight and the queen. Guinevere appeared to be crying and Lancelot was making no attempt to calm her. Now what would he do?

Kit crept close to the tent and heard the dandy knight talking to the queen, her answers punctuated by incessant sobbing. She rolled her eyes. Didn't that woman do anything but snivel?

"Guinevere, my pet, everything will be all right. Arthur will pay the ransom and then we'll be free. We can rule this land together. You will be my queen."

"Lancelot, when I left my homeland, I wanted so desperately to return. Now this land holds nothing but treachery. I . . . I want to go home to Arthur and Camelot."

"Your Highness, you know Arthur is an old man. He'll not rule for long. I am young and strong. Our kingdom will last for many, many years. We will rule together."

"Your words will not turn me against Arthur. I was foolish once. I'll not be so again."

Lancelot turned his back on her and scuffed his foot on the ground. "Trust me, Guinevere, I will build you a castle, finer even than Camelot. It will be the most magnificent structure in all of Ireland."

"I do not trust you. Nor should Arthur. And, if I ever see him again, I'll advise him never to trust your counsel. You have betrayed anyone who ever trusted you. I daresay you've played false with my dear sister-in-law as well. You should have care in dealing with her. She can do more harm than good if she feels betrayed."

Chapter Fifteen

Arthur strode to the door to greet the sorcerer. "Merlin, why have you returned so quickly? Were you able to learn anything, or is it hopeless?"

The sorcerer's face was solemn, but not dire. "I have found the search party and dispatched them to the Isle of Clare. The will arrive at break of day two days hence."

"Sire, what of the others?" Leigh asked. "Aaron? Kit? Did you see them as well?"

The wizard nodded, an enigmatic smile in his features.

"You are quite right, Leigh." Arthur stroked his beard and considered. "If these others are involved in the kidnapping or are themselves victims, we must know if their fate. What can you tell us?"

The old wizard closed his eyes and sank wearily into Lancelot's chair, which was pulled away from the table. Arthur leaned closer to the elderly gentleman, and asked softly, "Old friend, are you ill? You look very strange. Leigh, fetch some wine."

Merlin raised a restraining hand.

"I am not ill, only weary from the conflict with Morganna. Her presence is taxing."

Arthur placed his hand at his chin, his fingertips covering his mouth, as if to hold back any negative comment.

Leigh came to the arm of the chair and placed his hand on the wizard's arm.

Merlin looked down on the boy's slender fingers. Fingers untried in battle.

"Leigh, did Olyn ever have any encounters with Morganna while you were in his care?"

"He spoke of her as a foul influence, indicated her powers were greater than his own, and that she had stolen his skills."

The wizard looked up at the king.

"Arthur, your dear sister is endangering the future of two countries and your future with your chosen queen. What would you have me do?"

"Need you ask, Merlin? I would have you right all wrongs, but I fear it is a most complex task. Use whatever methods you have. Ruin the witch, if you must, but return my queen and save the *Sine Vitium*. All else can go up in smoke for all I care."

Leigh said, "Sire, you must consider another country other than England and another queen other than Guinevere. You cannot put your desires above what is just."

"I see the passion of justice burning in your eyes, lad." Arthur grinned, knowing he had overstepped from regent to man.

"Your Highness," Leigh said carefully, measuring his tone. "Perhaps I come from too simple a background. Right and wrong are very clear to me. I do not understand all the complexities of a kingdom, but while you rule, you must protect all those vassals in your realm. Is this not so?"

Arthur nodded. The boy was right. He was not thinking of anything but his queen and the salve. What most profited him. The elixir would make his the strongest kingdom in any of the known worlds. But was power all a regent should consider? Arthur knew he was being tested.

"Leigh, go to the kitchen and have some food prepared for us. Have it brought here. We will dine at the Round Table and consider the proper course of action that must be undertaken."

Leigh did as he was bid, leaving the sorcerer and the King to a private discussion.

Merlin rose from Lancelot's chair and pushed it disdainfully aside. The king took note of the wizard's discomfort and went to his side.

"Merlin, while you were gone that brief period, Leigh showed me the mark on his neck. This lad is truly the chosen one. He too must be protected. Is there any connection between the boy and the *Sine Vitium*?" he asked, wringing his hands.

"Whatever connection there might be is tenuous at best. They both simply come from the same land. I am certain Leigh does not know its location."

"The boy is so lacking in duplicity I'm sure he would reveal it to me. He only seeks to do what is right and just. I long for that fervor I once had as a lad. Where has my passion gone?" he asked, sinking back into his chair.

Merlin joined him in Gawain's chair, gently admonishing his king.

"Your true path has been cluttered with the trappings of a kingdom. Nothing is quite as simple as it once was."

"Quite so, Merlin. What are we to do?"

The moon was high and visibility was excellent. Baldy saw the outlines of the captive queen and that dandy of a knight in the witch's tent. He assembled the men on deck.

"I sez, we gets the queen and that knight on board this ship and gets away from this bewitched island as quick as possible."

The thin man, who always seemed to be to the back of the crowd, pushed his way forward. "Capt'n, we can't jest scoop 'em up. The witch sees all. She'll follow us to the edge of the sea. Ya can't hide from a witch."

Baldy paused to consider the thin man's words. "Mayhap yer right. We'll first find the fox woman and then the witch will want to stay on our good side. Why should she be master of this ship? It's my ship. Tricking a witch ain't easy, but if we're careful, we kin do it."

Again the thin man piped up. "Trick a witch? You've been at the rum stores too much, Capt'n. How yer gonna trick her? Tie garlic around her wrists?"

"Nah, we got ter be smarter than that. She'll have to think it's her idea to come aboard. It must be her plan, even if it ain't. You unnerstand? Drop the skiff. We'll find the fox woman now and settle with the witch when we can."

The skiff slipped silently into the water. The sea was calm and the oars dipping into the water made only the slightest noise. It was enough. Aaron's acute hearing picked up on it immediately. From his vantage point above the knoll he pressed his body deep into the grasses. Only an animal could detect his presence.

A nearby twig broke with a snap, sending Aaron's heartbeat racing. He spun his head around and met the liquid green eyes of Kit.

"Aaron, what have you learned?"

The boy pointed to the sea where the skiff was approaching through the placid water.

"I know, I heard them as well," Kit said, settling down on the ground beside him. "What are they up to?"

Merlin strode into the Council Room. Arthur stood at the table, maps laid out before him. His slender finger traced a route from Northern Ireland down to the southernmost coast. It would take him weeks to reach his search party. Merlin said the party had nearly reached the coast. They'd been on the move since the wizard had contacted them.

"Merlin," Arthur said, "Have you heard from Miroet and Kamelin?"

"Not directly, Sire, but trust those two are the best you could have sent. They know their homeland well, every tree and vale. They are just and honorable men. Their father instructed them well."

Moving back from the table, Arthur settled himself in his chair. "I have no doubts as to their competence for the search. My concern is the safety of the queen and the return of the traitor Lancelot. The three of them fought side-by-side many times. It may be difficult for them to take Lancelot into custody."

"Your concern is misplaced, Sire. The Irish princes are steadfast in their loyalty to you. They will do whatever you ask. You must not judge all of your knights with the same measure as Lancelot."

A firm knock on the oaken door drew their attention to the opening. Leigh pushed the door fully open. "Sire, have you heard from your search party? Are they near Clare? We must join them. Furthermore, we must do so with great haste. I fear the longer Guinevere is in the company of Lancelot, the greater danger she is in."

Arthur knitted his brows. He did not like a squire directing his course of action. Scowling at Merlin, he indicated his displeasure.

The old wizard cocked his eyebrow. "Arthur, this time your pride is the obstacle. The boy is right. We must take action and it must be taken without further delay."

Leigh, as if realizing he'd overstepped his bounds, walked contritely to the king and knelt before him. "Sire, I only choose to serve. But my cousin and the woman I am destined to be with are in grave danger. It is my duty to rescue them."

"Quite so, lad. I understand. So long ago, I, too, acted with the fervor and zeal of youth. We'll save them. However, we must utilize my sorcerer and all of his magic to overthrow this enemy. This cannot be resolved by might alone."

Leigh rose from his knee, taking the hand Arthur offered. "Forgive me, Sire, I have no wish to countermand your orders. I am but impatient to begin."

Merlin nodded and turned to the task at hand. "Come, gentlemen, we must prepare and meet with the Irish princes. Arthur, bring Excalibur and wear your finest armor. Join me in my workroom when you are prepared."

"Your Highness, may I have the honor of serving as your squire?" Leigh asked.

"You may, lad. Come, we must make haste."

Arthur and Leigh headed to the armory and Merlin went straight to his workroom.

It had been many years since Merlin had employed his skill of observing enemies without their knowledge. He'd never felt observation was totally noble. He preferred to confront his adversaries directly. However, those he was dealing with on this occasion were far less than noble.

Closing his eyes, he stood in the direct center of the room. A shaft of light poured down on the wizard. Throwing his head back, he looked up into the brilliance. Therein, he saw a scene so horrifying, he shook.

Morganna! Taking control. The queen was defying her sister-in-law and the man who took her from the king. Her foolhardiness had placed her in grave peril. Her defiance of Morganna was not wise. Lancelot was appeasing Morganna and trying to curry favor with the queen as well. If this scene could not be set aright, the fate of the two countries would be dashed against the rocks of civilization. It would be the end of the world as Arthur knew it.

Summoning all his power, he sent out a message to the queen.

Take heart, Guinevere, Arthur is coming. We will free you and restore your dignity.

At that moment, Arthur and Leigh entered the workroom. Merlin lowered his head and the light vanished.

Trying to shake off the unsettling images, Merlin noted how Arthur cut a dashing figure in his full armor. Leigh, similarly attired, stood straight and tall beside his king.

"Merlin, will we take mounts? We will have need of them."

"I am sure you will need horses, but horses do not have royal blood lines and will not be able to use the Travel Tunnel. We will find mounts when we arrive."

"Great Sorcerer," Leigh asked softly, "Can you not make horses out of mice or something?"

Arthur smiled, knowing Merlin did not like anyone to make sport of his skills.

"Lad, I will see mounts are provided, however, I do not prey on helpless animals for my own gain. Mice, indeed," he huffed.

"I guess our best course is to return to Olyn and see if he can use some spell or other to free the Queen," Kit said as they emerged from the tall grasses.

"Rut, Woof, Olyn rut." Though the boy was capable of more and more speech, he was frugal with his words.

Kit smiled and ruffled his hair. The boy returned her smile, took her hand, and they headed back to Olyn's workroom.

Olyn looked up from his table. His hair stuck out in all directions and his eyes were blazing. Waving his arms in the air, he pointed to the spirals of dust that were forming.

"What is it, Olyn? Is it the other sorcerer? That Merlin?" Kit asked, half fearful, half disbelieving.

The wizard seemed incapable of speech. He continued to wave his hands and twirled about. The spirals continued their upward journey. A fierce wind swept through the room and whipped the old gentleman's robe about his body. The coarse material flapped like a canvas sail. The noise was deafening.

Kit reached out to stop him, and all motion ceased. As violent as the action was, it became as still as death in a matter of seconds.

"Olyn, are you all right? You are not harmed, are you?"

He let out a long breath and sighed. "Yes, it is Merlin, he's nearby. But . . . but he's not coming here."

Kit scowled. "What do you mean, he's not coming here? Where is he going?"

"I'm not sure, lass, he's about the king's business. I sense someone else is with him. Who, I do not know."

"Well, if he's not coming, I guess it's up to us to save the queen and capture the dandy knight. He should be hung for mutiny," Kit said firmly. She held no respect for a disloyal crewman. She didn't tolerate it in her men, and she suspected the king would feel likewise.

"Kit, I don't know if I can save her by myself." Fear was evident in Olyn's voice. He lowered himself to a bench on the side wall of the workroom. His ample body seemed to diminish as he sat.

Kit came to his side and patted the old man's arm. "Don't worry, Olyn, we'll save her and capture him. You need not concern yourself. Aaron and I will handle the matter. I thought perhaps a spell would help, but it's not necessary."

"Kit girl, be very careful, something foreboding is in the air. I fear there is sorcery at work, and not Merlin's alone. She stripped me of power once before and I do not wish to tangle with her again. She's dangerous."

"Who? How dangerous can a woman be? Most are weak and expect all sorts of comforts."

"You're right about her wanting comforts. But her greater thirst is for power."

"I understand, Olyn. I, too, want power. I want my homeland free of English rule and I want my castle on my island, and I shall have it."

He shook his head and looked to the boy for understanding. Aaron held his head high and threw out his chest.

"Aaron serve Woof," he said proudly.

"We save, we capture."

Kit pressed the old wizard further.

"I need to know who this woman is that threatens you. What harm can a mere woman do to a wizard?"

"Her name is Morganna LeFay. She's the King's half-sister and she's all evil. She wants to have all the power here in Ireland that Arthur has in England. However, she won't be concerned for the welfare of those she rules, as is Arthur."

"As I said, I understand the desire for power, but how can she accomplish this? Is she a witch? Is her power like yours, but greater?"

"Her power is greater than mine by leagues and nearly rivals Merlin's. She is a force to be reckoned with. If you are to take her on, you will need to use every skill you've ever learned. You will need to transform and pray she hasn't learned that you can."

"Scilti, remember this, I am the most ruthless female pirate who ever roamed the Seven Seas."

Olyn nodded, noting she had called him by his sea name. She was marshaling her forces. He could almost see her thinking process. She focused on the matter at hand and allowed nothing to distract her from her goal.

"Aaron, can you sneak into the tent unnoticed?"

Firmly, he nodded, and proceeded to leave the workroom.

She caught him by his tunic.

"Not this instant, when I finish my plan." She smiled, knowing Aaron would do whatever she asked of him. "Olyn, can you handle an illusion spell? Nothing fancy, just to hide my human presence."

"You can't be thinking you can just appear as a fox and no one will be the wiser. I told you she is a witch, and she may even have knowledge of your transformation. It's too risky. Let's wait until Merlin returns."

"How can you even know he's coming back? You said he wasn't coming here. We must do this ourselves, Olyn." Kit paced back and forth, and her footsteps made no more sound than a wild creature in a forest.

"Please, Kit, let me try again to reach Merlin. We need his help against Morganna."

"Olyn, did you not tell me I am to be a queen in this land and that my reign is ordained by the Ancient Druids? The Druids are more powerful than any witch. Nothing will happen that can break that ordination."

"You're right, lass, but how do you plan to free the queen and capture Lancelot? The Druids won't come down and tie him up for you."

"Have no fear, Olyn, it can be done. Aaron, you will go into the tent and make sure no one sees you. Free the queen's hands, but tell her not to move. Then have her ask for wine. Can you do this?"

"I can," Aaron said.

"Good. Olyn, you are to hide me with an illusion spell and I will invite Lancelot to share the wine with Guinevere. He will see no one and believe it is his own thought. When I enter the tent I will drug the wine so Dandy Knight will fall asleep with the first sip."

"Once he's asleep, Aaron, you will lead the queen to the castle and Olyn's protection. I will transform at the edge of the sea and find my mutinous crew. They will chase me, knowing I am valuable. I believe they think I am a bewitched fox, and they will try to capture me."

"Remember, Kit," the old man cautioned, "You can be trapped as can any fox. You do not have any protection as a fox. You must be careful."

"Trust me, Olyn, I will be most careful." Kit was concerned, but not frightened. She'd never been in a situation where she had to be wary as a fox. Most of her time as a fox was spent with Leigh. *Oh, how I miss him.* Bit by bit it was coming back to her and her own memories startled her.

Aaron tilted his head expectantly at Kit. "Is now the time?"

"Aaron? How is it you speak so well?" Olyn asked, wide-eyed.

"I've been listening. Kit once told me it is better to save words than waste them."

"Quite right, boy." Olyn grabbed the boy and embraced him.

"This is not the time for celebrations. We must act swiftly. I will leave after you raise the illusion, Olyn. Aaron, you follow keeping out of sight. Understand?" Kit asked.

"I do," he replied.

Morganna heard the approach of the tunnel and used an illusion spell to hide her presence. Tall and silent she stood, as still as the tree she seemed to be, an oak standing beside the castle wall. No one had noticed the tree hadn't been there the day before. She watched as the boy sneaked over the castle wall and down to the knoll above the cliff. Olyn would not be able to hide from her for long. She'd seen to that, years before. But where was he?

Though neither could see the other, Olyn sensed her presence.

"Beware, Kit, she is about."

The young woman nodded, and the illusion swept over her like a velvet cloak. At once she was gone. Or, so it seemed. Carefully taking the potion Olyn had given her, she approached the tent.

Lancelot was sitting, his head in his hands, on an upturned pail. Kit could smell fear on him. Gone was the proud knight who had defied her. This was a broken man.

Her keen hearing picked up the almost imperceptible sound of Aaron's arrival. He slit the tent wall with his knife and slipped in behind the Queen. She sat, her head thrown back in despair.

"Your Highness?" Aaron whispered.

"Fear not, I will save you. Do as I say."

Giving her head a slight nod, she listened to his instruction. She ran her tongue over her lips. "Lancelot, can you not give me some wine? One would do that for any captive. Please?"

"What?" he said, distracted.

"Wine, please."

He reached to the table behind him and found the wine flask.

"That is a good idea, Highness, I believe I will join you." He poured himself a goblet and took a deep draught. Pouring a second, he extended his hand and offered it to the captive queen. Before it reached her lips, he'd fallen into a deep stupor.

The sound of the Travel Tunnel ceased, and only the metallic clatter of the assembled horsemen remained.

Miroet and Kamelin sat proud and tall in their saddles. Merlin, Leigh, and the king stood before them. They recognized Arthur, dismounted, and knelt before him.

"Sire, what brings you to this land? As yet, we've not found what we seek." Miroet looked to his brother for confirmation.

"Quite right, Sire, we have searched nearly the entire country and have found nothing."

"I know that, just as I know you will continue to search until you find what I seek. We are here on another matter. Do you have any spare mounts?"

Kamelin rose and went to the rear of their party. He took a huge black horse from the string of extra mounts and handed the reins to the king.

"This is Damien. He is strong as the devil and rides with the fury of hell."

"He is most fitting for me," Arthur said.

"The journey I undertake is from the bowels of the most vile."

Leigh looked at the great stallion and blanched.

"Merlin, do I need a mount so large and fierce?"

"Fear not, lad," said the Irish prince, "I have selected a tamer mount for you. He is strong and will do your bidding, but he responds better to handling. Damien requires a strong hand."

"Sire, I am able-bodied, but unfamiliar with riding in battle. Cathaoimore is the only horse I am acquainted with."

The king nodded and handed the reins of a smaller dappled horse over to the lad.

"I understand, Leigh, but this horse will serve you well. Come, mount up. we must hurry."

Merlin raised a restraining hand. "Arthur, she is here and she is dangerous. You must have a plan in place before you go running into a situation I cannot control."

"Your Highness, what is the situation that must be controlled? Are you in danger? We will gladly assist you. What is your bidding?" the princes asked in unison.

"Your father, Alverez, would be most proud of you. I wish you to continue in my service and aid me in recovering the queen and capturing Lancelot."

"As you wish, Sire, but who has the queen and why must your most trusted knight be captured?"

Merlin again spoke. "Good Sirs, your loyalty to the king is beyond question, but the same is no longer true for Lancelot. He has captured Guinevere and plans to rule Ireland with her as his queen."

Both the Irish princes looked down at the wizard in disbelief. "How can this be? Our father is king and though he is old and we do not wish the throne, we have been told the Druids will select our next ruler."

"They have already done so. He is here before you."

"You're Arthur?" Miroet asked incredulously.

Merlin stepped between the king and the knights.

"The Druids have selected this lad and a woman who calls this isle home. The matter of rule is of no import at the moment. We must rescue Guinevere and the woman chosen to rule with Leigh. We do not know exactly where the queen is being held, but fear she is held by pirates."

Though he was weary, a fire stirred in Arthur's breast. A yearning for the woman he loved, Guinevere, his queen. Even though she had betrayed him, he loved her still, and could forgive her youthful indiscretion.

Leigh recognized the fire burning in Arthur's eyes. A similar flame burned in his heart. He would have the woman, Kit, if she was found. Carefully, he mounted the dapple and pulled up on the reins. Nudging the horse with his knees, he rode alongside of Arthur.

Damien reared back and Arthur held his head high.

Leigh looked down the hill to the grassy area above the tent at the edge of the cliff. There he saw Aaron tugging on the arms of Lancelot. The knight was dead weight for the boy. Some force seemed to be holding the man's feet. He pointed.

"There, Highness, isn't that Lancelot being pulled by Aaron?"

"I do not know this Aaron, but someone appears to be pulling him along the ground. Strange, his feet seem to be floating in midair. How can this be, Merlin?"

"My old friend, Olyn, seems to have the matter well in hand. I must congratulate him. Come, we will find him at once," Merlin said, mounting a small donkey.

Bouncing along on the back of the small animal, Merlin was most awkward and uncomfortable. Arthur rode ahead with Leigh following close behind him. The princes fell in line after the boy and Merlin trailed the parade.

Kit heard the approaching horsemen and stopped abruptly, causing Aaron to stumble.

"Wrong?" Aaron asked, knowing she wouldn't stop because the man was heavy. She was strong enough to carry him by herself.

"Men are approaching on horseback. Direct him behind the tree until I can see who they are."

Aaron did has he was bid and leaned the traitor against a tall oak.

Merlin slapped the reluctant donkey with its reins and pulled in front of the line.

"Leigh, is that our lad of little speech?"

"It is, Merlin, but where is the woman? He would not leave her somewhere."

"From what I've learned of young Kit, her comings and goings concern no one but herself. Olyn has, no doubt, given her an illusion spell. It is one of the few he has left."

Arthur nodded. "That would explain the feet seeming to move above the ground with no support. What are we to do, Merlin?"

Though Aaron and Kit hid behind the tree, Merlin discerned their location. He signaled the men to follow him around the back of the oak.

Aaron heard the horses and turned to see them. "Woof, look, the wizard." Kit dropped the illusion and stood in plain view at the side of the tree. She kicked the sleeping Lancelot in disdain. "Well, sorcerer, we captured the fop and rescued the queen without all your magic spells or ancient omens from the Druids. What have you to say now? Kit O'Malley is a match for any man, even a Knight of the Round Table."

Aaron nodded in agreement, his chest puffed with pride for his part in the rescue.

Leigh saw himself in the boy. *We are very alike. Kit was right. He could be my brother.*

He walked to the boy and grasped him about the shoulders. "Well done, Aaron." Inclining his gaze, he looked at the woman as she stood, her green eyes blazing, daring anyone to challenge her.

Guinevere ran up, clutching a robe about her shoulders. "Oh, thank heavens you've come. Dear Arthur, I beg your forgiveness. I've sorely wronged you. Please find it in your heart to love me once again."

Arthur released the breath he'd been holding since he saw her draw near. "Forgiveness may take a while, but I've never stopped loving you."

Guinevere dropped to her knees.

Merlin went to the stricken girl. She was a child once more, leaning again on Arthur's protection.

"Guinevere, you must never trust anyone who plots against Arthur. Arthur is a true and just king. He only seeks what is needed to sustain his kingdom."

Chapter Sixteen

Aaron and Kit crept away as the king and Merlin were consoling the frightened queen. They were unobserved save for Leigh. He was not about to let this woman out of his sight. Several paces back, he followed.

"Aaron, you run on ahead to the workroom. Tell Olyn and Helga I'll be coming soon. I'm going to swim and wash off the stench of that traitor."

The boy nodded and continued to the castle. Kit sat back against the steep bank and slid down into the sea. The sweet, salty taste lingered on her tongue. She paddled about the gentle waves and climbed out onto the bank. Shaking herself, she nearly knocked herself off her four feet.

Though he'd seen her transformation once before, this time it was in broad daylight and he was sure no one else caused the transformation. He'd been hesitant to accept it when it'd happened in the wizard's presence. But this woman was truly Kit. His Kit. There would never be another fox with vermilion fur and liquid green eyes. His body warmed with satisfaction. *If this is my chosen queen, I am well pleased with the selection.*

Free as an animal of the field, Kit ran and poked in the tall grasses for signs of rodents. She was hungry, and a mouse would sate her hunger. Catching a delicious scent, she followed the tantalizing odor. *Just ahead in that dense thicket.* She raced in.

Darkness came, sudden and swift, as four wooden walls closed down around her. She'd been trapped! And no one knew exactly where she was. Aaron would miss her and retrace his steps, but how much time would pass before he would begin his search?

"Skinny, make sure yer got a net around thet box. She's a slippery one. And she's bewitched, thet's fer certain. Don't take any chances."

"Aye, Capt'n, I've got the net good and tight. She ain't gonn' nowhere."

It was one thing to be a wild creature and outwit those who would make you dinner, but it was quite another to be trapped by men. Men took unfair advantage. For her, there was no escape. At least not while they held her in the box. But she'd been in worse situations and come out the winner. She ceased struggling, allowing them to believe she'd gone into shock.

Baldy gently lifted the box lid and peered at her. Though she was in fact not frightened, she trembled.

"Well, I guess we gots ya now, miss Foxy. Thet wizard and his king will pay dearly fer the likes of you. Won't they now, dearie?"

She withdrew and cowered before the rough crew. The same men she'd commanded. Though it was a sham, she hated giving in to these mutineers.

Leigh had seen it all. Kit's obvious joy of being free in her animal form, then the terrible capture, the loud snap of the falling box, which had trapped her in the confining space she dreaded so. Within moments, the men from Lancelot's ship swarmed the box. It became clear these seamen were not taking any chances on her escape. The net was secure around the box. Perhaps, if they let her free of the box, she could chew her way out of the net.

He watched in mounting horror. *I have to do something. I cannot stand by and watch her made a prisoner, held in some rough cage like a dangerous animal.*

Though she was, at the moment, an animal, even these ruffians should be able to see Kit was no ordinary fox. Her fur was a deeper red than any other wild fox. *If only I could signal her and divert their attention, she can free herself.*

Gathering all his courage, Leigh revealed himself and addressed the scurvy crew. "Ahoy there, men. What treasure have you found? You must give it up to the king, you know."

The men raised their heads in surprise.

Baldy stepped in front of the box. "What yer mean, it's the king's? He didn't find it. We did. And what we finds, we keeps."

"Gentlemen, I'm sure that such a rule is in force on the high seas, but this is Arthur's kingdom. These lands owe him homage. You have no right to any treasure found on Arthur's land. I suggest you turn it over to me for transport to Camelot." The men advanced on him.

Leigh let out a soft whistle.

Kit's ears pricked up at the familiar sound. Leigh! She emerged slowly and began to gnaw at the netting. Within moments, she was free. Free to run to the tide cave and become a woman once more.

Leigh saw the blazing streak of red and pressed the sailors further. "You understand if it is found you stole from the High King, you could be keelhauled, and if you survive, be subject to life imprisonment. Though Arthur's dungeons are far less terrible than those of the infidels, I'm sure men of the sea would prefer freedom."

The men advanced once again. Baldy bore down on Leigh with a vengeance. "Look, little man. I ain't turning nothing over to no King Arthur nor any other. Thet fox is mine and I'm keeping it," he said, in time to catch the blaze of Kit's fur disappearing down the knoll to the sea.

"You fools, you was supposed to watch it," he bellowed. "Now we gots nothing. After it. It can't have gotten far. It won't jump into the sea. Critters don't usually like water. It'll be trapped along the shore. Cut it off from above. Now move."

Certain Kit was safe, Leigh took a different route to the tide cave. The men were too busy to notice his departure.

Down into the ground he went, to the upper ledge of the cave. He heard the soft ripple of the water as Kit swam through it. He whistled. She turned her head and smiled. Something deep within Leigh stirred, a longing for something, someone. A feeling he'd never experienced before. He watched her eyes as he removed his armor and stripped down to his chausses.

Pulling Aaron's tackle from the niche, he swung down and dropped into the water. With swift, sure strokes, he quickly swam to her. The seawater clung to her eyelashes framing the liquid emerald with diamonds. Leigh had never seen or even dreamed of a more magnificent woman. Not only was she beautiful, she was smart and clever as well. This woman was worthy of a kingdom. In fact, she was worth every kingdom on earth.

He reached out his hand to her. She took hold of it and treaded water to stay above the surface. His heart pounded so loudly, he was certain she could see it trying to leap from his chest. Though she was naked, she showed no shame. Nor should she. She was the true royal here. And most definitely regal.

She was neither timid nor fearful. With clean sweeps of her strong arms, she swam easily in the pool. Turning her body to swim on her back, she tantalized him with a slow, languid smile. And then she was gone. He heard the rush of a running waterfall. *Oh, God don't let her change before I reach her. I cannot be separated from her again.*

Around the slight bend of the cave wall the waterfall was ahead of him. Kit was nowhere in sight. Then a musical tone as clear as the finest silver bell sounded. She was laughing? Laughing at him?

"Kit, where are you? Why do you hide from me?"

An arm reached through the waterfall. "I hide only to tempt you, Leigh." Relief poured over him as sure as the water when he went through it.

She'd found some twigs and built a small fire to take the chill from the damp air. He moved to the edge of the fire, briskly rubbing his arms.

"Kit, you must be more careful. When I saw you trapped, it tore my heart to shreds. I can't bear you being caged."

"I'm not too fond of it myself. But I escaped."

"Yes, you did. This time, but what will happen if I'm not around to distract your captors?" He sought to scold her, but was so drawn by her nude body and the vermilion hair spilling over her shoulders, his admonition became a plea.

He reached out to her and she moved into him. The feel of her skin next to his was intoxicating. Pushing him gently back, she studied him. Though sex was new to her, she had an animal's natural instinct, unbound by civilized reserve. She reached for his manhood and stroked him; strong, confident strokes. He'd never felt this urgency in his loins. Kit blended into him, her nose nuzzling his throat, the ecstasy so great it was near pain.

Gently, he reached down and lifted her chin to place his lips on hers. Her kiss was the opening of another universe. Soft and pliant, he lips met his with an urgency of their own. He held her face tenderly in his hands, gave her a light kiss on her forehead, swept her off her feet and then searched the ledge for the blanket he knew was here so many years ago. The one he'd left when he first discovered the fall.

"It's over there near the wall."

"You minx, you know of my intent."

"I am a vixen, not a minx, and my intent is the same as yours."

"You would mate with me then?"

"Mate? You are not a seaman and I, at the moment, am not an animal. I would make love with you, Leigh."

"This is a new experience for me. I am not sure how to state my desire," Leigh said shyly. His hands were bold. He ran them over her soft smooth breasts, down over her back to cup her buttocks. Eyes tightly closed, he let the passion wash over him.

She emitted a soft low growl. His eyes flew open wide. Was she turning again? *I can't lose her now. I need her.* His desire grew stronger than a gale wind. No force on earth, at sea, not even in the vast skies, could compare.

Oh, God, she's still a woman, and what a woman.

Carefully, he entered her. His touch was tender with restrained urgency. Kit rose to meet him without hesitation of any sort. She arched her body up to his and urged him, aiding his thrust home, wrapping her legs about his torso and drawing her arms around his muscular back, meeting each stroke eagerly, their bodies perfectly matching spasm for exquisite spasm.

Together, they joined in the dance as old as time, reaching the height of ecstasy simultaneously.

When it was over, his passion spent, Leigh reluctantly broke from her. "Kit, I must be dead, for this is heaven," he said, falling back onto the blanket, peering into the deep green pools of her eyes.

"You're not dead, just complete. We are destined to be one," she said, seemingly contented.

"That's a relief, because I look forward to experiencing this many times over. To you, I make this pledge. No matter the passage of time or distance between us, I will always love you."

"Why? Because the Druids say so?"

"No, this is a love that cannot be compelled. I love you because every fiber of my being, mind, soul, and heart belong to you. My greatest hope is to be yours in the same fashion."

Kit rolled to her side on the rough blanket, the flames of the fire casting gentle shadows on her naked body.

Leigh watched her with the diligence of a sentinel. While he was alive, no harm would come to her. He swore this on his life. This allegiance was stronger, even, than his loyalty to Arthur.

Chapter Seventeen

Morganna could feel the magic in the air. She'd not spent her entire life around sorcery and learning from the masters not to be aware of the presence of a wizard at work. The feeling was stronger than Olyn's dwindling powers. It could only mean one thing. Merlin was in this land. And close by. Again she took up her post outside the crumbling castle wall. A majestic oak, seemingly as trustworthy as the tree she purported to be, she listened, watching the queen's cousin and a young lass approach.

"Leigh, are Merlin and Arthur both at my castle?"

He raised an eyebrow.

"Your castle? Kit, the castle belongs to the king."

"Not so. I will make it the splendid structure it once was and I will rule here. Not some English king."

Leigh shook his head, smiling, and said, "Kit, you are most stubborn. This is something you have no control over. This isle owes allegiance to Arthur. A treaty with my cousin's family pledges this land to the High King of England. That is Arthur."

Impatiently, she stamped her foot. "No, this is my land and no one can turn it over to the English, just because some foolish girl wanted to be a queen."

"I can see there is no way to make you understand the reality of the situation. I'll leave the explanations to Olyn."

"Well," she said guardedly, "Scilti will not forget his loyalty to me."

"Scilti? And who is he?"

"You know him as Olyn, but he served as my first mate aboard my pirate ship."

Leigh stretched to the brink of incredulity. "Pirate ship? And, of course, you were the captain?"

Her nostrils flared. "Yes, I am a captain, and men do my bidding."

Resigned, Leigh took her hand in his and led the way up the grassy knoll to the only standing wall. "We'll talk about it after we meet with Arthur and Merlin."

"Then they are in my castle."

"Who?"

"Arthur and Merlin. As I asked in the first place."

Leigh laughed to himself. How can a woman so perfect be so obtuse? The pair passed so closely by her, Morganna could have touched them.

She fought back a chuckle at her good fortunate. Both Arthur and Merlin within her clutches.

Using the powers of observation she had no compunction utilizing, she drew her mind to the interior of the castle. Only the fat foolish cook was in the kitchen. There was little else standing at ground level. *This means they are below grade. Probably in that dank dungeon Olyn uses as a workroom.*

At the edge of the castle grounds, Kit asked, "What are they going to do with that useless fool of a knight?"

Shaking his head, Leigh answered sadly, "I don't know. I suppose it will be up to Arthur's council at the Round Table. It's hard to believe such a knight as Lancelot could be a traitor."

This turn of events was even more to the liking of Morganna. She could dispose of the worrisome knight and keep the balm herself. All she had to do was find it.

She forced her powers deep beneath the earth. She was certain the queen's cousin and this redheaded lass were heading to Olyn's workroom. Merlin and Arthur were there as well. *How nice to have all my fish in one basket.*

Olyn stood before the senior wizard, unable to understand what was taking place. All events were spinning in the old man's brain.

"Merlin, what are we to do? We are not even sure if Leigh and Kit are safe. Aaron, where did you leave her? Why did she not come with you?"

Aaron faced the king, smiled, and said, "He knows."

"The lad is right, Olyn. I'm sure the two are together and are happy to be as one, as are Guinevere and I. Whatever the forces of battle or sorcery, nothing is stronger than the power of love."

Merlin sighed. Everything seemed to be falling into its proper place according to the tenets of the Ancient Druids. And yet, there was a strange foreboding in the air, something cold, damp, and evil.

"Arthur, I think it best if we return to Camelot. As soon as Leigh arrives, we will set out at once."

Olyn asked, "What of Kit? What is my task in her life? Am I to remain her guardian? She is past needing guidance."

The large door of the workroom opened and Leigh ushered Kit through the opening.

Arthur nodded a greeting. "Thanks be praised, you're safe. And you too, lass. I'm much comforted you are well."

"It is true they are safe, for the moment," Merlin said.

"I fear there is evil nearby and danger will again touch the lives of these two."

Guinevere sat huddled on a bench on the side of the workroom, softly sobbing.

Arthur went to her. "Fear not, my queen. You are safe and we will be back in Camelot, quite soon.

"If only I hadn't been so foolish. I should have honored my vows and not given in to childish infatuation. I've thrown everyone's lives into turmoil."

Merlin crossed the narrow room and placed his hand upon the shoulder of the young queen. "Fear not, child, we all do foolish things in the name of love. And only when we learn true love is not foolish do we share in the full measure." Arthur nodded solemnly.

"Quite so."

Tears streaming down her face, she looked up to her husband.

"Arthur, I beg your forgiveness and will never cause you harm again."

Knowing that would likely not be so, he still gently took her in his arms as he would a young child.

In the open courtyard, Lancelot sat on the same chair Kit and Aaron had placed him in before his escape. Miroet rode his horse around and around the knight, binding him with a stout rope.

"Good sirs," Lancelot protested, "How can you treat me thus? We fought side-by-side. This is most unjust. In the name of your oaths as knights, release me."

"It saddens my brother and me that you have played false with the king. We believed you to be the most noble of Arthur's champions. We cannot forget we rode together, but neither can we forget you broke your oath as a knight and as a member of the Round Table."

Kamelin gazed at the bound knight and spoke with great sorrow.

"Lancelot, it has long been my dream to sit beside you at Arthur's Round Table. You have disgraced yourself and the other champions. It is no longer an honor to be your companion."

Once they were certain the knight was tightly bound and had no means of escape, they mounted their horses and stood with their backs to him.

The brothers were weary and longed to make camp for the night. Aaron came into the courtyard and bid them join the others for the evening meal.

The prince bowed low to the urchin. "We would be most privileged to join you for a meal. It's been months since we sat at table. Lead the way, lad."

Aaron took the horse's reins and pointed to the kitchen.

"There, I will take care of your mounts."

When they entered the kitchen, they found Merlin, Olyn, and Arthur poring over maps of the region.

Arthur raised a hand in greeting. "Miroet, Kamelin, do come join us. Helga has prepared a wonderful supper for us. Your search most likely has sharpened your hunger."

Morganna observed unseen. *So, these are the princes who found the balm. I must have it.* Though she had no proof, she could see no other reason for their presence. They must have it. All were above ground, making it easier to see their plans. Once the princes ate and received their instructions from Arthur, she would cause them to fall into a deep sleep and take their charts and maps. Surely, they noted the location on something.

Helga bustled about the kitchen placing trenchers at the table into which she poured a rich thick stew. Kit had caught a rabbit for her that morning. The old woman looked up and saw Kit and Leigh approaching. She nodded knowingly.

"Did you two have a nice swim now?"

Morganna was certain the princes had the balm in their possession. *I will leave them and prepare for my own journey.* Returning to her grand tent on the knoll, she ordered the pirate captain to make ready to sail.

"Listen, Missy, I don't follow no orders what don't profit me. What'cha gots to say ter thet?" Baldy stepped up, his hands on his hips.

Morganna nodded, drew her eyes narrow, and said in her most seductive tone, "Well, good captain. Gain is not the only motive for action. Loss must too be considered."

Baldy scowled and said, "What yer mean, loss? I ain't about to lose nothing."

Now enraged, Morganna flared her nostrils and drew down on the man she towered over. "You foolish little man. Think you to best me? I can turn you into a toad with a simple snap of my fingers. You will do as I say, else you will not have time to consider any other action. You will be dead. Do you understand?"

A crowd of the crewmen gathered and all were nodding solemnly. Save the skinny man to the rear of the group.

"I told you not to mess with a witch. She'll turn us into swine, every one of us."

Baldy nodded his acquiescence and tried to make it appear it was his plan all the while. He swaggered in front of his men.

"Now, you men, understand we're goin' ter help the lady. Whatever she sez. Now hop to it, men."

Smiling to herself, Morganna thought, *Wise choice, little man.*

"I could be most helpful to those plundering the high seas."

Baldy's eyes bulged with anticipation.

"Thet would be jest fine now, wouldn't it, lads?"

The skinny doubter spoke up once again. "And what does we hafta do fer you?"

Barely able to contain her disgust for these simpletons, she smiled coyly and said, "It's quite simple. All I require is the capture of two men. They will not give you any trouble as I will put them under a spell."

"I told ya, I told ya. Ya gotta watch out, she's a witch. Yer gots to have a care she don't bewitch us too," the skinny loquacious seaman yelled.

'Spell' was far too simple a term to label what she would do to the Irish princes. But spell was all these stupid men understand.

"I assure you, gentlemen, I will not harm you. All I require is the capture of two men in the castle courtyard. They will do as you bid them."

Baldy eyed her skeptically. "And then what's we to do with 'em?"

"Bind them and bring them to me. Then there is the matter of the man bound in the chair in the same courtyard."

"Yer mean that fool, Lancelot?"

Secretly, she found herself pleased this rough seaman had the same opinion of the knight as she.

"Yes. Kill him." She had no use for him any longer.

Merlin approached the future royals, hands extended.

"Come, you two. We have much to do."

"Merlin, do not trouble yourself with the Irish crown at the moment," Arthur interrupted. "We must return Guinevere to Camelot and prepare a full council trial for Lancelot."

"But what of the balm the princes seek?" Leigh asked.

"Balm? What is it? Some kind of healing potion?" Kit asked.

Merlin turned his steel blue gaze at the impudent woman.

"Miss O'Malley, you will learn to hold your tongue in the presence of sorcerers."

Offended, Kit returned a flint hard green stare back at the wizard.

"Oh, Great Wizard of the Third Realm to the High King Arthur, I do most humbly beg your pardon."

Kit's sarcasm was not lost on Aaron or Leigh. Both covered their mouths to stifle giggles.

Even Olyn smiled. Merlin was becoming more and more pompous. Arthur laughed and clapped his old friend on the shoulder.

"Truly, Merlin, you take your obligations too seriously."

Merlin would not be so easily placated. "This is no cause for levity. The trust of the Round Table has been broken. This deed must not go unpunished."

"Nor will it, Merlin," Arthur assured his wisest council. He turned to Aaron. "Lad, I need you to stay here on Clare and protect the future Irish Queen."

Aaron nodded skeptically. "Woof Queen?"

Leigh placed his arm about the shoulders of the boy he was certain was his brother. "Aaron, I trust you to care for Kit until I return and make her my queen."

"Wait a moment. I will have a hand it whatever decision that effects my future," Kit said vehemently.

Leigh found that heart tore at him to remain with the woman he loved, yet he'd pledged service to Arthur.

"Kit, please," he implored.

"I must attend the trial for Lancelot or compromise the Knights of the Round Table."

Her deep green eyes revealed that, in her opinion, he was selecting the wrong path. "Do what you will. I will rule in my own land in my own way. As chieftain. I have the tools to lead. I shall see to the welfare of the people."

Olyn nodded at the headstrong young woman. Kit returned his nod and promptly became still.

"Arthur, we must prepare Lancelot for a return journey to Camelot. We will transport him in the Travel Tunnel," Merlin said firmly.

"I'm certain, Sire, you once said only royals and wizards can use the Travel Tunnel. How are we going to transport Lancelot?"

Arthur smiled, pleased Leigh understood each of the many duties of one who rules. A king, above all, must listen. Merlin, too, was pleased. "Quite so, Leigh. Alone, Lancelot could not travel. However, Excalibur will be bound to his back to serve as a royal transport."

Kit had been edging her way along the wall to be near her trusted Scilti. Lowering her voice to a whisper, she asked, "Can you use this tunnel by yourself, since you are a wizard and, by the king's own statement, I am a royal?"

Olyn narrowed his eyes disapprovingly at his young ward.

"Kit, you cannot think to use this high power for personal gain?"

"Leigh," the king interjected,

"Would you and this young lad be able to carry the traitor from the courtyard?"

Eager to please, Aaron said quickly, "We can," nodding to his brother for conformation.

"Yes, Sire," Leigh affirmed.

"Have a care, fools," Morganna said angrily.

"I don't wish to be heard."

The crew crept slowly to the men guarding Lancelot. He found himself bound tightly in a chair. Not his chair at the Round Table, but a crudely built chair, little more than a stool. The outrage!

He heard the ship's crew approach.

Lifting his head, Lancelot watched Morganna raise her arms and a strange mist settled down upon the princes. It was clear they were aware something had happened to them, yet they were powerless. They could neither move nor speak. Baldy and his men quickly bound Miroet and Kamaelin and threw them across their horses' backs.

Once the princes left, Lancelot looked to Morganna for deliverance. *Surely she will rescue me. She wants the Irish crown as much as I.*

"Morganna, release me."

Her eyes narrowed to ominous slits. "Oh, I will release you, Lancelot. Release you into the next world."

In all his years in service to Arthur, no matter who the foe, nor how strong the defense, Lancelot had never known fear. In a matter of moments, he became well acquainted, and fear was not his friend.

"Please, you cannot mean to harm me. I care deeply for you. You are to be my queen."

"I shall be queen, but I will reign alone. I have no need of you."

He began to rock the chair, fighting against the bonds. A strong firm hand reached up and held him fast.

Aaron swiftly cut the bonds and said softly, "Position your hands as if they are still tied. She shall not kill you."

Lancelot stilled his struggling and fought against himself to spring his hands out to freedom.

Morganna appeared to be warming to the task of eliminating him. "Well, knight, we will dispose of you and continue our search with the two princes. I am certain they will reveal the whereabouts of the *Sine Vitium.*"

"*Sine Vitium*, is that what you seek? And how will my demise aid you in that search?"

"It will not, but ridding the kingdom of one so foolish as you will give me great pleasure." She smiled almost coyly. Sweeping her wide skirts over the dirt in the desolate courtyard, she turned her back on the unfortunate champion. "Now I will show Arthur how this land is to be ruled."

The princes were secure in the hold of the boat and Baldy returned to the courtyard. "Beggin' yer pardon, sorceress, what am I ter do? Does ya stil want me ter kill 'em?"

Without the slightest hesitation, she closed her eyes and nodded. Baldy approached the chair.

Aaron whispered, "Now," and Lancelot leapt to his feet and swiftly grabbed the sailor's knife.

"I guess the deed with not be done this eve," Lancelot said, holding the man about the throat.

"I didn't mean no harm, Sir, I was jes doin' what I was ordered to do. Don't kill me. I spy on her fer ya. Then you can gets that medicine she so sure of getting. Please."

Aaron shook his head. Strange how loyalties shifted in moments. He knew Kit would not change alliances with the will of the wind.

Lancelot began to swagger and menace the captain. "I guess you thought you had the better of me, eh? Well, Sir Lancelot is not about to be bested by the likes of you."

Aaron quickly secured the sailor and tied him loosely to a tree. Baldy offered no resistance.

"So, lad? You've saved me again. I thank you. You shall be rewarded when I return to Camelot," Lancelot said.

Again, Aaron shook his head. This man did not realize the peril he had placed himself in by kidnapping the Queen. Aaron took the knight's hands and quickly bound them in front of him.

"What's the meaning of this? You save me just to capture me? Who are you and by whose orders do you bind me?"

"I saved you to stand trial. I am Aaron, Leigh's brother."

"Leigh has no authority to put me on trial, nor have you. I demand to be released."

"No." Leigh approached the knight he'd once served.

"Lancelot, I am ashamed I squired with you. You have fallen lower than the rats in the hold of a ship. You have lost everything you once held dear. Arthur will return you to Camelot to stand trial before all the Knights of the Round Table."

Faced with disgrace and possible imprisonment, Lancelot began to softly weep.

Merlin and the King drew closer. Arthur, too, wept to see his most favored champion little more than a thief. His trusted companion, his confidant, stripped of all, even his dignity, wounded Arthur deeply.

Merlin appeared much less affected, knowing this, too, was the Ordination's path. "Arthur, we must return to Camelot at once. He should be tried before the sun rises on another day."

Arthur wiped his eyes with the back of his hand. Placing his hand on Lancelot's shoulder, he said, "It saddens me more than you can imagine, Lancelot. My trusted champion and my queen. Guinevere is young, but youth is not an excuse for you. You will be tried by the full council as soon as the knights are gathered."

Arthur slid Excalibur from the sheath at his side and handed the sword to Merlin. "Let us make haste. Bind the sword to him."

Aaron looked wide-eyed at the wizard as the sword suspended above and behind Lancelot. Slowly, it lowered and a golden cord wrapped the blade close to the body of the fallen knight.

Leigh approached the king.

"Sire, what are your directions for my brother and Kit?"

Aaron stood, ready to do whatever the king ordered.

Kit, angered Leigh would suggest the king had any right to give her instruction, said, "Leigh, no one gives me commands. This is my land and I will give whatever orders are necessary to accomplish whatever tasks need doing."

Aaron and Olyn stood quietly, their faces neither frightened nor angered. Olyn knew it was fruitless to argue with the king. Aaron moved to Kit's side and placed a gentle hand on her arm.

"Woof?" he begged, knowing she would deny him nothing. And he was right. She would do whatever this strange, and for the most part silent, boy asked of her.

Chapter Eighteen

Though it took many years and a great deal of labor, Kit finally secured the throne, through clever alliances. The castle itself seemed to draw the people of the countryside to its restoration. They were once again assisted by the rightful installation of 'The O'Malley'. She sat in the center of the Great Hall she'd restored. The walls, clean and repaired, gave not a hint of the former ruin. Tapestries depicting great hunts lined the hall. The furnishings were heavy, cut and hewn of the finest wood on the island. Trades of every sort offered their services to the one who would restore their homeland to its greatest glory. She had fulfilled her promise.

"You do not bow and cower before me. I am a leader, not a goddess. What is your petition?" Kit asked firmly, but not unkindly.

"Madam," the farmer said, "I cannot pay the tax levied against me."

"And what reason do you give not to honor your duty? The tax on this isle is meager, only what is required to run the isle as a profitable and comfortable land for us all."

"I know, Madam, and though I wish to pay, my livestock have sickened and many are dead."

"Do you know the cause for these deaths?"

"I fear the well near my farm has been tainted."

"Tainted? By whom? What gain could one hope to attain from poisoning a well?"

"I do not know, but I fear it is the work of a witch."

Kit, somewhat discomforted by the response, carefully considered what could be done if in fact the tainting had been done by a witch.

"Very well, for the moment you owe no tax, but you must assist in the discovery of the culprit who poisoned the well. This could affect many of you," she said, addressing all those who assembled in the Great Hall.

Olyn, sitting to the right of Kit, reached out and touched her hand.

Gazing down on the old man's hand, she felt a tender pang for the man she loved. But this must come before any matters of the heart. Who would be so foul to poison a well? What possible gain would dead animals provide? The villager was right. No person would do such a thing. It had to be the work of a witch.

Why did I waste my time on these fools? Morganna wondered. No spell, no torture, not even an outright bribe would loosen the lips of the two Irish princes. These remained steadfast and loyal, not easily swayed by any of her magic, potions, or seductions.

Miroet, the younger, would not even speak. His older brother spoke only to advise Morganna of their pledge to Arthur. She spent most of her powers trying to extract information about the *Sine Vitium*.

Baldy approached the sorceress tentatively, barely daring to address her. "Cuse me, Yer Magicness, couldn't we jes let them go?"

"Let them go? Are you daft? What would that gain?"

"Beggin' yer pardon, but if we lets them free, they'll go find yer medicine. Alls we hafta do is follow 'em."

Her amber eyes glowed with hell fire. *By the fates, the fool has actually gotten a good idea.* She'd exhausted every other method and time was not her friend.

"Very good, Captain, that is a wise decision. Free them but don't follow them too closely. We must keep them in sight, but not alert them to our presence." Going to the edge of the cliff where the princes were tied, she made a show of compassion. "It is apparent you will not reveal anything that would endanger Arthur and that is admirable. I wish I had such fine knights in my employ. Therefore, I set you free to return to your family. You have nothing further to fear from me. I, too, value loyalty, and yours is above reproach. God speed, good knights."

Miroet and Kamelin eyed each other in total disbelief. Quickly, they mounted their horses and sped from her.

Morganna found her strength waning daily. She had to find the balm. Now she needed it not only to protect the army she would raise, but to restore her own powers. Using her power of observation, she'd depleted most of her reserves. But she had to know where that damned Kit and that simple boy were. She had to also find the old wizard. Somehow, he was getting stronger as she grew weaker. *I should have listened more closely when Merlin was willing to teach me.* Now the senior wizard stood staunchly against her. She could feel his power waged against her own.

Gathering all at her disposal, she focused all her remaining power on observing Kit in her great hall.

Aaron announced the arrival of the Irish princes.

"Woof, Miroet, and Kamelin are in the courtyard. Shall I show them in?"

"Of course, and don't call me Woof. You can say my name."

"Yes, but I like Woof."

Exasperated, Kit shook her head at the only person on earth she fully tolerated. Arranging the folds of her robe about her, she spotted the princes approaching. "Good day, gentlemen. How are the king and Leigh? Have you seen them recently?"

"No, Madam, when you left the courtyard we were taken prisoner and have been held for six long months."

"Who could capture the finest of Ireland's knights? Tales of your valor abound the countryside."

Miroet blushed and shuffled his toe in the rushes on the floor of the Great Hall. "Thank you for your kind words. It's true mere men could not have captured us, but we were not taken by men. A witch cast a spell on us. We were unable to move as she continually questioned us. Once in her domain, she lifted the speaking part and questioned us endlessly about our mission for King Arthur."

Kit leaned forward in the tall chair on the dais in the center of the large room. "I am certain you revealed nothing. No one, not even a witch, can turn an Irish knight from his duty. I am proud of you. As your father would have been proud."

"Would have been? Why do you say it thus?"

Kit nodded solemnly. "I am sorry. I received word only this morning your father passed away."

"Our father was hale and hearty when we left to seek the *Sine Vitium.*

Mother passed, many years earlier and we have no other living relatives."

Miroet advanced to the edge of the dais and took the hem of Kit's robe in his hand. "Then it has come to pass the ordination of the Druids is to be fulfilled. Please, Madam, have we your leave to bury our father?"

"Good knights, you owe no allegiance to me. Do make haste to see to your father's funeral. Olyn has sent word to Arthur of your father's death. I feel certain he will wish to attend any service you have in mind."

Kamelin said, "While it is true we have not sworn allegiance to you, once the Ordination is in place, you will be our queen."

"Thank you for your kind words, particularly in your time of sorrow, but I am not truly a royal. I'm simply a sailor who is enjoying the fruits of her labors."

Aaron stepped out from behind a stout post near the entrance of the Great Hall. Purposefully, he stepped to the center of the room. "No, Kit, I believe you have no choice but to honor the Ordination. You will be powerless to do otherwise."

"Aaron, mind your tongue and see these knights are provided with supplies for their journey. Their home is several days ride from here."

Aaron smiled and left to provide the supplies the weary travelers would need. He passed Olyn on his way to the kitchen. "Olyn, the Irish princes arrived and have just learned of their father's death."

Olyn had relayed the information regarding their father's passing to Merlin, but was unaware Alverez's sons did not know.

"Aaron, do they plan to set out at once? Or will they remain to freshen themselves and dine with us?"

"I think they are anxious to leave. Their father has been dead several days and it is not wise to have a body unburied so long."

"That is true. Perhaps I should ask Merlin to transport them in the tunnel. They are royals, even if they do not follow in their father's footsteps."

As Aaron continued to the kitchen, Olyn walked into the Great Hall and saw Kit conversing with the knights. She no longer took her place on the raised dais. Stepping down, she spoke with the princes on the same level. She had no pretensions of royalty or grandeur. This was her home and she was doing what she could to make the princes welcome, even in such a trying time for them.

"Kit, you are most gracious and we thank you for your consideration."

Olyn put his arms about the young men. "Lads, I'm sorry about your father. He was a fine man."

Kamelin looked at the old wizard and a single tear fell upon his cheek. "My father spoke of you often. He felt you were unjustly punished by the witch, thus I am gratified you are to be part of the lives of the new royals." Olyn felt his eyes grow wide. "How do you know such a thing to be true? I've not been told."

Miroet placed a restraining hand on his brother. "Kamelin, what little we know of the Druids Ordination is not to be expounded upon. My brother is only assuming you would be part of the royal household, since you are so close to Kit and Leigh."

Still incredulous, Olyn asked, "How is it you know of the Druid's Ordination?"

Miroet said, "When my brother and I became of age, our father asked if we wished his kingdom or to serve Arthur. Since we are close friends, as well as brothers, we chose service to Arthur rather than one of us rule the other."

Kamelin continued his brother's tale. "He then told us of the little he knew about the Ordination. We do not know the whole of it, but know the royals are not from current royal families and I must admit we surmise your young lady here to be a future queen."

"Most astute, Kamelin. She is in fact one of the royals, but she is most stubborn about the issue."

"Scilti," Kit scolded, "I am not stubborn."

Aaron reentered the room. "Maybe not stubborn, but most certainly steadfast," he commented jovially.

"Aaron, since you learned to speak, you say too much," she said, her green eyes flashing. There was no way she could contradict the boy she thought of as part of her family.

The princes spoke in unison. "We will take our leave and return to Camelot after our father is laid to rest."

Olyn raised his arms and shook his hands. "No, no, I will transport you with Merlin's help. You have been through much and a long ride is not what you need."

The knights looked at each other and nodded agreement. They followed the old wizard as he descended to his workroom in the dungeon, each assisting the old man along the way. Though he had spent many hours in the workroom since Kit had restored the castle, his area did not show any signs of improvement. The cobwebs festooned the walls and bugs scuttled along the wet ground. Today, the dampness hung in the air with a somber mist as if the walls were crying for the dead king.

"Yer Witchness, me men followed them princes and they went back to thet castle where we took 'em," Baldy informed Morganna, from a safe distance.

The dimwit obviously knew enough to realize he sorely tried her patience.

The skinny sailor, remaining at an even greater distance, spoke timidly. "I overherred 'em said their pap was dead. Must a come fer a funeral."

Damn their eyes, she thought. Trying to sound social and receptive of the information, Morganna lowered her lashes and moved nearer to the captain. "I suppose that must be the case. However, I appreciate your efforts."

As if not convinced she was truly benign, Baldy stepped back. "What does yer want now?"

What do I want? I want to be rid of these fools. Majestically, she lifted her long dress and swept into her tent, effectively dismissing them.

She tapped a slender finger against her chin. *If the princes are attending their father's funeral, surely Arthur will attend. Nothing is going to stop me now.* The Irish princes would surely hand over the balm to Arthur at the funeral. She had to attend that service, but she must be unnoticed. No tree disguise this time. Trees did not grow in great halls.

Using her powers of observation, she spied on Olyn deep in the dungeon workroom. These days she had to restrict her observations to short periods. She needed to rest between her sessions of observation. The activity was proving very taxing. Her strength was waning. She needed that balm.

Olyn opened the Master Tome in the center of his worktable. The once pristine pages were covered with dust formed during his stint as Scilti at sea with Kit. Not that he had bothered to clean even after they returned to the castle. The transformation of the castle above was nothing short of miraculous, but similar marvels did not reach to his workroom.

Grabbing a rag, Olyn swatted dust from the book and began in earnest to contact Merlin. This calling upon the Greatest Sorcerer of all time was not taken lightly, and it was not the full moon when Merlin requested he was to be called upon. Truly, he had incurred his wrath when he informed Merlin of the death of the Irish King. Yet, contact him he must. Merlin was focused on the matter of the trial and would not be aware of the arrival of the Irish King's sons.

He opened the book, raised his arms, and closed his eyes, hoping against hope Merlin would not shut him out as a nuisance. At once, the familiar spirals rose and hung suspended over the book.

The deep resonant voice boomed from the walls. "Olyn, why do you call upon me thus? I am aware of the death and the impending fulfillment of the Druid's Ordination. I will handle all these matters in due time."

"I know, Great Wizard, but his sons have arrived here on Clare and need a quick conveyance to their home that they might bury their father. He has been dead several days and must be interred as befits a king."

The image of Merlin appeared among the spirals. The great wizard closed his eyes and stroked his long white beard as was his habit when contemplating. "Quite so, Olyn. What do you propose?"

Flattered the Great Wizard would ask his opinion on a matter of such great import, Olyn hesitated, then cleared his throat and spoke in hushed respectful tones. "Sire, they are royals, even if they do not wish to rule. Could they not be transported in the Travel Tunnel? 'Twould save time and allow them to quickly return to Camelot for the trial."

"Olyn, I am well pleased with you. You are right, the king must be buried with the proper respect. Arthur, Leigh, and I will come at once to Clare. You and Kit will join us to attend the service for Alverez."

Chapter Nineteen

"Merlin, Merlin, please answer me," Arthur asked gravely.

"Are you all right?" Merlin blinked his eyes.

"I'm fine, Arthur. You need not trouble yourself."

Not convinced his old friend was well, Arthur pressed him further.

"You look as if you're not really here with me. What is happening to you?"

"In truth, Arthur, I was not with you. I was conferring with Olyn regarding Alverez's funeral."

"Have you word of his sons? Their father's death seems rather sudden. When we spoke last spring he seemed in excellent health."

Merlin nodded. "The king's death, though unexpected by men, is a part of the Druid's Ordination."

"Yes, yes, I understand. Where do the princes wish to hold the service?" the king asked.

"Olyn informed me they are planning to return to their home and bury their father as soon as possible. He asked to use the Travel Tunnel."

"Is that wise, Merlin? True, they are royals, but it seems we have used the Tunnel a great deal of late. Is there not a danger in its overuse?"

Merlin considered Arthur's question. "You are wise to be cautious, but Olyn pointed out that the King should be interred in a manner that befits a king. The poor man has been dead for many days. He must be buried as soon as possible."

Arthur nodded. "Yes, quite so. I will prepare for the journey. I trust young Leigh will accompany us, since Alverez was King of his land."

"Yes, Leigh should attend. Do you think Guinevere will desire to attend also?"

Merlin closed his eyes, drew a deep breath, then spoke. "Your Highness, in most cases I would say the queen of one land should attend the funeral of a king of another land. However, in view of recent events I deem it wise she remain here at Camelot."

Arthur did not wish his relief to show, but he felt deeply relieved. He didn't want to expose his queen to any further discomfort. She had suffered enough.

"I agree. Lancelot will not be able to trouble her during our absence. I have posted Gawain at his cell door."

"Very well, Your Highness. Please inform Leigh of our journey. I'm certain he will welcome the prospect of seeing his lady love."

Arthur laughed, his blue eyes twinkling. "Lady love, is it, Merlin? I think this attraction is more than a passing fancy. This is a love ordained."

Merlin nodded solemnly. What the King had stated was quite so. Theirs was a love so deep and abiding, nothing and no one could tear it asunder.

First it was a whisper, a roar, then the fury of ten thousand horses. Morganna listened carefully to determine the course the Travel Tunnel was taking. It had to be Merlin returning to the castle. What should have been her castle for these horrible months. The castle that bitch restored. Morganna clenched her fists tightly and, trembling, she drew her own blood.

The castle above the knoll was a magnificent structure. And it could have been hers, if only she didn't have to deal with such incompetents. Angrily, she paced. *Why am I forced to suffer the presence of fools?* Lancelot's men obeyed her only slightly better than they followed the knight's orders, and that only because they were frightened. She wanted undying devotion and true admiration. Here in this forsaken place on a windswept knoll above the sea, she was nothing. Her powers all but gone, daily she plotted how to regain them.

The deafening roar of the Travel Tunnel was now directly overhead. If it only dipped slightly, she could reach the tail. As it swooped low over the knoll, she deftly caught the end. Up it swept her and then settled low on the grass just outside the courtyard. She ducked beneath the newly cultivated shrubs. There was no time for an illusion.

The swirling of the Tunnel ceased and from its core stepped Merlin, Leigh, and her half-brother, Arthur. All were dressed in their finest clothes and all in somber hues. At least that wimp Guinevere wasn't with them. Morganna watched as the three men entered the courtyard and were greeted warmly by Olyn.

"It's good to see you all. I only wish it were under happier circumstances."

Alverez was a good king, probably the best among the many warring factions that cluttered Ireland. Arthur could have dealt better with Alverez than any of the other chieftains, who had no rules or order of any kind. Arthur extended his hand to Olyn.

"Yes, old friend, it is good to see you as well, and I, too, wish it were for a more joyous occasion."

"Olyn," Merlin began, "Are you ready to make the journey to the Princes' home?"

Olyn nodded solemnly. "Yes, Helga has made provisions, since there will be little staff at the princes' home. The princes are ready to leave at once."

Merlin drew his brows together. "And what of Kit? As a future queen, it is her duty to attend as well."

Olyn shook his head. "I know, Great Wizard, and I clearly pointed that fact to her, but she will not leave her castle and denies that she is to be queen of any land. She says her land is Ireland and Clare is her home. She will serve the island and someday extend her influences to the mainland. In her mind, a free country should rule itself. The only form of government she believes in is one that serves the people honestly. Thus far, she's seen little evidence of that."

Merlin drew in a deep breath. "I understand her feelings. But, for the moment, her feelings must be set aside. The very reason she has been chosen is to eliminate the chaos throughout her country. She cannot defy her duty."

All the while, Leigh stood silent beside the King. His heart felt like it breaking within his chest. Kit would not change her mind. Nothing he said would convince her. People died everyday. Just because the man was a king and his funeral would be an affair of state did not convince her to accompany him.

As stubborn as she was, dee couldn't help but feel his breaking heart swell with pride for her accomplishments. She had taken a crude pile of stones and created a castle that very nearly rivaled

Camelot. Not only had she restored the castle, she'd invigorated the local economy.

Despite the nearly overwhelming desire to smite them all, Morganna knew she had to focus on the fact Arthur was present and must have the balm with him. The funeral had had even less impact on her than Kit. Kit could understand sorrow. Morganna felt it only as an impediment to her goal.

Carefully, she listened to the group of mourners. Try as he would, Olyn had been unable to convince Kit to accompany the party of grief-stricken knights and sorcerers.

This was her chance! *I'll capture that fool woman and make Arthur ransom her with the balm.*

As though reading her mind, Merlin said, "Olyn, I know you wish to attend this funeral service for King Alverez, but I feel danger in the air. I want you to stay with our reluctant queen. Until the coronation, there is a risk to the Proclamation of the Druids. And, dear old friend, it is our duty above all to honor that Proclamation. We do not have another option," Merlin said with sadness in his heart.

Olyn nodded and walked to the princes' mounts. Taking Miroet's hand in his own, he said, "Young man, I am sure your father was deeply proud of you and rightfully so. You and your brother are fine, admirable knights. I deeply regret I am unable to come to the service. Your father and I understood the burdens of rule, and I am certain he would know I mean him no disrespect by remaining here to protect the future queen."

Kamelin nodded. "Good sorcerer, our father spoke of you highly and he would understand duty must come first."

Morganna overheard this conversation with glee. Even with her dwindling powers, she could best this fool wizard. She rubbed her hands together. *I took most of his powers years ago. Now I will strip him of the remainder.*

Kit watched Leigh and his companions step into the Travel Tunnel with a heavy heart. He should have stayed there with her. *We belong together. Why must he let his so-called duty to the king come before us?*

From her hiding place beneath the lush shrubs in the restored courtyard, Morganna watched Kit shake her head and disappear from the window.

This is the time, Morganna thought. *If I am able to trap her as a woman, ransom will be easy to extract from my dear brother.* He'd be as soft with her as he is with his own queen. Kit had remained, unwisely to her thinking, at the castle she coveted.

Olyn looked wistfully at the departing Travel Tunnel. He turned and reentered the castle, just as he saw his ward leave the tower window. He silently wished his friend Alverez God speed and slowly shuffled to the kitchen. Helga was kneading bread at the table in the center of the room. "I thought you were going to the funeral with the others. Why do you remain?"

"Merlin felt Kit might be in some danger and requested I look after her."

Helga laughed, the flour flying about her. "Look after Kit? I think the good King misjudges our lass."

Olyn smiled. He, too, felt Kit could more than take care of herself. She welcomed danger, if only for the joy of defeating it. "You could very well be correct, but I fear Merlin warns of a danger a sorcerer must handle."

The old woman wiped a fallen lock of hair from her floured face and again bent to the task of pounding the dough into a loaf.

"Does Kit know you are to watch her as if she is a helpless child?"

"No," Olyn replied, "And I don't think it's wise to inform her."

"You need not worry. I would be the last to tell her she is being watched like a babe." Helga suddenly became silent as Kit entered the kitchen and slid her graceful body onto the bench at the far side of the table. Olyn noticed that her smile seemed forced. Fidgeting, she appeared to find great difficult remaining still.

"What babe needs watching?" she asked, reaching across the table and pulling a small piece of dough from the loaf. She turned it over and over in her hands, then began to tear it into even smaller segments.

Helga threw a quick look at Olyn. He slid onto the bench beside Kit. "All babes need watching. Wouldn't you agree?"

"Why did you not go with the others? I recall you said you and Alverez were old friends."

"Yes, we were friends, but my duty is to you, Kit. Merlin requested I remain here with you."

"Why? I am not a motherless child who needs constant care. I have handled myself for many years. True, I would miss your guidance, but I am sure I could survive for a few weeks without you."

Helga laughed again, throwing billows of flour clouds. She coughed as she inhaled the particles. "I just informed our friend, the sorcerer, you could take care of yourself. He seemed certain it was his duty to look out for you."

Olyn drew in a long breath, waiting for the tirade he expected from his ward. None was forthcoming. Puzzled, he cocked his head, pointed his index finger at her, and tried to speak. The words would not come. He lowered his finger and shook his head.

Kit looked at him, her deep green eyes questioning.

"You seem to be expecting something. What is it?"

"I'm not sure. You are different somehow. More mature, less volatile."

"Perhaps. I have a home and the responsibilities of my people. I suppose it is somewhat sobering."

"Kit, you behave in every aspect like a queen. Yet you refuse to accept the tenets of the Druid's Ordination. Can you tell me your reasoning?"

"I do not like being told what to do. What is expected of me. The future is mine to determine. No one or nothing decides my path. My destiny is within my control."

Olyn shook his head. There seemed to be no reasoning with her. He tried another tactic. "I see, yet your selected destiny and the Ordination of the Druids seems on the same path."

"Perhaps," she said, "perhaps," then left him to wonder what had changed her. Damn her. Did she have to be so beautiful and so smart? *How will I ever be able to trick her?*

Enviously, Morganna watched Kit comb her long, thick red tresses, the sun lighting on the copper mane. Kit's neck arched as she pulled the silver comb through her hair.

Every inch a queen, no matter how she denied it. The girl stood, dropped her clothing, kicked it to a corner. Putting on a page's tunic, she quickly exited her tower room. As she entered the courtyard, she looked around to see if anyone had discovered her. Not a soul seemed to be present.

Save her, of course. Morganna knew how to hide her presence carefully, her heart pulling at her to find some means to acquire the *Sine Vitium*. Morganna drew as close as she dared to Kit. *I mustn't let her escape again. I will cut her off from her foolish wizard.* Not that Morganna thought Olyn was a threat. He was a nuisance, a bothersome person she didn't wish to deal with.

Kit looked about the courtyard one final time, then sprinted for the grassy knoll. She loved the feeling of the wind in her hair, just to feel it whistling past the fur on her muzzle. Down the sheer face of the cliff, she ventured. At the water's edge she stopped to see her reflection. Her hair was long and bright. Perhaps she shouldn't have covered it all these years. Then maybe she would have been content to be some man's lovely wife.

Shaking her head, knowing she would not have been content to be at anyone's bid and call, she dove into the cold seawater. Careful not to swim far from shore, she climbed up the cliff and began to run on all fours in the open fields. She wasn't hungry for food, only for freedom to have her own land, as free as the animals of the field. Not to have warring tribes try to establish rule solely for personal gain. Her land deserved to be free. Free from foreign rule and free to make its mark on the pages of history. If only, she wished, her land could be free and wealthy and could serve the peoples too long plagued by countless wars. She ran as fast and as long as her strength allowed. Returning to the courtyard, she leapt into the wide fountain in the center. Emerging from the water, she was soaked but happy.

Morganna remained close by her side throughout her romp. Now she had the means to capture Kit and separate her dear brother from the balm. *I'm sure he will pay any price to get back the one his precious Leigh treasures.*

For three days, Morganna watched and waited. Each day the routine was the same. Kit would comb her hair, strip off her fine gown, and put on a simple tunic. Then run to the water to become a fox.

Since water was the key, now all she had to do was figure how to keep her in a state of foxhood, and extract the ransom from Arthur.

Chapter Twenty

Kit sank into the chair beside the tower window and began to brush her hair. Time seemed to be standing still. It had been weeks since Leigh and the others had left for the funeral. Kit knew the warm weather would force them to hold the services quickly, but she did not know how long it would take to settle the king's affairs. Daily, she hoped to hear the Travel Tunnel sweep over the land. *Stop it, you fool. You never mooned over anyone, and you are not going to start now, when your goal is very nearly in sight.*

A gentle knock sounded at the door. A young maid stuck her head into the room.

"Madam, do you wish refreshment with your bath?"

Momentarily, Kit stopped her brushing and nodded to the girl to place the drink on the table. The girl did so and quickly exited.

Kit reached for the drink and sipped deeply. With a strange sense of lethargy, she set the goblet back on the table. The room seemed to move in slow, continuous circles. Dizzy, she fell to the floor with a soft cry.

Outside Kit's bedroom door, Morganna listened carefully, hoping against hope the fall would be unheard by anyone other than herself. Hearing the soft thud as Kit's body hit the floor, Morganna let herself into the tower room.

Struggling, she pulled the sleeping Kit to a tub filled with water. The tepid water did not arouse her. Morganna gleefully pushed her beneath the surface. Remaining asleep, Kit changed form. She lifted the sodden fox from the tub and placed her in the small cage she'd brought with her. The cage, made entirely of metal with only a tiny opening in the hinged lid, was just large enough to hold the slumbering animal. She propped the fox so its head was against the side and poured water into the opening. *I'm not sure how the water works, so I won't cover its head again. It won't pay to drown the damned thing.*

Carefully, she set the box in the center of the wash stand then listened for a sign the fox was awakening.

Kit sneezed. Groggily, she woke. She was inside a cage, and her head hurt and her stomach roiled. She could not move. *God, how I hate being enclosed. I'm trapped for sure this time. Leigh warned me.*

Realizing it would not be productive to dwell on what had happened, she tried to move her shoulder, hoping for a more comfortable position. The corner of the cage scraped against her fur. Fur? It had to be the witch. Her crew wasn't that smart. Morganna changed her. How? And how could she possibly escape? She certainly couldn't reason with her. She'd have to use tricks to escape.

After taking a deep breath, Kit began to bark and howl. On and on, Kit howled, hour after hour. Howling until she could endure the sound herself no longer. Suddenly, she stopped and gave a loud gasping breath.

"Don't you dare die on me. You . . . you cur." Kit maintained her silence. Endless minutes passed and Kit heard the chair scrape across the wooden floor. The witch lifted the lid of the cage. Taking advantage of the slim opportunity Kit forced her muzzle through the tiny opening and bit down on Morganna's finger. Howling in pain, Morganna withdrew her finger and Kit leapt to freedom. Enraged, the sorceress grabbed her cloak and quickly threw it over Kit and held her tightly within its folds.

Aaron had followed the maid to Kit's quarters. He entered stealthy behind her. Watching, he saw her become the evil sorceress Olyn had warned him about. His eyes grew wide as his beloved Kit was pushed in the water while she slept. His brother had given him charge of caring for her in his absence.

Aaron, like his brother, placed high value on duty and pledges. He had to rescue Kit, but he would need help. Carefully opening the door, he peered into the passageway. Empty. Placing his feet in particular locations, so not a squeak would alert anyone to his presence, he descended the worn stair. Using his own private entrance to Olyn's workroom, he tapped on the door. Olyn's voice bid him enter.

"Come in, lad," Olyn said, a puzzled expression on his face.

"You look distraught. What is wrong, Aaron?"

Still one of little speech, Aaron replied, "She's taken her."

"Taken her? Taken who? And who has taken her?"

"Kit, the evil woman has taken her." The boy offered the explanation without any show of emotion.

"By the evil woman, you mean Morganna, the witch?"

"Yes."

"How?" Olyn asked.

"I need to know if Morganna has used witchcraft or took her by simple trickery."

Aaron's chest heaved. He drew in a deep breath and began to relate exactly what had taken place in the tower.

Olyn closed his eyes and shook his head. "We have to rescue Kit. By the fates, Morganna has subjected Kit to the one thing she dreads. Confined spaces."

Aaron nodded. "I know." A deep chill came over Olyn. The cold held its own foreboding.

"What can we do? We must save her. Leigh will be angry I did not keep her safe as I promised."

"Don't fault yourself, Aaron. The witch has powers Leigh did not foresee. I cannot trouble Merlin this time. I must do it alone."

"Alone? I will help." Olyn gave the boy a pleased smile.

"Of course, lad, I merely meant I will be the only sorcerer. You will assist me."

"How? What am I to do?"

Deep in thought, Olyn lowered himself onto the bench alongside his worktable. Rising, he opened the Master Tome. This time he was not seeking the mantle, but instead turned to a page that seemed untouched by time. There was no yellowing of the pages. The ink was crisp and clear.

Running his plump finger down the page, he stopped at a paragraph that almost seemed to leap from the page. 'A Power Duel' .

Aaron could not yet read words, but he clearly read his intent.

"Can you best her?" the lad asked. There was no response.

Aaron asked again, "Well, can you?"

"Lad. It is not a matter of can, but one of must. It will take some time, and I will need your help, but we will do it. We must do it." Aaron sat on the bench and waited.

"Boy, go up and see if you can find the witch. I must know her exact location."

Aaron hurried to do the wizard's bidding. Taking his own special route, he was quickly at the surface and into the courtyard. His keen eyes scanned the horizon. There she was, carrying her cloak in her arms. The material seemed to have a life of its own, wriggling as if something was alive within its folds.

Not wishing to waste a moment, he hurried down the stair route the wizard used, in case he might meet him on the way. Nearly to the door, he saw Olyn working his way up the passage.

"Have you found her, boy?"

"Yes, she's on the knoll struggling with her cloak."

"Struggling with her cloak? Why would she do such a thing?"

"I believe Kit is within the cloak and has escaped the cage. The witch must have recaptured her by throwing it over her."

Aaron put his sturdy arm around him and together they entered the courtyard. Olyn peered into the distance and spotted Morganna, still visible in the morning mist.

Olyn brushed his hands over his robe, cupped them over his mouth, and yelled. Though the distance was great, he was certain he would be heard. "Stop, you hag. Release the fox."

Morganna spun around so quickly, she nearly fell over her own feet. Eyes blazing, she clutched the cloak tighter. "You foolish little man, how dare you call me hag?"

Baiting her further, Olyn slowly walked toward her. "Morganna, you must face it, the years are beginning to show. Your beauty fades and your step is much slower. The power you once held is dwindling. You can no longer call yourself sorceress. You have not the skills."

"I have skill enough to rob you of yours."

Olyn smiled wickedly, and moved closer to the furious woman. "Perhaps we should test your skills?"

"Think you to best me?" she asked angrily, throwing the cloak aside.

"You will never be half the sorcerer I am. I stole most of your powers once, and now I will have the remainder." Rapidly, she approached the wizard, meeting him toe-to-toe, and glaring fire into his eyes.

"Think twice, woman, are you willing to risk all for your vanity? Your comely looks will not save you this time. I am not some foolish knight easily swayed by your beauty. Though, in truth, most of your beauty flees in the face of your rage." Olyn smiled confidently, knowing the taunting was increasing her ire.

"My powers always exceeded yours, and those have dwindled further with time," she yelled.

Olyn nodded solemnly. She was very nearly correct, yet he still had that power of illusion. Her power was at its very lowest ebb, since she was so fond of the use of observation and her anger would cloud her mind. As a wizard he was privy to the degree of another's powers. Boldly, Olyn stepped back from the hot breath on his face. Facing the sun, he threw up the illusion of great height. Through the mist, he became larger than any man had ever been.

Morganna's eyes widened. Startled, she stepped back, tripping on the hem of her gown. She sank to the ground. As quickly as Kit had eluded Morganna's grasp, Aaron snatched the fox up in his sturdy arms. Kit was not sure who had recaptured her, but she wasn't taking any chances and, turning quickly, she nipped the hand that held her.

"Ow, that's not fair. I'm trying to save you," he said, as the fox jumped to the ground. Properly chastised, Kit licked the boy's hand and sat back on her haunches.

"I supposed you didn't know it was me. I forgive you," he said, stroking her fur.

Together they looked back to the knoll where she'd first escaped. There, upon the knoll, Olyn stood, bigger than the great oak outside the courtyard.

Morganna regained her composure. "So it's to be a duel, eh, wizard? You first-level fool. There is no way you can best me." She directed her long slender finger to the ground beneath his feet. Hot blistering bubbles of brown mud spewed forth. Olyn sidestepped with an agility belied by his girth. Morganna stomped her feet in rage. From beneath her feet, fissures split through the ground. Again, Olyn averted disaster, leaping back, narrowly avoiding the chasm. She felt her anger reached a fever pitch. She began to twirl, creating a gale force wind.

The giant Olyn never moved. Not a hair did he move. Gathering all her reserve strength, she narrowed her eyes. She knew the orbs within them glowed with an amber fire.

Once more, Olyn withstood her magic. As the great rainbow after a summer rain is pure illusion, so did Olyn appear. His height exceeded even that of the castle. Her ire changed to fear. She sank to the ground curling her body into a compact ball. She became as tiny as a field mouse. In fact, she was a field mouse, quickly fleeing the giant Olyn.

Kit reacted instantly, scampering after the mouse in a most fox-like manner. In a few short leaps, she pounced on the hapless animal. Holding the witch between her teeth, she felt sorely tempted to eat her and be done with her, once and for all. Just as she was about to take a little nip, Aaron ran to her side, holding Morganna's cage.

Kit couldn't hold back a satisfied smile. *How fitting, to enclose her in this tiny space that once held me.*

Aaron gently took the mouse from Kit's jaws. Softly, she growled.

"I know, I don't like her either," Aaron said as he placed the mouse within the cage. "Besides, she'd probably give you a stomachache."

Chapter Twenty-one

Olyn held the cage and peered into the tiny slit. The mouse lay breathing heavily, clearly frightened.

"Well, all powerful sorceress, for all your folly, you have rendered yourself ineffectual. How pleased Arthur will be to see you. And, I'm sure, even Merlin will be surprised to see how the mighty have fallen."

Aaron stood beside Kit, petting her head. "I think Kit wanted to eat her. She held her fast in her teeth and didn't want to give her to me."

Olyn grinned. He hadn't felt so empowered in years. Looking down on Kit, he said, "Perhaps you should join us as a woman?"

Kit nodded and headed off to the knoll and down to the shore. Aaron's keen hearing picked up the sound of the Travel Tunnel. Roaring, it swooped low and ceased its swirling.

From the vortex, Arthur emerged, followed by Merlin and Leigh. Kit, too, heard the thundering noise and hastened to the sea. *I will be as his love when he first sees me.* Even as a fox, the urge to mate was strong. Her desire coursed through her veins as swiftly as her hot blood. Before diving into the cool water, she paused only a moment, to observe herself as a fox. Would she ever use this guise again?

A few short strokes brought her to the edge of the tide cave. There, in the shadows reflecting off the crystal pool, stood her love. How like a king he stood. Tall, proud, and totally honorable, Leigh would make a good king. She watched him as he removed his mourning attire, revealing a well-muscled body.

He dove into the water and swam to meet her. The diamond drops of water clung to her smooth white shoulders. He placed his arms about her and kissed the droplets from them.

Lowering her lashes, she gave a flirtatious smile then dove beneath the surface, the move calculated to turn her into a fox once again.

"Kit, why do you toy with me? You know I came to see you as the woman I love, not as a favorite pet. I love you with a love far greater than any man ever loved a woman."

The animal darted along the shoreline and paused. In an instant, she walked straight into the tide pool and when the surface reached her shoulders, she plunged her head in.

Breaking the surface, she tossed her shining red tresses and sprayed the droplets on Leigh. He swam closer and held her tightly in his strong arms.

"This time, you will remain a woman. The woman I love," he said, as if confident she would agree. Gently, he wiped the wet hair from the side of her face.

With a modicum of respect, she answered, "Yes, I will be a woman for you, but I wish to make love where we spent so many years together. In the tower."

"I take it you prefer a bed for your lovemaking. How many other locations have you tried?"

Kit narrowed her eyes, not sure if Leigh spoke in jest or in earnest. Leigh laughed. "Kit, I know you have been faithful to me during my absence. I sought to taunt you, as you teased me."

"Well, say what you mean and say it plain, so there are no misunderstandings."

He closed his eyes and nodded. "Kit, I love you and will never desire another."

"You have a fine way of showing it, leaving me for a silly funeral. People die every day. Why was it so important for you to attend this particular funeral?"

He shook his head in obvious exasperation. "I told you, love, the duty I have to the crown is greater even than you and I."

Petulantly, she swam to the shore and emerged from the water. With the grace of a queen, she wiped the water from her body with a small linen cloth.

Leigh followed her and took the scrap of material from her. "Is this the same rag we used to play tug of war?"

Her mouth in a firm straight line, she seized the linen from him. "What if it is? Can I not have things than mean something to me? You hold your duty sacrosanct. This scrap of cloth holds the same for me as does your duty for you."

"Kit, my darling, duty does not come before my feelings for you. It is just a large part of who I am." He enfolded her in his arms, tilted up her chin and placed his lips against hers. Gently at first, then with deepening passion he pressed his lips more firmly down on hers.

Her long sensual arms snaked around his neck and she wrapped her legs about his torso. "Now, Sir Knight, I have you, and you will never escape me again."

"This is such a divine prison, I have no wish to escape. I will remain your captive the rest of my life."

Kit's eyes flooded with desire. "Leigh, let's go to the tower. I want to mate in my own bed. As sweet as the tide pool is, the blanket on my bed is softer than the one we found here in the cave."

"Only a few short months and you have grown soft, my pretty?" he said, mocking her gently.

Arthur and Merlin rejoined Olyn after they washed and changed their clothes.

"Olyn, old friend, what have you there?" Merlin asked.

Arthur approached and said, "Looks to be a rather intricate cage. How did you happen to come by it, Olyn?"

Olyn smiled. "Actually, good king, the box belongs to your dear sister. Or, I should say, half-sister."

Aaron said, "She's less than even half now." Puzzled, Merlin took the box from Olyn and peered into the slit. "What is in here?"

"The box holds Morganna. I duped her into a 'Power Duel', and she lost. At present she is a tiny field mouse, and since the cage would not hold her if she attempted to regain her natural size, she is helpless. The cage will withstand any pressure."

"Well, Olyn, I am impressed. That is quite a feat for a first-level sorcerer."

Arthur nodded in agreement. Taking the cage from Merlin, he looked in at the small mouse and said, "Morganna, now you see what all your scheming has gained you. I deem it your punishment to remain as a mouse in this complicated trap you designed for another."

Aaron nodded solemnly. "Yes, Kit was in there."

Merlin's eyes flew open wider. "She held Kit captive in this cage?"

"Yes, for a time. Morganna drugged her and forced a change. If it had not been for Aaron, she would most probably be dead or held for ransom," Olyn related.

Merlin drew on his long beard. "Morganna, no doubt, wanted something more than a dead fox. She has made no secret of her desire for the Irish crown."

Merlin again peered into the cage. The mouse had begun to run in fruitless circles. "Arthur, I feel Morganna should be tried along with Lancelot for treason. She did hope to overthrow your rule in Ireland, and Lancelot is most certainly a co-conspirator. Both should be tried for their crimes."

"Quite so, Merlin. We will leave on the morrow. All the Knights of the Round Table should be at Camelot by the following day."

Olyn looked expectantly at the senior wizard. "Sire, would it be possible for me to attend the trial? I have witnessed many of Morganna's foul deeds. I know, for a certainty, Lancelot captured the queen. Leigh should testify as well."

Arthur smiled broadly. "I think it would most fitting if we all return to Camelot."

"All? Are we all to go to Camelot? Helga as well?" Aaron asked, as he had grown increasingly fond of the woman who prepared sweets for him.

Merlin winked at Olyn. "Well, lad, do you have something to add to the trial? Can you testify? Olyn tells me you are a reluctant speaker."

Immediately on his guard, Aaron angrily replied, "One does not need to use many words to tell the truth about a fiend."

Olyn hurried to the boy's side. "Aaron, the king is merely having a jest with you. Your Highness, Aaron's loyalties are as deep and abiding as Leigh's. He has many of his brother's traits.

"Leigh is your brother?"

Olyn answered on the boy's behalf. "Yes, Sire, they share the same father. When Leigh's parents were poisoned by Morganna, his father survived and took another to wife. Aaron is the child of that union."

"Then you have even greater reason to speak against Morganna and Lancelot," the king responded.

"I remember little of my father. But, Helga, Olyn, Leigh, and Kit are my family now, and those two have wronged them. I will testify."

High above in the tower, Kit listened to the gulls screaming outside the window as she dropped her clothing at the edge of the large bed. Leigh watched her with hungry eyes.

"How I love that sound. Don't you miss it at Camelot?"

"Camelot is not quite as near the sea as this, so yes, sometimes I do miss their cries. But not nearly as much as I miss you. Each day I awaken and reach for you, only to have my dreams dashed to dust." He threw his garments on top of her and pulled her to him as he sat on the bed.

Believing she had the upper hand, she raised her chin and looked down her patrician nose at her love. "If such is the case, you should remain here with me and not return to Camelot. After all, this is your homeland as well as mine."

He touched her cheek with the back of his calloused hand. "Kit, you know I love you, and would love to remain here on this island for the rest of my days, but I have to serve Arthur, as I promised."

"We'll think about Arthur and his court another time. This is our time, and I don't wish to waste it talking about others."

"Then what do you wish to talk about?" he asked, throwing himself back on the wide bed in the center of the tower. Casually placing his hands behind his head, he grinned at his love.

"Oh, stop looking like a cat that swallowed a bird. We have little time to enjoy one another. Let's not waste it."

"Any time I spend with you is a minute to be treasured, even if I do talk about others."

Further conversation was halted by the onslaught of her urgent lips pressed on his. She straddled his body, her knees at his sides. Pressing him tighter within her thighs, she grinned. "Now you really are my prisoner, and I will never free you."

His body was reacting in a way he'd come to welcome. He reached up to her head and held her face within his hands, softly smothering her with ever- intensifying kisses. As she relaxed her knees, he rolled her onto her side and held her in his tender grasp.

"Kit, this truly is some sort of magic. Never have I felt so exhilarated and so fulfilled at the same time. You complete me."

"As it should be. Isn't that what the Druids' Ordination says?"

"Since when do you accept the words of the Ancient Druids?"

Raising up on her elbow, she grinned saucily at him. "Since I have found it suits me."

"Then you will rule with me as my queen?"

She rose from her position and turned her back to him. He stopped her by grasping her arm.

Kit glanced back at him over her shoulder, and said, "You must convince me."

"Convince you? And what will that take?"

She leapt on him with the ferocity of a wild beast, playfully nipping at his neck, as he lay naked on her bed. "I'm sure, oh great one, you will think of something."

"Kit, why do you mock me?" he asked, tantalized by the ever-changing vixen before him.

Uncharacteristically, she lowered her eyes and stole a glance at him from beneath her thick fringe of eyelashes. "I do not mock you, Leigh. I love you."

"Then, if you love me, you will come with me to Camelot?"

Cocking an eyebrow and suppressing a smile, she said, "Convince me."

Chapter Twenty-two

Kit and Leigh had passed many hours alone, together in the old tower and now lay together in the bed, tired and happy. Leigh's stomach rumbled. "I think, my love, we need to eat."

"I thought I was all you need to satisfy you?"

"I'm speaking of another hunger. We haven't eaten at all today. I would rather live to love another day, than starve and die."

"Most wise, oh great king," she mocked.

Scooping up his clothes, she threw them at him and began to don her own garments.

He reached to his head where the clothes had landed and began to dress. "I wonder what the others will think of our extended absence?" he mused.

"I don't believe they will waste their time thinking of us. They have more important issues on their minds."

"Oh, now you agree something other than you can be important?"

"Of course. I have learned a great deal about responsibility in the re- making of this manor."

"Then you will accompany me to Camelot for Lancelot's trial?"

Drawing herself up to her full height, she tossed her copper hair back over her shoulder. "I will, provided you agree to convince me often."

"Rest assured, my queen, you will receive daily convincing."

The magnificent Great Hall bustled with activity. Helga seemed to be everywhere, making sure all had their fill. Olyn reached up and touched her arm as she placed a trencher before him. "Dear lady, do rest and enjoy the beautiful meal you have prepared."

Merlin looked up and noticed all were present.

"Well, Miss Kit, have you decided to accompany us to Camelot and testify at the trial of Lancelot?"

"I have agreed to accompany Leigh and remain for a time in Camelot, but I will not abandon my home or the people who live and work here."

Arthur nodded in approval. "Of course you would not be expected to live at Camelot, but I would deeply appreciate your testimony as to the foul deeds of Lancelot and Morganna."

A frown passed over her features. Leigh noted her discomfort and reached out to hold her hand. "Kit, I know I did not mention that your validation of the wrongs committed by Lancelot and Morganna would be expected of you. If you don't wish to speak, I am sure there is enough evidence without your verification."

Merlin spoke up. "Leigh is quite right, young lady. Whichever you feel must be done will be done. The Ordination of the Druids supersedes everything. You are to be a queen, with all the rights and responsibilities of a regent. Please consider your answer carefully."

Gracefully, she swept her broad skirts aside and took a seat in the large dining chair Leigh had pulled from the table for her. She clasped her hands in front of her and regally looked down upon them. She cleared her throat and said, "I will speak at the trial. However, it must be taken into account that I have no reason of revenge for doing so."

Olyn's chest puffed with pride for the girl who had become as much to him as his beloved Leigh. Again, he nodded his approval. "You are going to be a very wise ruler. I can see the peoples of your homeland will be well pleased with your regency. You have much to learn, but a just heart is the most important thing a ruler must have."

All preparation for the journey was completed. The group stood on the knoll outside the courtyard in their finest raiment. Arthur carried his half- sister, still in the small cage.

Merlin warned, "Arthur, do be wary and don't listen to any pleas from that witch. She will play on your sense of fairness."

Arthur smiled, looking into the small slit. "This cat has come to the end of her nine lives. I shall not give an inch."

Helga wiped a tear from her eye with her apron. "Do be careful and hurry home. I shall miss you."

Aaron looked sorrowfully at the woman, who was the only mother he'd known. He'd come to care for her deeply and was sore wounded to see her cry. Stepping apart from those prepared to enter the Travel Tunnel, he ran to her. She enfolded him in her ample arms. He looked up at her, his own eyes misting.

"I'm not leaving. Helga needs me. It is my duty to stay with her."

Leigh, equally conflicted, smiled at his brother. "Thank you, Aaron. I don't wish to leave the dear woman either, but my duty to the crown is clear."

Aaron gave his brother a slight bow. "And mine is to Helga."

The five then entered the swiftly forming Travel Tunnel. Kit was the last swept within its spirals. Gently she blew the boy and Helga a kiss.

The council room was quietly hushed. Arthur's champions filed into the room, carefully averting their eyes from the accused. There was little noise, save the soft metallic clink of ceremonial chainmail against each sturdy oaken chair as the knights took their seats at the Round Table.

Arthur sat beside the empty chair at the renowned table. Leigh and Kit stood silent behind the king.

Merlin, with Olyn at his side, opened the proceedings. "Gentlemen, as we are gathered for this sad and solemn occasion, I must remind you, even though you served and fought with Lancelot, it is your duty to carefully assess the charges and render a fair and just verdict."

Arthur rose from his chair and faced the accused. "Lancelot, Morganna, you are charged with treason, kidnapping, and misuse of powers and authorities. How do you plead?"

Kit watched carefully as every eye in the room focused on Lancelot and the small cage on the table beside him. His eyes darted around the council room, no doubt seeking some measure of sympathy.

He may find some comrade who will be lenient with him, but he'll not find any tenderness from me, Kit thought ruefully. She assessed each man in turn around the table. Most were tall, sturdy men. All directed their gazes at Arthur.

Leaning toward Leigh, she whispered, "What will happen to them when they are convicted?"

"Kit," he admonished, "all the evidence must be presented, weighed, and voted upon before they can be convicted. Don't be too quick to judge."

"You mean they will go through a meaningless trial even though we all know they are guilty?"

Drawing his index finger across his lips, he glared her into silence. Kit crossed her arms in front of her and drew her mouth to a thin firm line.

Timidly, Lancelot addressed the champions and the King. "Sire, I sought only to extend your influence to an unruly land. I meant no harm to this assemblage."

Leigh drew in an audible breath.

"He meant no harm?" Kit hissed.

"Explain your intentions," Merlin demanded. "Everything I've learned tells quite clearly you did intend to harm this regency. You planned to establish your own kingdom and rule with Morganna."

He leaned forward and pointed his finger at the now trembling knight. Glowering at the accused, he ordered, "Defend yourself."

Kit muttered, "Defend himself? His actions are indefensible." She started to step forward and felt Leigh's hand on her arm.

"Wait, Kit, you have no authority at these proceedings."

"We can't tell them what a heinous slug he is?" she asked incredulously. "Watch, you will learn."

"I do not need to learn. They must be told what this traitor had done. Any man who would turn on his lord is worse than a seaman who would mutiny against his captain."

"You are right, Kit, but you must learn you are not the only one who has information. You will be asked in turn. Be patient."

"Patient? You fool, if someone doesn't speak up as to his treachery, that damned witch'll turn us all into frogs."

Leigh stifled a laugh. "Don't worry, Kit, the witch is rendered harmless while she remains in the little cage. Arthur will not free her."

Not convinced, Kit cocked an eyebrow and said, "Well, what about her defense? He gave the fool knight a chance to defend himself. If he's a just ruler, as you say, he must give the witch time to defend herself as well."

Kit watched Leigh closely as he pondered her question.

He drew his brows together in a frown. "You're right, but I know Arthur will never chance releasing her."

Merlin again addressed the accused. "Morganna, I know you can hear me. I will listen to your defense and translate for the members of this distinguished group."

A series of high-pitched squeaks emanated from the tiny cage. Merlin's expression changed from tolerance to intense rage. Olyn reached up to his mentor's shoulder.

"Great Wizard, I understand how the woman is baiting you, but you must not give in to your desire to challenge her to another duel. While you are stronger, she is more devious than you are powerful."

Merlin closed his eyes and drew in a deep breath. "Quite so, Olyn, quite so. I thank you, old friend."

Arthur took over the questioning. "Does anyone here have anything to say in defense of these two?"

Kit could not believe even one single person would speak on their behalf. A small figure peered around the large oak door at the entrance of the council room. All heads turned in the direction of the diversion. Guinevere stepped into the room.

"Gentlemen, while I have nothing to say in defense of the accused, I would like to remind you that to completely disgrace a Knight of the Round Table, disgraces the Round Table as well. Please be kind in your punishment." Arthur nodded his assent.

Kit began to feel a slight softening toward the queen. She was considerate in her condemnation. As badly as she'd been used, she was now able to see the larger picture and how unjust actions could affect the crown.

This must be what Leigh meant I had to learn. Kit reached for Leigh's hand and pressed her own into it.

He closed his eyes, smiled, and gently squeezed her hand. Arthur continued. "Since there appears to be no defense, let us present and examine the evidence against Morganna and Lancelot."

Merlin, who had gathered his composure, raised his hand. "Sire, I feel the traitors should be tried together. While there is some reason to believe Morganna duped Lancelot, as a member of the Round Table, he should have recognized her treachery."

"I agree, so say you all?" The king addressed the champions. All present signified assent.

Miroet rose and addressed the group. "My brother and I witnessed firsthand the traitorous acts of the witch Morganna and the knight Lancelot. He is not fit to be a Knight of the Round Table, nor should she be allowed to practice her witchcraft. They are both dangerous to the crown and the person of King Arthur. My vote is for condemnation."

Arthur addressed each of the knights in turn. Those who knew of Morganna's treachery spoke against her. There was not a single voice to speak in her defense.

Leigh took his turn and told of the treatment the queen had endured at the hand of Lancelot and how meanly she'd been treated aboard the pirate ship.

Kit addressed the group. "These two have committed crimes against the king, against me, and against both Ireland and England. The witch Morganna poisoned me and placed me in the cage you see before you. When I was free, I overheard her and Lancelot conspire to seize control of Ireland and to keep for themselves, something called *Sine Vitium*. I have since learned this is a balm King Arthur prizes. They indicated it would make them invincible."

Elegantly, Kit stepped back behind the king's throne. Leigh bent down and placed a soft kiss on her cheek. Kit watched as Lancelot realized his fate would not be pleasant. The kingdom he desired would never be his. He would never be a ruler in his own land. His face grew ashen, and his eyes sank back into their sockets, giving him the appearance of death itself. Beside him on the table, whimpers and squeaks came from the little cage. After all the evidence was heard, a vote was taken and recorded. Merlin read the knights' findings.

"Lancelot, you will never again be allowed to call yourself a Knight of the Round Table. You will be banished from any and all British holdings. You will surrender your armor and sword. The ceremonial sword at your former seat at the table will be re-forged in preparation for the next seated knight."

Merlin gazed sadly at the parchment in his hand, whereupon the witch's verdict was written. He cleared his throat and spoke softly. In a voice barely audible, Kit could hear the pain in his tone. This was not an easy task.

"Morganna," he said.

"You will remain here at Camelot in my care. You will be fed and cared for, but you will remain a mouse for the remainder of your life. And, beware, lest you think you can change into a smaller creature and effect your escape. As you may have forgotten, when you deplete your powers, you must return to your original form before implementing another change. I shall be with you forever. I will wear your prison on a cord about my waist."

Kit swore she heard the mouse scream. *Serves her right. There are limits to what can be done in the name of greed.* Kit had no feelings of remorse for her piracy, but kidnapping a queen was way beyond the limits. Arthur had graciously turned a blind eye.

In unison, the knights rose and filed from the council room as quietly as they had entered.

Arthur sank back into his chair. "This was a sad commentary on the state of this country. When a Knight of the Round Table commits treachery such as this, what can the people expect of their ruler?"

From the open area in the center of the table where Lancelot stood, a cry emanated, like that of a wounded animal, a creature in severe pain.

Arthur's eyes glazed with tears. "Lancelot, how could you do this to me, to the crown, to Guinevere? Have I not treated you as well as I would a natural son?"

"Oh, God forgive me," Lancelot beseeched.

"I can offer no reasonable explanation. I am gravely sorry and though I am forced to wander in other lands, you will remain in my heart for the rest of my days."

"And, you in mine," Arthur replied.

Chapter Twenty-three

Arthur stood in the center of the large room, admiring the handiwork of many people.

The smell of the apple wood burning in the large fireplace sweetened, as well as warmed, the air in the Grand Hall at Camelot. The finest linen draped on the long sideboard that would serve as a presentation table for the re- forged sword of Lancelot. There was much speculation surrounding the sword. The blade had not been designed for battle, and thus was very ornate and beautiful. The finest smith had traveled from Germany to create the most intricate of designs. Ownership hinged on several factors. One must be brave, strong and, above all, honorable.

"Excuse me, Arthur," Merlin asked, entering the room. "Do you have a moment? I have learned two of your champions are, in fact, related to the woman at Kit's castle."

"Oh, so now you are referring to the Castle Clare as Kit's, in the same manner she does?"

"Sire, even when she rules with Leigh, she will claim it as hers." Arthur smiled.

"Of course she will. It's what makes her Kit, and most probably why the Druids selected her."

"You are quite right, Sire. However, the castle's ownership is not the question at hand."

"What is the question?"

"Helga, the woman who remained on the island with Leigh's half brother. She is the mother of Dinan and Braynor the Black."

"I had no idea they were brothers, and certainly did not know their mother was alive. I was told she was taken in a Viking raid when her children were small."

Merlin nodded. "I believe it was Braynor who told me his mother was taken. I'm not even sure he knows Dinan is his brother."

"How is it you come to such information?" Arthur asked, his head cocked.

"Olyn was admiring the crests of the champions and noted the similarities between the two, then recalled seeing a medallion of Helga's that seemed to blend the crests of both."

"I trust you have more proof than the musings of a lower-level wizard?"

Merlin looked crossly at him. "Arthur, you know I would not come to you without first having checked it thoroughly. I am certain these are the facts."

"Very well, what do you wish to do with the information?"

"Your Highness, Olyn feels strongly his ward, Leigh, will be the one you select to hold the next seat at the Round Table."

Arthur's eyes twinkled. "And of course you said nothing that would indicate he might be wrong?"

"Sire, we both know it is the most logical step in the Druids Ordination. Besides, he is the most worthy candidate," Merlin said with firm conviction.

"I see." Arthur nodded benevolently. "I gather you wish to use this occasion to bring Helga and her sons together as well as to seat the next champion?"

"Arthur, you know selecting Leigh as the next seated knight is only the first in the sequence of events. If he is to be a knight of the Round Table, he must, of course, be knighted. And I believe he will then feel the next step will be to wed Kit and return to Clare to establish their regency."

"I assume you feel certain this will be the case?" Arthur looked at his old friend, as the wizard smiled and stroked his long white beard.

"Do not toy with me, Arthur," Merlin warned. He knew Arthur would not venture to incur his wrath.

"Very well, arrange for her and Leigh's brother to arrive in time for the presentation. Use the Travel Tunnel, since Helga is relation to members of the Round Table and Aaron has some royal blood, there should be no problem. They would not need a dispensation as was required when we transported Lancelot.

"A very wise decision, Sire."

"I'm glad you approve, since it was, in fact, your decision. Do you wish me to inform the brothers their mother is alive and coming here?"

Merlin looked down at the clean rushes on the floor and scuffed his toe against them. "Arthur, I would like to ask Olyn to inform them. Over the years, he and Helga have become true friends. I'm sure he would like to do this for her."

"Very good." Arthur nodded in agreement. "Friendship is a most valuable commodity. I'm sure Olyn will take great pleasure in imparting this information. Please ask him to do so, with my blessing."

"Thank you, Sire."

Olyn walked as swiftly as his girth would allow down the long corridor where the champions stayed while they were at Camelot. Softly, he knocked at the door Merlin told him was the quarters of Dinan.

"Enter," a voice said from within.

The knight seated on the shelf that served as a bed was reading from a worn scroll.

"Good day, Sir Knight. I am Olyn, an old friend to Merlin, and I have news to impart."

"Certainly, Sir, proceed."

"Dinan, I have reason to believe your brother is another knight of the Round Table, and that your mother is still alive."

The knight jumped up with a start. "I have a brother? Here? How can this be so?"

"Have you ever noticed your crest and that of Braynor the Black are very similar?"

The knight narrowed his eyes and scowled at Olyn. "No, I've never taken particular notice. Just a similarity would not indicate relationship. Many crests are the same as others."

"This is true and were that the only reason for my revelation it would be small chance, at best."

"What further reason do you have?"

"For many years I have shared a castle with a woman who was taken from her children in a Viking raid long ago. She wears a medallion that is a perfect blending of the crests of both you and Braynor. I asked Merlin to research the medallion and your crests. He has found the three of you are related."

"By the heavens!" He exclaimed. "Have you told Braynor of this revelation?"

"No, as your room was the first I found. Perhaps you would like to join me while I tell him." Olyn's heart swelled with joy, just imagining the look of wonder on his old friend's face when she realized her sons were alive.

Dinan dropped the scroll and grabbed Olyn about the waist, swinging him around as if he were a small child. "Come, let's tell him now. Where is my mother?" Questions poured from the champion with the force of a raging river.

"Of course, we will go to him straight away. Your mother resides in a castle on the Isle of Clare off the coast of Ireland. She is well and I know she misses you."

"Does she speak of us often?"

The wizard nodded. Olyn only wished Helga could see the joy on the face of her son. He hoped the other brother would react in similar fashion. Braynor was called 'the Black' due largely to his dark foreboding manner. He did not seem to be one who could easily be overjoyed.

Together Olyn and Dinan went down the corridor and knocked gently on the door of the room assigned to Braynor the Black.

A deep resonant voice bid them enter. The knight, seated in like manner to Dinan, on his bed, was reading. Raising his head, he looked at the two. "Yes, gentlemen? Is there something I can do for you?"

Unable to contain himself, Dinan grabbed the man and began to hug him furiously.

"What's wrong with you? Are you daft?" Braynor asked angrily.

Abruptly, Dinan released the knight and stepped back. "No, Sir, I'm not daft. I've just learned I have a brother and my mother is alive."

"How nice for you. What does this have to do with me? Why are you here?" His eyes narrowed and his shoulders squared in his usual adversarial manner.

Olyn stepped between the two men. Placing a firm hand on Braynor's chest, he said, "We are not here for combat. We bring good news. Can you recall when you were taken in the Viking raid?"

He nodded. "Yes, dimly. I was a child and I've done my best to forget the incident."

"Yes, yes, you were younger than I and we were pulled from our mother's arms."

"Our mother? We are brothers?"

Dinan smiled widely and bobbed his head up and down furiously. "We are, we are. And our mother is alive."

"How is it," Braynor asked Olyn, "You know of this?"

"I observed your crest and Dinan's are quite similar and when they are blended they depict the medallion that is worn by an old friend of mine. I asked Merlin to see if there was some connection. By whatever means, he learned the three of you are a family. He was unable to learn anything about your father."

Vehemently, Braynor spat on the floor. "I have no wish to ever see him again. If, indeed, he's still alive. I have no doubt someone ran him through for his thievery. The man was no good."

Dinan looked solemnly at his brother. "How is it you know of our father? I was older, yet I have no memory of him after that awful day."

"I was taken to the same village as he. He remained with our group until I was about eight or so. He was mean, he enjoyed hurting anyone, anything. It didn't matter to him if it were a rabbit or a child. Just to inflict pain."

Olyn came to the man's side and placed his hand on his shoulder. "No wonder you're called black. With that memory, how could anyone be other than black?"

"'Tis nothing, I am over it now. It makes me a better warrior."

Dinan put his arm about his brother's shoulder on the opposite side of Olyn. "You truly are a valiant warrior. I've fought in many battles beside you, but you are a man as well, a brother and a son. There is joy in this, is there not?"

"I suppose. I've often admired your skills as a soldier. It is heartwarming to have a brother I can be proud of, even if I was never proud of my father."

Olyn stepped back and said, "Your mother will be overjoyed to see you. I cannot tell you how many times I saw her weep for the two of you."

"You know our mother well then, wizard?"

"I do."

"When will we see her? We must remain here at Camelot until the next champion is seated and Clare is several weeks travel from here," Dinan said.

Olyn nearly burst with excitement. "Quite so, good sirs, but she will be present here at the presentation ceremony. Merlin will bring her here."

"The king's sorcerer? Is this a trick?" Braynor asked suspiciously.

Olyn smiled and shook his head. "It is no trick. Your mother will be here tomorrow. Merlin has seen to it. I will leave the two of you to catch up on each other's lives. Good day to you both."

Neither man saw Olyn slip quietly from the room. Helga looked awestruck at the magnificence of the hall. This Camelot was more beautiful than anything she had ever imagined; the brilliant wall hangings, the graceful carved benches, even the rushes on the floor were something out of a dream. In fact, she was not sure she was not dreaming. It had all happened so fast. One moment, she was tending her garden, and the next, she found herself swept up in that thing that swirled. She and Aaron had left Castle Clare without any preparations. They came with the clothes on their backs.

Aaron stepped beside her and tugged at her sleeve. "Helga, why are we here? Did Leigh send for us? Have we done something wrong?"

"Goodness, lad, so many questions. I have many myself, but we must do whatever they ask. We certainly are being treated well. Look at these clothes, we never had anything so grand back home."

"I suppose, but I hate these shoes. I prefer to go barefoot."

"I am well aware of that, Aaron, but you certainly do look handsome. Leigh will be proud of his brother."

"When will we see him?"

"I don't know," she said, glancing about the large room.

Servants were bringing in food of every size and description, the tables heavily laden. Helga saw the door open and Olyn came into the room.

"Helga, so good to see you. Did you like your Travel Tunnel journey?"

"It was not quite what I expected, but then I never expected to be in one at all." She leaned her head toward the wizard and whispered, "Do you know why we are here? No one has told us anything. They fed us, gave us these beautiful clothes, and left us here in this huge room."

"Have no fear, woman. Everything that will happen will bring you joy, I promise," he said, patting her arm. His eyes were unusually bright and his smile broader than she'd ever seen before.

That man has a secret. She nodded and stepped to the side, her arm about Aaron.

The double doors of the main entrance opened by two knights, flanking each side. The members of the Round Table entered. Their mail created a soft, somewhat tinny sound as each of them sat in their assigned seats. A trumpet sounded, Arthur entered with Guinevere on his arm. He took his place at the Round Table. She sat on a throne above and behind him.

Merlin entered carrying a large pillow covered with gold velvet. Each corner of the pillow had a large tassel. The tassels swayed gently, as the old man approached the presentation table. There, on the table lay the sword, covered with a white cloth. Merlin placed the pillow in front of the table on the floor.

Arthur rose and bid the knights rise as well. All his champions stood silently at their places. Arthur approached the presentation table and addressed the group.

"Ladies and gentlemen, I have a far more pleasant duty to perform than the last time I was at the Round Table."

The knights looked at one another and nodded, each wondering who would be selected to receive Lancelot's sword. Though re-forged, many would think of it as Lancelot's though the knight's betrayal would weigh heavy on the hearts of many.

Arthur sighed, cleared his throat, and began to speak. "Leigh Longwurth, please step forward."

Leigh stood at Olyn and Helga's side. He looked anxiously at the couple he had come to treat as parents.

Olyn placed a friendly hand at the young man's back and gently urged him to go to the table where Arthur stood.

Arthur extended his hand. "Leigh, in honor of your valiant rescue of the queen and other services to the crown, I am knighting you."

Helga reached down to the front of her dress for a handkerchief then realized she was not wearing her apron. The tears of pride were falling fast. She sniffed. Olyn offered her a piece of cloth to dry her eyes. The only thing that would bring her more joy would be to see her sons.

Woman, get a hold of yourself. You are very fortunate to see two of the boys you raised so well. There should be no tears for what might have been. Helga's heart caught in her throat. How proud Leigh's father would have been, if only he'd lived to see this day.

Leigh, of average stature, seemed dwarfed by the king. Arthur bid him kneel on the gold pillow placed before him. Turning his back to the group, he reached to the table and drew back the white cloth covering the re-forged sword. He held it high, the sun streaming through the high narrow windows glinting off the blade.

Gently, Arthur placed it on Leigh's left shoulder and then on his right. "In the name of God and England, I dub thee knight."

Kit stood silently apart from the others. Though she'd always hated and feared everything English, she had to admit this was an impressive honor.

Leigh stepped back and rejoined Olyn and Helga. His brother grinned with pride.

Kit began to assess where she would fit in the scheme of things, when Arthur's voice interrupted her train of thought.

"Kit O'Malley, please step forward."

Quickly, she glanced about the room. Olyn was nodding his head furiously, urging her to step up.

"Miss O'Malley?" Arthur again called. "Please come here. You have nothing to fear, child. You, too, are to be honored for your part in Guinevere's rescue. What is it you desire? Since I cannot make you a knight, how may I honor you?"

And why can I not be a knight? Knowing it would be foolhardy to make such a request, Kit carefully pondered her answer. Gracefully, she approached the king. She placed her hand in his extended one and curtsied.

"Sire, I have learned much in my short stay here at Camelot. Your rule and the care of your peoples impress me. What I truly desire is to create a similar situation for my people. I need your authority since I am told you consider my homeland yours." She had to rein in her tongue. To ask someone for what she felt was hers rankled her. Yet, she would appear humble if it served her purpose.

She gazed directly King Arthur, defying him to do other than grant her request.

Arthur nodded and spoke. "What you desire is admirable. I'm sure you are aware of the Ordination of the Ancient Druids, and thus in the name of fulfillment of that ordination I hereby grant your request. Your holdings are your own and no one will challenge what has been decreed."

Unable to contain her joy, her eyes flew wide and she searched the room for Leigh. Quickly, she ran to him.

"Now we have everything. You can come home with me," she said as she held Leigh fast in her embrace.

Merlin raised his hand to his mouth, coughed loudly, and said, "See here, young woman. Leigh has obligations to the crown."

"What obligations? The king made him a knight. He can be a knight in Ireland as well as England."

Guinevere rose from her chair and proceeded to the presentation table. The sword had been returned to its position. She fondled the hilt with slender fingers. "Kit, there is more to this ceremony. It would be wise to listen, before you make any rash declarations."

Before I make rash declarations? Guinevere is in no position to make that statement. Yet, reason caused Kit to hold her tongue.

"Leigh, would you please return to the presentation table?"

Leigh again approached the regent. He started to kneel once more on the gold pillow. Arthur bid him rise.

"Leigh, you come from a royal family and your presence here at this court is a joy for all of us. Therefore, I have chosen you as the next seated knight at the Round Table."

Again, he raised the sword, lowered it, then placed it in Leigh's outstretched hands.

The two walked to the Round Table. Arthur drew out the chair beside his own and indicated Leigh was to sit. Carefully, Leigh placed the sword, with the blade's tip pointing center in the blank space on the table and took his place beside the king.

The entire hall burst into applause. One person in the Great Hall was not happy, Kit decided as she exited as quickly as she dared. Now Leigh would never leave the pretty palace. Feeling her hopes dashed, she raced to the room they had provided for her.

She called for a bath to be drawn. A servant girl answered. This was not her usual assignment. All the other servants were at the ceremony. The girl moved as fast as she was able and dragged the large tub into Kit's room. After what seemed like an eternity, the tub filled. Kit waited impatiently for the serving girl to finish, then removed her splendid gown quickly and in her frenzied anger, she threw the clothes to the floor and kicked them aside. She sank into the warm tub up to her neck. Vigorously scrubbing her arms, she was unable to decide whether to cry or howl. *This is unfair. For all Arthur's pomp and ceremony, he's still a damned Englishman. And now Leigh's one, too.*

"I wish I could take Scilti and return to the sea. I'm a pirate and a damned good one at that."

She hesitated only a moment, then plunged her head below the surface.

She pawed her way up and leapt out of the tub. Vigorously, she shook herself, purposely throwing water on her discarded finery. He fur nearly dry, she crept out of the room and down the vacant corridor. As everyone had gathered in the large hall, no one would see her exit. She raced as fast as her four legs would carry her. Out into the open courtyard, over the drawbridge, and out onto the rolling meadow. She ran aimlessly, just to feel the wind coursing through her fur.

Freedom!

Hurrying across the unfamiliar meadow, she began to search for a mouse or a hapless mole. She wasn't really hungry, she just felt like hunting. *Oh, for the days when Leigh and I ran together just for the joy of running.*

Why can't things always be that simple? Now everything is duty, responsibility, and honor. Damn his honor.

Carelessly, she darted this way and that. Fueled by her anger, she took dangerous chances. The scent of a mouse drew her to a small stream. The mouse ran over a fallen tree branch that hung over the water. She pounced and missed the rodent by mere inches. Suddenly, she felt a sharp pain in her hind leg. A spring trap staked to the bank of the stream! The pain grew intense. How could she be so foolish?

The Great Hall was nearly empty. Most of the guests had departed. Leigh remained seated in his chair at the Round Table. Two other knights were still seated as well.

Merlin, Olyn, Aaron, and Helga stood near the side door. The old woman seemed unable to cease her crying. She did not sob aloud, but tears of joy fell unfettered down her plump cheeks.

"Olyn, I want to thank you for bringing me here to see our Leigh knighted. I've often wondered if my sons ever became knights."

Olyn's features became almost cherubic. A grin spread over his face like rain over a spring flower. "Well, Helga, I think you have every reason to be as proud of your sons as you are of Leigh."

Carefully dabbing at the tears with the cloth Olyn provided, she smiled and said, "I know, Olyn, but I do wish I knew how they turned out. They didn't have a great start in life, being stolen when they were but wee lads."

Helga eyed the two men who remained at the Round Table with Leigh. They rose and approached the group by the side door.

"Good day to you, Ma'am," they said with a slight bow to the woman.

"Good day to you as well, gentlemen. Do you know our Leigh? The one who was just made a Knight of the Round Table?"

"We do," Dinan said.

"We have been members as well for several years. May we introduce ourselves?"

Helga was flustered by the attention of the two knights. She had not known much formality at the Castle Clare. "But, of course. I am Helga Rahn, and you are?"

"I am Dinan Rahn and this is my brother, known as Braynor the Black." Helga's eyes flew wide in surprise. "Your name is the same as mine. Is Braynor's surname Rahn as well?"

"It is, dear lady, but I never use it because I hated my father for what he became when we were captured," Braynor the Black said.

Helga's eyes rolled back in her head, her skin turned ashen, and she fell in a heap at the feet of the two knights.

Olyn rushed to her aid. "Oh, dear, look what I've done. I've frightened the poor woman." He reached under her large shoulders and supported her on his knee. "Helga?" he said, patting her cheek to rouse her from her faint.

Both Dinan and Braynor rushed to help. "Mother, are you all right?"

"I can't believe it's really you. So many years have passed. You were just babies," she said, sobbing in earnest.

Braynor knelt at her side and supported her body, taking her from Olyn. The old wizard stood and watched the reunited family. The other lads, Leigh and Aaron, came to his side.

"Olyn are they truly her sons? How did you find them?" Leigh said.

"I had help from Merlin. It's too bad she missed so many years. Thankfully she'll be able to spend some time with them before we must return to Clare."

Aaron looked up at his older brother. "Does this mean she will not take care of us any longer?"

Helga began to stir. "Aaron, you need never fear that I might give up your care. I lost two sons for many years, but I shan't lose you. I will bake and cook for you, until you find a wife."

Aaron winced. "A wife? What do I need one of them for?"

Leigh laughed. "Some day, little brother, you will want a woman in your life, more than you want Helga's cakes."

"Well, perhaps, if she could cook as good as Helga."

The color returning to Helga's cheeks, she struggled to right herself. "Boys, you are truly my sons. The heavens be praised."

Leigh looked about the Great Hall. Save for the five of them, there was no one. "Aaron, have you seen Kit? She was here only moments ago. Where could she have gone?"

Merlin, who had been quietly observing the happenings, lifted his eyebrows, closed his eyes and said, "Leigh, I believe your ladylove was hurt when Arthur did not make her a knight as well. And your rebuff was not taken kindly."

"Rebuff? I merely stated I have a duty to Arthur until he directs me otherwise."

Olyn shook his head. "Merlin is quite right, Leigh, she felt set aside. You did not explain yourself. You alluded you will remain here at Camelot forever. You did not tell her that someday you will return to Clare."

Leigh eyed the wizard with a look of pure incredulity. "I cannot believe she would think such a thing. Of course, I will return. I quite simply do not know when."

Merlin nodded. "Leigh, you have a great deal to learn about women. They do not assume you mean something unless you have actually said it, and said it plainly."

Helga, now fully erect, turned to Olyn. "If Kit believes Leigh is lost to her, there is no telling what she may do."

Aaron looked from his brother to Olyn. "Woof?"

"By all that's holy, she wouldn't change herself and run off would she?" Leigh rushed about, looking for a trace of her. He found nothing, no hair ribbon, not even a whiff of her scent.

"Aaron, we have to find her. Gentlemen," he said, addressing Helga's sons, "could you please assist us?"

"Certainly, Leigh, how can we help?"

Aaron looked out the side door up the corridor leading to the stairs. "Leigh, I think it would be better if I searched alone. If she sees you and the others, she might flee. She still trusts me."

"Thank you, Aaron, but the knights and I will find her. It is not a job for a boy," Leigh said, dismissing him.

Aaron drew his mouth into a straight line, then narrowed his eyes and confronted his brother. "Now I know why she ran off. You are careless with the feelings of others. I will find her and make sure she is safe. If she's smart, and you know she is, she'll hide from you." With a finality that halted further discussion, Aaron left the room.

Pain seared through Kit's leg with a mind-numbing force. The stake, driven high on the stream bank, was out of reach of the water. Try as she would, she could not reach it. *If only I could transform, I could pull the damned thing off myself.* But the more she pulled, the more severe the pain. When she could endure no longer, she passed out.

Aaron looked everywhere. It was harder here. Here, Kit's hiding places were not familiar. He found himself in strange territory. He certainly understood Kit's anger. Leigh had made him mad, too. But, why would she run off so no one could find her? What about all the people at home? She called them her people, didn't she? *That's not how you treat your people.*

A rustling of the grasses near a stream caught his attention. Then he heard a soft mewing, an animal in distress. Back on Clare, he'd had the same fascination for animals as his brother, and he recognized the call of pain. Again, he heard the sound and stooped to the bank to hear it more clearly.

Pushing aside the leaves, he found a fox, its eyes shut tightly in fear, its leg caught in a spring trap. Could it be Kit? Carefully he lifted the fox's eyelid. His heart soared. Yes, a deep emerald green. He'd found Kit!

With every ounce of his strength, he pulled against the bands of the trap. He could not free her. *I need tools.* He braced himself against the sapling along the bank and placed his feet on the stake. He pushed and kicked until the stake was free. Taking off his shirt, he wrapped Kit in it and held her wound tightly to prevent further bleeding. He scrambled up the bank and headed toward the castle. *I can't take her in there. Someone will find us.*

The stables. There I can find a tool to pry her free and she can rest on the clean straw.

It seemed forever until he reached the stable. No one was around. They were all still celebrating Leigh's knighting.

Aaron snorted. *You'd think Leigh had been made a saint instead of a knight. Who does he think he is that he can ignore our homeland?*

Aaron placed Kit on the straw in the last stall. There were few horses in the stable and several stalls were empty. Here he would not be risking discovery.

The fox mewed in pain.

"Relax, Kit. I'll get the trap off as soon as I find a pry bar." Her eyes, flooded with pain, looked wildly at him.

"Shh, Kit, we'll have you free very soon." Looking around, he found a furrier tool, used for extracting horseshoe nails. It was strong and long enough to give him the leverage he needed to pry the jaw of the trap. Nudging her gently with his foot, he urged her to move her leg. She pulled up on her leg convulsively.

Instantly, she was free. As soon as he was certain she was out of harm's way, Aaron released the bar and the jaws snapped tightly shut. He threw the trap disdainfully at the side of the stall.

Kit seemed to be regaining consciousness. She tried to lift her head. The pain was too much and her head lolled back onto Aaron's shirt. Carefully, he petted her and cooed softly to her.

"You'll be all right. I'll wash your wound and you will be fine in a day or so."

She looked at him, imploring him to understand. "Woof."

"You want me to change you?"

She closed her eyes and nodded.

Aaron looked around the stable and could not find a suitable container large enough for Kit to fit as a woman.

"You rest, I'll find something," he said, looking anxiously about. There was nothing, except the horse trough. It could work. He could carry her as a fox and when she changed, she could help herself.

Confident his plan would work, he hurried to the last stall. There, he found Kit conscious. Her eyes darted feverishly about.

"Don't worry, you'll soon be a woman."

Tenderly, he lifted the wounded fox and carried her to the trough. No one was in the area. He placed her gently in the water. As weak as she was, she splashed joyfully in the redeeming fluid.

"Thank you, Aaron, I didn't think I'd ever get out of there."

Though it took all her strength, slowly she rose from the trough and tried to get her legs under her. She stumbled, and Aaron reached for her, then half carried her back to the last stall. He laid her down on the fresh straw. A quick search of the remaining stalls revealed the softest horse blanket he'd ever seen. Gently, he placed it around her. She was shivering, but her body seemed to be on fire.

"Aaron, please, you must find some moss."

"Moss?"

"To draw out the infection. Please, hurry," she said weakly.

He wrapped her tightly in the soft blanket and slipped out of the stable. *Where am I supposed to find moss?*

Baylor and Dinan searched the complex labyrinth of corridors in the magnificent Camelot. Leigh's queen was nowhere to be found.

"I don't want to be the one to tell him we can't find her. The man is daft with grief." The Black Knight sighed.

"I know what you mean, Braynor. I've never seen a man so guilt ridden. I guess we all have a lesson to learn about understanding one another."

"Quite so, but that is not the matter at hand. We have to find his Kit."

"Who is this woman anyway? She seems to have the undivided attentions of many powerful men. Even the King is concerned."

"Do you think her attraction has anything to do with the search the Irish Princes undertook for Arthur?"

Dinan shook his head. "I don't know, but there is definitely more to the woman than most believe."

Baylor did not seem to be paying attention to his brother. He looked down a dark hallway. "There, do you see him?"

"See who?" his brother replied, following his gaze. "Yes, now I do. It appears to be a small boy, and he's crying."

Slowly the knight approached the lad, who was sitting in an unlit corner with his head on his knees.

"See here, lad, what is troubling you? Why do you weep?"

Immediately, Aaron rose to his feet and wiped his tears with his forearm. "I ain't crying." He glared, daring them to refute his statement.

Dinan stooped down to the boy's height and spoke gently.

"Of course you weren't sobbing like a girl, but something is distressing you. Isn't it now?"

"Yeah, no. Don't you worry none. I'll handle it."

Baylor took the boy's arm in his hand and spoke rather gruffly. "Do you know where the new knight's lady is?"

Aaron wrenched his arm from the Black Knight. "No, I don't and if I did I wouldn't tell you. Nor Leigh neither." He met the knight's cold stare, turned, and ran.

"Braynor, you frightened him. Now we'll never find him. I'm certain he knows where she is."

The Black Knight closed his eyes and nodded. "You're probably right. I've been cynical for so long, I know no other way to speak."

"You'll learn, brother. But, for now, we must find the lad."

Chapter Twenty-four

Olyn paced back and forth, his mind confused. He tried to force himself to concentrate. He had to use an observation spell if he was to learn of Kit's whereabouts. It would be unthinkable to ask Merlin for assistance.

Merlin had entrusted him with the care of Kit, and he'd betrayed that trust by allowing her a free hand in her life decisions. The Druid Ordination demanded complete compliance. *I am a failure. I was simply to safeguard the future queen of my homeland and I couldn't even discharge that basic duty.* His despair enveloped his entire body as he sat dejectedly, with his head in his hands on the large bench in the Great Hall. He was so consumed by his own shortcomings, he failed to hear the king's wizard enter.

"Olyn, old friend, what is troubling you so?"

"I'm a failure as a wizard, as a guardian, and even as a friend."

"That simply is not true," Merlin said. He put his long arm about the shoulder of the other man.

Unable to control his grief, Olyn began to weep.

"She's gone, Merlin, I've failed once again. We'll never be able to find her if she chooses not to be found."

"She will be found when the time is right. The Ordination of the Druids will be fulfilled, no matter the workings of mere mortals."

"Kit is anything but a mere mortal, even discounting her unique ability to change into an animal. She is unlike any other mortal whoever lived."

"While you are correct, she is vastly different from any other mortal. She is not the first so affected by the Druids Ordination."

Olyn looked up in complete surprise. "She isn't? How can this be so?"

"The Ordination of the Ancient Druids is older than time itself. Peace, war, and rulers all come within the scope of the Druids. While people think they have control of such situations, the fact of the matter is, humans are mere pawns. It is only by following the tenets set forth that men run the way of the world."

At the far end of the Great Hall, the large center door opened, and Queen Guinevere entered, looking anxiously at the two wizards. "Gentlemen, has there been any news of Kit?"

Merlin moved to her side. "No, Your Highness, there's been no sign of her."

"Nothing? Leigh is beside himself with grief. Is nothing being done to find her?"

Merlin guided the Queen to the end of the bench where Olyn was sitting. "Guinevere, Arthur has search parties looking for her. She will be found, as she is part of something larger than herself. I cannot tell you more, but it will resolve itself."

Braynor hurried along the hallway following the swift-moving boy. He darted this way and that, ducking into hidden niches and scurrying into places so small, the knight could not follow.

"Dinan, he's coming toward you. Catch him. He knows where she is. I'm certain of it."

"You'll never get him to come out if you frighten him. You have to talk to him, make him understand we want to help Kit, not hurt her."

Baylor's gaze softened. "You're right, I guess I don't remember what it's like to be a child."

The Black Knight searched where he thought the lad had run to no avail. Dinan hissed to get his brother's attention. "Psst, Braynor," he said, pointing to the elaborate paneling in the corridor. "This panel seems to have a life, as I hear a breath."

Braynor nodded and gently tapped the wood. "I believe this is hollow. Could a person be in here?" he asked loudly, so that Aaron might hear him. The only sound emanating was the sniffles of a frightened boy.

Dinan tried a softer approach. "Are you ill, lad? Please come out, and we will help you."

"Don't need help. I'm not sick," he whimpered.

"Well," Dinan said, "perhaps someone else is sick? Someone you care for?"

"Mayhap Helga will know what to do. I'll only come out if you bring Helga."

"Helga? Our Mother?"

Vehemently, the boy cried out, "She's not your mother. She's mine! Mine and my sister's."

"Dinan, have you two found Kit?"

Dinan turned as Leigh entered the room. "No, Sir."

"Then why are you talking to the wall?"

Dinan shook his head. "We've not found her, but we did find the boy, and we believe he knows where she is."

Braynor rose from his stooped position at the wall and asked, "Leigh, does the boy have a sister? He claims Helga is mother to him, and his sister."

At once, Leigh understood. "He hasn't a sister, just a woman who is like sister to him. Isn't that right, Aaron?" he asked, addressing the panel.

"She is so my sister, and Helga will take care of us. No one else." Leigh smiled, confident Aaron would come out and allow Helga to help him. "Aaron, I will get Helga, and then you will tell us where Kit is."

"No, I won't. You only hurt her feelings. I'll tell Helga, no one else. Just Helga."

Frantic, Leigh pounded on Helga's door. "Helga, please come quickly. I need your help."

The old woman hurried to the door as fast as her girth would allow, though it seemed ages to Leigh.

"Yes, lad, what is it? How can I help?" she asked.

Leigh stood at the door's opening. "Helga, Aaron knows where Kit is, and he will tell no one except you. He is frightened. I think she may be hurt or ill. Can you come and get him to tell where she is?"

"I don't know, Leigh, he was pretty angry at you for her running off in the first place." Helga grabbed a shawl and he led her down the corridor where he'd left the two knights. As they approached the panel Aaron had chosen as a hiding place, they now heard more anger than fear coming from behind the wall.

"I won't tell you," he screamed, "only Helga, only Helga."

"Lad, we mean Kit no harm. Leigh just has to explain some things to her."

"Why didn't he just tell her plain? His stinky duty is more important than me or Kit, more even than his friendship with Olyn."

Leigh knelt down, so he was only a thin piece of veneer away from his brother. "Aaron, that is not so. You, Kit, Olyn, and Helga are my family. The only family I've ever known. You are important, and I've been foolish not to realize that."

A defiant voice from behind the panel said, "Yes you are. And I'm glad you know it, but I still will only tell Helga where Kit is."

Helga's eyes crinkled. "It seems the boy is a bit stubborn. Perhaps it would be better if you all left, and I talk to Aaron."

Helga knelt down on her ample haunches. "Aaron, you simply must come out this moment. I'm an old woman and you shouldn't make me squat to speak to you."

A voice slightly less hostile emerged from the panel. "I'm sorry, but you are the only one I can trust."

"No one means to harm Kit. Now come out here and tell me what is wrong."

Slowly, he came out from the wall. "It's Kit, and I think she's sick."

"Why do you feel she's sick? Did she vomit?" Helga asked.

"No, but she's all hot and her leg is puffed up."

"Oh dear, that sounds bad. Where is she?"

Aaron looked furtively around the corridor. Seeing no one, he said, "She's in the stables."

"In the stables? That's no place for a sick person. Why did you not bring her back to her quarters?"

"'Cause, I didn't want Leigh to find her. He tells her lies."

"Now, Aaron, that is not true. Leigh would never lie, especially not to Kit. He loves her."

"Well, he sure has a funny way of showing it."

"Enough, Aaron, take me to Kit."

Helga peered into the dark stable, the warmth enveloping her like a cloak. "Aaron, where is she?"

Aaron looked around to see if they were unobserved. "Come this way," he said, leading her down to the end of the row of stalls.

Helga looked into the last compartment, the pungent odor of damp straw assailing her nostrils. "Oh, good heavens, Kit," the old woman said, dropping to her knees beside her. She placed a palm on Kit's forehead.

"Aaron, she's burning up. We have to get her into a proper bed."

"How? I can't carry her myself, even the two of us can't move her without being seen. We need help, but we can't trust anyone."

Helga nodded. "I understand, but I believe I have the answer. Find my son, Braynor."

"The big, mean man? He's really your son?" Aaron asked incredulously.

"Yes, now go and find him quickly. Tell no one else, he will come with you and carry Kit to her quarters."

"He won't tell the others?"

"No, Braynor is silent, as he is strong."

Helga tried to cool the feverish Kit while she waited for Aaron and her son to return.

Fetching cool water from the trough, she bathed Kit's pale face. Delirious, Kit ranted, "Scilti, we have to get off this boat. The men are mutinying, we have to jump ship."

Helga tried to soothe her, to no avail. Kit thrashed and threw the soft horse blanket off her body. Astounded at the sight of her nakedness, Helga quickly covered her. Where were the girl's clothes?

Kit's eyes flew open. She looked horrified, turning this was and that, yelling out orders. "Stop, you. I'll have you flogged, you cur."

Braynor stepped into the stall. "Mother, is she lucid? She seems to be talking about being at sea."

Helga looked up at her son. "Yes, Braynor, she is raving, however, she was once a sea captain, among other things."

"A woman sea captain? She's so small. How could she control her men?" the large knight asked. "What other unusual occupations has she held?"

"You wouldn't believe me if I told you," Helga responded. Aaron spoke up. "Yup, she's a fox, too."

Swiftly Helga turned. "Aaron, hold your tongue."

Braynor looked to his mother for confirmation. "Does he speak the truth?"

Glaring at Aaron, Helga nodded. "He does, but you must never repeat what he said."

"I shall not. People would think I was daft," Braynor said, shaking his head.

Though Olyn knew Kit was within the castle walls, and that she was well cared for, he was beginning to worry. Helga wouldn't allow anyone into the room, but she'd apprised Olyn of the dire situation.

Kit's wound wasn't responding to conventional treatment. Time was passing all too quickly. Her fever raged on. The infection from the deep gash on her leg was spreading. A sickening purple covered her lower limb.

A gentle tap at the chamber door alerted Helga. Hurrying to prevent an unwanted visit, Helga cracked the door open. "Who is there?"

Seeing no one in the corridor, Olyn said, "It's Olyn, Helga. How does Kit fare? Is there any improvement?"

Helga hung her head. "No, Olyn, and I fear for her life."

Olyn crossed to the bed in the center of the room and looked down on his ward. Her hair was wet and stringy against the sweat-soaked pillow, her leg, festered and putrid.

Olyn shook his head woefully. "Helga, I am sure you have done all you can, but we must seek a higher power if we are to cure her. Merlin must be informed of the severity of her condition."

Helga nodded. "As much as I don't want to break a confidence, something must be done to save the girl. It's beyond my herbs and healing cloths. But Aaron will object, you know."

"He may, but I'm certain he would not wish Kit to die."

With great trepidation, Olyn knocked on Merlin's workroom door. The senior wizard bid him enter. "Olyn, old friend, you look distressed. Is there a problem? How can I help?"

"I only pray you can, great sorcerer. It's Kit. She is gravely ill from an infection. I fear she is near death."

Merlin's eyebrows raised, his eyes dark with anger. "You fear she is near death, and now you inform me? Why was I not told when she first became ill?"

Olyn hung his head. "I only learned of the severity of the situation moments ago. I suspected she had returned to the castle when Aaron no longer skulked about the hallways. Aaron feels Leigh is responsible for her condition and swore Helga to secrecy."

"This does not bode well, Olyn. The anger of the Druids will be fearsome if this woman dies. I dare not contemplate the revenge they will extract from mankind."

Olyn bowed his head. "I know."

Merlin grabbed the heavy wizard about the waist then pulled him into a quickly forming Travel Tunnel.

"Merlin, where are we going? You must stay here at Camelot to help Kit. If this is a journey that must be undertaken, I will go, but you must be here for Kit."

"Fear not, Olyn. We will help Kit, but we cannot do it alone. This needs the strength of a higher power. We must face the Druids," Merlin said with such apprehension his voice shook.

As before, the Tunnel swirled upward to the room without substance. There was no physical presence, but the wizards knew they were in the company of the Ancient Druids.

"How dare you enter this company?" a voice boomed apparently from nowhere.

"Oh, Great Ancient Ones, I beg your understanding," Merlin said. "The woman chosen to fulfill the Ordination of this august body is gravely ill. We come to you for the power to heal her, that the Ordination be completed."

A single voice, with a different timber, addressed the wizards. "In his search, has Arthur found the *Sine Vitium*?"

Puzzled, Merlin knitted his brows together and said, "I know not." He started to form a question, but the visage halted him.

"Return to Camelot. All will be made aright."

"But her fever rages. She is delirious! By what magic can she be healed?" Olyn asked.

Merlin glared at him and spoke softly out of the side of his mouth. "We are in no position to ask what manner of magic they employ."

In a stronger voice, Merlin addressed the company of Druids. "It will be done according to your direction."

Chapter Twenty-five

Merlin came slowly down the long corridor to the War Room. Pausing only a moment, he pushed the large door open. Arthur sat at the Round Table in his accustomed seat. The king seemed to be going over the castle accounts.

Olyn cleared his throat and said, "Sire, may I speak with you?"

Surprised, Arthur looked up. "You seek my council? For the most part, it is I who seek yours."

"Quite so, Your Highness, however this is a matter of grave concern and I would like your thoughts on the matter." Merlin hesitated, looked down to the floor, and began to speak. "You recall the Ordination of the Ancient Druids?"

"Most certainly. Has something happened that would alter the Ordination?" Arthur asked.

Merlin closed his eyes and continued to speak. "It is Kit. Sire, she is in a deep coma, and Olyn fears for her life."

"Is nothing being done to heal her? This cannot be. Should she perish, the Druids' anger could decimate all of England, Ireland, and perhaps the remainder of the civilized world."

"I know. Olyn and I consulted with them, and they sent us away, saying all will be aright. This magic is far greater than mine, and I dare not question it."

"Most wise, Merlin," the king agreed. "However, I believe young Leigh must be informed of her condition. He's beside himself with grief, as Helga will not admit him to Kit's chamber. Aaron sleeps outside the door, so no one can get past him. He is very loyal to her."

At that moment, a tap sounded at the large oaken door.

"Excuse me, Sire, may I have a word with you?" Leigh asked.

"I am increasingly worried over the duration of Kit's illness. Something more must be done. Please, Sire?"

The tall, thin wizard closed his eyes, and drew in a deep breath. "I understand your concern, lad. Arthur and I were just speaking of the situation. We are agreed Aaron should allow you to see her, and you should know the Druids say all will be well."

"He is my brother, and I understand his loyalty. In fact, I admire his unrelenting watch over her. But I love her. Would you intervene that I might see her?"

Arthur glanced at Merlin and nodded. "We will make certain you are admitted to her chamber."

Leigh approached Kit's chamber and found Aaron sleeping across the threshold, barring the way.

Leigh prodded him with the toe of his boot.

"What? Oh, it's you." The boy bristled. "You can't come in."

Arthur stepped out from behind Leigh and said, "Young man, this is my castle, and I am the king. I will say who is admitted where."

Aaron's eyes flew open wide. "Yes, Sire. Of course. As you say, Sire." Quickly he stood, and moved aside that they might enter.

Helga was sitting beside the bed, sponging Kit's head with cool cloths. "Oh, Leigh, thank the fates you've come. I fear our girl will not last the night."

Stunned, Leigh dropped to his knees and began to pray.

"Oh, Lord, forgive my vanity. I placed what I perceived as duty above my love for her. Please, please, save her."

Merlin placed a long thin hand on Leigh's shoulder.

"Do not fear, young knight, your lady will recover."

"How can you know this? Do you know of some magic potion that can save her?"

"No, lad, I am repeating the answer of the Druids. They say all will be aright."

"What can I do?" Leigh pleaded.

Arthur walked to the bed and looked down on the silent figure. "Some things take time, lad, some things take time, and all we can do is wait."

Helga bustled about, clearing the room of the discarded cloths, and moved aside to allow Leigh to sit at Kit's bedside.

"Come along now, Aaron," she said.

"I will get you something to eat."

"I ain't hungry," he spat.

"Nevertheless, you will eat," she said firmly, taking him by the arm and leading him from the room.

"It's not right. Leigh lied, and if he hadn't, she wouldn't have been hurt. I'm going back and make him leave."

"No, you are not. You cannot defy the king. Arthur wants Leigh with Kit, and nothing you say can change that. Now finish the biscuits and go find me more herbs. The ones I showed you yesterday. They seem to soothe her."

Placated, Aaron set out to the fields to locate the required herbs. The ones Helga requested grew at the edge of a stream. The same stream where Kit was captured. Carefully, he went to the water's edge lest he be caught in a like manner. There, on the edge of the bank were the herbs Helga had shown him. He reached out for them, holding on to the gnarled roots on a tree that hung over the water. But the roots were old and dried, barely holding to the soil. They gave way under Aaron's weight. He plunged into the stream.

The water ran swift and cold, but not very deep. Getting off his knees, he felt something strike the back of his leg. An intricately carved box floated up the stream. Aaron took it from the water. Setting the box up on the stream's edge, he continued to harvest the plants. Dusk was setting in when he completed his task. He removed his tunic and wrapped the medicine and the carved box in the cloth. The shadows were quickly lengthening, and he hastened back to Camelot. Kit's fever would be worse after the sun set.

Aaron returned to Kit's room. The door sat ajar. Leigh sat, his head in his hands, at her bedside. Helga continued to bathe her forehead. She looked up and saw Aaron enter.

"Come in, Aaron. Did you find the medicine? The pungent mint seems to soothe her."

"Yes, here they are," he said, thrusting his tunic at her. Helga opened the bundle.

"What is this?"

"I don't know. I found the box in the stream. It's pretty. I thought Kit might like it."

She turned the box over in her hands. "Yes, it is very beautiful. It has some writing on the side. I wonder what it says. Perhaps Olyn can read it."

Hearing his name as he approached, Olyn asked, "Read? What have you that needs reading?"

Helga thrust the box at him. "This. Aaron found it while gathering herbs for me. Can you read the inscription?"

Olyn took the carved box and turned it over and over in his hands. "My Latin is dormant from lack of use. I will take it to Merlin. It seems strange such an intricate piece of work would be left in the open and not safeguarded."

Merlin, too, was checking on Kit's condition and entered the room.

"So, Helga, is there any improvement?"

"Sadly, no," she said.

"But Kit is no worse either. That is little hope at best. But, better than none."

The senior wizard nodded and turned to his colleague. "What have you there, Olyn?"

"It's a box Aaron found in a stream not far from here."

Merlin inclined his head and took the carved piece from him. At once his eyes flew open wide, the pupils dilated. "Have you any idea what the boy has found?"

"No. Aaron though it might be a discarded trinket Kit would enjoy."

Merlin went to the edge of the bed and placed a hand on Leigh's shoulder. "You must fetch King Arthur at once."

"Please, Merlin, I don't wish to leave her side. Please send someone else."

"Trust me, lad, this time your duty to the crown will not harm Kit. It will save her. Now, go quickly."

In a daze, Leigh hastened to do Merlin's bidding, returning moments later with Arthur.

Merlin stood over Kit, beaming. Judging by the look on Merlin's face he expected to see her improved. But there she lay, still as ever.

Merlin came to the king's side. "Arthur, have you any word from the Irish princes? Have they made any discovery of the *Sine Vitium*?"

"Alas, no. It would surely be of great aid to our future queen, if it were in our possession," he said, his tone laced with hopelessness.

"Arthur, come here. Look at the box the boy found floating in the stream at the edge of the meadow."

"Quite attractive. What does the inscription say?"

Merlin's countenance was one of pure joy. "It says *Emandatus*."

"Emandatus? I've not used Latin of late. How does that translate?" Arthur asked.

"It means 'flawless'," Merlin replied giddily. "Open it, here we will find the balm to heal her wound, and thus she will carry out the Ordination. The Druids said all would be aright."

Leigh looked incredulously at the wizard. "Can this be so? Will she truly be healed?"

Olyn bobbed his head foolishly. "Yes, yes, Leigh. She will be well!"

Aaron looked at the wizard, his eyes as wide as they could open. "Truly? She will be her old self?"

Olyn clapped the boy on the back. "Yes, truly she will be well. Back to her old self."

Leigh ran to Merlin's side. "By the fates, can this be so? She is near death."

Ceremoniously, the wizard opened the carved box. Within lay a translucent substance that smelled strongly of foxmoor. Merlin motioned to Helga to bring him a clean cloth. He dipped it in the balm and smeared it over the gash on Kit's leg. Wondrously, the wound closed back upon itself, the inflammation subsided and the redness disappeared. Helga watched, astounded.

Merlin handed the cloth to Helga. "Take this and wring the cloth over clean water and use it to bathe her forehead. The fever will ebb."

Dumbfounded, Helga did as she was bid. All that night she bathed Kit, never stopping, not even to rest. Nor would she allow another to relieve her of the task. Leigh and Aaron stayed at her side, the younger nodding off from time to time.

As the dawn broke, Helga, unable to fight the fatigue a moment longer, fell asleep.

Leigh stared at his love. Leigh alone was awake in the room. Her eyelashes fluttered. He bent down and gently kissed her cheek.

"Oh, Kit, thank the Lord, you are better. I could not have gone on without you." He felt her forehead, no longer fevered.

She awoke and turned to look about the room. "Where am I? Aaron took me to the stables. Where is he?"

Hearing her voice, Aaron jumped to his feet. "You're awake!"

Kit reached out and ruffled his hair. "You can't get rid of me that easily." All Leigh could do was bow his head and offer thanks.

"Leigh," she said, "Aren't you going to speak to me? Or are your services required by the king?"

He raised his head. "Even the King shall never take me from your side again. I promise you. Now I can hold you in my arms, I shall never let you go."

Aaron spoke up. "If he does, I'll marry you, and that will serve him right."

Kit laughed. "But I have yet to agree."

"Little brother, have no fear, I will marry Kit, and though she's not your sister, she will be your sister-in-law."

Aaron smiled broadly. "Good!"

The celebration of Kit's recovery ended and Helga, insisting Kit rest, bustled everyone out of the room. As she tried to shoo Leigh, he embraced gave her a hearty embrace. "I'll only stay with her until she falls asleep. I promise I won't tire her. Run along now, Helga, please."

The old woman smiled. The corners of her eyes crinkled, and tears of joy slipped down her cheek.

Leigh stepped to the edge of the bed, then bent down and kissed the dozing Kit on her parted lips.

Awakening, she asked, "Leigh, do you truly care for me, above the king?"

"Kit, duty is important, but nothing is more important than love. And I love you, Vixen, I truly do," he said, taking her into his arms. "No power of wizard nor might of kings shall wrench me from your side. Though I've always loved you, it is only now I comprehend the responsibilities of that love. As a unit, we are stronger than either of us separate, we shall love and rule wisely."

"Well then, convince me."

"Oh, my darling vixen, when you are stronger, I promise to convince you. I shall convince you for the rest of my days."

Meet Dee Carey

Dee Carey began her writing career when she first could hold a pen Her tales features as a lead character a shape-shifting fox. She now lives in the Chicago area you can contact her at careydee639@gmail.com or www.careyfoxlady.com

If you enjoyed the fox 'tale' please leave a review on Amazon. It is much appreciated.

www.ingramcontent.com/pod-product-compliance
Lightning Source LLC
Chambersburg PA
CBHW032234050726
47591CB00001B/387